THE SECRET OF PROPHET HOUSE

By

Mary Rice

Solasta Books

The Secret of Prophet House

By

Mary Rice

The characters, places, and events in this book are solely from the author's imagination and any resemblance to actual events, locations, and persons, living or dead, is purely coincidental.

Cover Art courtesy of Island Art.

Solasta Books
Charlotte, North Carolina

ISBN: 979-8-9902524-0-0

Other Books by Mary Rice

Written as

M H RICE

THE SWITCH TRILOGY

SWITCH

FORSAKEN

RETURN

CHAPTER 1

Prophet House didn't look at all like the former home of a sea captain—especially not one rumored to be haunted. Sadie felt a tinge of disappointment as her eyes traveled up three stories of crisp white clapboard towering regally over a lush landscape of flowering plants and enormous blooming magnolia trees.

Sadie's mother gasped. "Dean, this is…"

"Pretty cool, huh?" Sadie's dad grinned. He stopped the car about ten feet from stone steps leading up to the grand porch that stretched across the entire width of the house.

Surveying the lush grounds, Sadie's mom sighed. "How will we ever manage to keep it up?"

"It's all taken care of, Meg. As long as we keep everything as it is and host a community event four times a year the town will maintain it for us."

Sadie's mother frowned. "What kind of events?"

"Nothing too crazy. I promise."

She didn't seem convinced. "Not seances, I hope."

"Of course not. At least, I don't think so." He winked at Sadie in the rearview mirror.

Sadie slumped in the back seat. "It doesn't look haunted anyway."

Sadie's dad raised his eyebrows. "Are you disappointed?"

Sadie shrugged. "A little, I guess. I thought it would be more…"

He chuckled. "Crumbling walls? Vines growing everywhere? Gargoyles on the roof?"

Sadie nodded. "Something like that." Even though the rain had let up, streaks of water still clung to the car window, distorting her view. She pressed her nose against the glass and tried to make out an odd structure on the roof. "Is that the tower Grandpa used to talk about?"

"It's called a widow's walk." Her dad switched off the engine. "Sea captains built them so their wives could look out to sea and watch their ships returning. Of course, sometimes they never came home. Hence the name."

Sadie's mom shuddered. "That's morbid. Let's call it something else."

"It's what they've been called since the 1700s, babe."

Sadie was intrigued. "How do you get up there?"

Her dad smiled. "There's a ladder in the attic that leads to a trapdoor. When I was a kid, I used to play up there whenever we came to check on the place."

Sadie could picture her ancestor, the first Sarah Prophet keeping watch, hoping to see her husband Nathanial's ship on the horizon. She wondered how long Sarah had waited that last time before realizing he was gone for good.

"What are you thinking about back there, squirt?"

Sadie sat back in the seat, arms crossed. "I was wondering if we're really gonna live here."

"That's the plan. I think it's about time we connected with our family's history. It's pretty fascinating, you know. Your great-great-great-grandfather built this house almost two hundred years ago."

Sadie rolled her eyes. "With treasure he took off a Spanish ship. I know." Something dawned on her and she sat up straight. "Please tell me there's indoor plumbing!"

"What fun would that be? But don't worry. There's a chamber pot in each bedroom."

"Dad, no!"

He threw his head back and laughed. "Just kidding. Your grandfather took the chamber pots out years ago. He converted the second maid's quarters on the first floor into a bathroom and added two more—one on the second floor and one on the third. He renovated existing bedrooms. Since the house had so many, it wasn't a problem losing a few. Satisfied?"

"I guess," Sadie grumbled.

"Well, the town wasn't too happy when he added them. Made the house lose some of its authenticity, especially since he'd added electricity and central heat years before. But the historical society minded the bathrooms most of all. They still have the chamber pots somewhere and maintain a four-seat outhouse in back for the tourists."

"Yuck." Sadie grimaced.

Her mom sighed. "I suppose it'll eventually feel like home. I just wish we could have our own things."

"The house is beautiful, Meg. Some of the furniture isn't really that old. They're reproductions of the original pieces. I think you'll be surprised once you see inside." He reached for her hand and gave it a reassuring squeeze. "The Davenport house doesn't go on the market until August. If you don't like it here, we'll move back. I promise."

"All right." She sighed. "So, tell me about these events we're expected to host."

"The one at the end of the summer is an historical reenactment," Sadie's dad said cheerfully. "Practically everyone in town dresses up in period costumes to recreate daily life at Prophet House as it was back in Nathaniel's day. Apparently, visitors come from all over for it. The historical society is excited to have real Prophets participating this year. That could be fun, don't you think?"

"If you say so." Meg's skeptical expression didn't waver. "How long do the events last? One or two days?"

"Most of them last a week, but the reenactment is ten days." Dean cleared his throat. "And we have to store our car off the property and hide anything in the house that wouldn't have been around in Nathaniel's day. No modern conveniences."

"Dean Prophet!"

Sadie felt an argument coming on, so she stepped out of the car. She could understand how her mom felt. They were leaving everything behind, literally. She half expected her mother to refuse to get out of the car.

Her dad pulled several bags from the trunk and tossed one to Sadie. "This one's yours, squirt."

"Dad!"

"Sorry." He grinned.

Sadie's mom got out of the car carrying a small bag. She seemed to have softened a little. "Don't embarrass her, Dean."

He gave his wife a quick kiss on the cheek. "I'll try not to, but it comes naturally."

Sadie's mom rolled her eyes. "Tell me something we don't know."

A portly woman emerged from the house, carrying a stack of papers and wearing a pinched expression. "You must be the Prophets."

A gust of wind rustled the papers, but not a hair on the woman's perfectly coiffed head moved. Sadie wondered how much hairspray it took to plaster it in place like that.

"I'm Dean Prophet." Sadie's dad stuck out his hand, but the woman hugged the papers to her chest as if protecting them from a would-be thief.

"I'm Mrs. Northrup, president of the Everleigh Historical Society. I'm glad to meet you." She didn't seem glad to meet them at all, but when she turned her attention to Sadie, she brightened considerably. "You must be the one who's named for her."

Sadie took a step back, in case the woman was thinking of making physical contact after all. "Her?"

"Your third-great-grandmother. You must be Sarah Elizabeth." Her red nails made a clicking noise as she fiddled with one of the gold buttons on her pink jacket. "You resemble her. There's a portrait of Sarah in the parlor. She was quite a beauty. She had dark hair like yours and the most riveting blue eyes."

"Mine are hazel."

"So they are." Mrs. Northrup sniffed. "And I'm guessing you're… eleven?"

"Thirteen last week. And everybody calls me Sadie."

Mrs. Northrup's pinched expression returned. "I see…"

She started to hand the stack of papers to Sadie's dad, but yanked them back and eyed him suspiciously. "These documents are for a Declan Nathaniel Prophet."

Sadie's dad gave her what he clearly thought was a charming smile. "That's me."

Her eyes narrowed. "I'd like to see some identification."

Obviously amused, Dean pulled his wallet from his back pocket and handed her his driver's license.

"Our family's big on nicknames," Sadie offered, regretting it when her comment earned her another stern look from Mrs. Northrup.

"I can see that, Miss Prophet. How nice." Mrs. Northrup handed back the license and wiped her hand on her pink skirt.

Sadie's mom appeared from the back of the car. "At least the rain stopped."

Mrs. Northrup gave her a wooden smile. "You must be Margaret Prophet."

Sadie's mom smiled warmly. "I'm Meg."

Mrs. Northrup turned her nose up a bit. "Of course you are."

Dean's eyes narrowed. "Don't let us keep you, Mrs. Northrup. You must have other things to do." He looked over his shoulder at Sadie and whispered, "Other people to torture…"

Sadie snickered, then looked away when Mrs. Northrup eyed them both suspiciously.

"Humph." Mrs. Northrup grudgingly handed over the papers. She managed a smile, but it looked painful and there were traces of red lipstick on her teeth. "These are your copies of our agreement. Honestly, we had hoped… I mean, we'd assumed that no one from the family would ever show up to claim the property. Except for that one summer three years ago, your father was perfectly content to let it remain under the care of the town." She shook her head. "All those unfortunate additions and he barely stayed three months. Your mother was only here that last night. I credit her with bringing him to his senses and making him realize that Prophet House is an important historical treasure. The town has spent a great deal of money and effort maintaining it. I myself have provided many of the authentic touches around the house. And as you can see, all that work has paid off. It's one of the most beautiful historic homes in the country and people come from all over to see it. The governor himself was here just last month. In the spring, summer, and fall, I give tours every weekend." She hesitated, perhaps hoping they'd come to their senses and give up the preposterous idea of moving in. But after a tense few moments, she sniffed. "But here you are…"

"Yep, here we are," Dean replied flatly.

Her fake smile vanished. "Yes."

Sadie picked up her backpack but dropped it when a shutter overhead banged against the house. A curtain fluttered from an open window on the third floor and Sadie caught a glimpse of a face looking out at them. "Who's that?"

Mrs. Northrup jerked around, dropping her over-stuffed purse on the ground with a thud. An ornate letter opener fell out and she scrambled to pick it up. Sadie wondered if she'd pilfered it from the house. Mrs. Northrup quickly stuck the letter opener back inside her purse and proceeded to smooth imaginary wrinkles from her skirt.

"There's no one in the house." Mrs. Northrup's voice had taken on a shrill tone.

"I just saw someone! Right up there." Sadie pointed to the open window next to the third-floor balcony.

"I've been here all morning and I can assure you there's no one inside," Mrs. Northrup snapped. "Maybe you saw one of the ghosts."

Sadie's breath caught in her throat. "Ghosts?"

"Some people have claimed to see the ghost of Captain Prophet. Others swear they've seen his poor wife up there on the widow's walk… or maybe even—"

"Have you seen them?" Sadie blurted out.

Mrs. Northrup smiled slyly. "I'm here almost every day, so I've seen quite a few things that were out of the ordinary. And others have claimed to see not just the captain and his wife, but–
–"

Dean cleared his throat loudly. "Don't feel you have to hang around on our account, Mrs. Northrup. We need to get settled in, so…"

Mrs. Northrup glanced back at the house, and Sadie thought she saw a flicker of fear cross the woman's face before she collected herself. "I'll just be going then. The caretaker will come by later. Let me know if you have any questions. I know this house better than anyone else. I'm here almost every day." Her voice took on an authoritative tone. "As president of the historical society, it's been up to me to keep an eye on things."

Dean raised his eyebrows. "You must have a key then." He stuck out his hand.

Mrs. Northrup's mouth fell open. "I—I thought you might want me to keep it… just in case, um—"

"That won't be necessary."

Mrs. Northrup stepped back and glared at him for a moment before rooting around in her bulging handbag and pulling out a keychain in the shape of a pineapple. Dangling from it was a large brass key with the letter P delicately etched into the head. It took her a couple of minutes to work it free. At first, Sadie didn't think Mrs. Northrup was actually going to hand it over, but she finally placed it in Dean's hand and watched him drop it in his pocket. After an awkward moment, she collected herself.

"Welcome to Everleigh, Mr. and Mrs. Prophet. Let's hope you'll be happy here." She glanced at Sadie disapprovingly, then turned on her heel and stomped off. Before driving away, she rolled down her window and called out. "Don't forget, the first reenactment meeting is tomorrow." She rolled up her window and stepped forcefully on the gas, kicking up gravel behind her.

"That was a little scary." Sadie's mom appeared shaken. "I hope everyone's not like her."

Dean put his arm around her. "Maybe she'll be nicer once she gets to know us." Meg gripped the car door handle to steady herself. "What are we supposed to do at the meeting on Tuesday?"

"Don't worry about that. I'll call and tell her you can't come since I'll be in Davenport and you'll have your hands full settling in."

Meg took a step and winced, rubbing her leg. "Dean, you don't think Mrs. Northrup really believes all that nonsense about ghosts, do you?"

He rubbed his chin thoughtfully. "I don't know. Maybe it isn't nonsense. I wouldn't mind meeting the old captain. I'd like to ask him what he did with all those gold coins."

Meg poked him playfully in his side. "Stop! Obviously, it's just an old legend. There probably never was a treasure. Or if there was, it's long gone." Her expression turned serious. "I don't like all this talk of ghosts though."

He chuckled. "I'm sure it's just a story to bring in tourists. Besides, ghosts are like snakes. If you leave them alone, they'll leave you alone."

"That's easy for you to say. You'll only be here on weekends."

His face lost its humor. "I know this is a lot to ask." He looked at the house and sighed. "Maybe I should give up the summer classes. I think we could manage until my job starts here in August."

Sadie's mom shook her head. "No. We need the money. Maybe it's time for me to think about going back to work too."

"Absolutely not. Your only job is to get better. Sadie can help around here during the week. What do you say, squirt?"

Sadie nodded. "No problem." All that mattered was getting her mom back—the way she was before the accident. She gave her mother what she hoped was a convincing smile. "It'll be great."

The shutter banged overhead again, and they all looked up. This time, the window was empty except for the curtain blowing in the ocean breeze. Sadie felt the hairs stand up on the back of her neck as she watched it flap in the wind. She picked up her bag and started up the steps, but not before glancing at the window again. Still empty. *I know what I saw…*

CHAPTER 2

Sadie dragged her suitcase into a grand entry hall large enough to comfortably fit twenty people. A formal dining room on the left and a parlor on the right were blocked off by velvet ropes, as were the hallway that led to the back of the house and the staircase that led to the second level. On a round table in the middle of the foyer were stacks of brochures.

Meg walked past the ropes to explore while Sadie and her dad approached the table.

"We're not giving tours, are we?" Sadie was mortified by the thought.

"No. I guess Mrs. Northrup forgot to take all this with her." Dean didn't seem at all pleased. "Or maybe she was making a point."

Sadie picked up one of the brochures. The cover had a photo of the house with Mrs. Northrup standing on the porch, wearing the same pink suit and a big smile. Inside were photos of other rooms with captions underneath.

A Prophet family tree filled the back cover, listing each generation starting with Nathaniel Alexander Prophet and Sarah Elizabeth Everleigh. Their children were Sarah Elizabeth, who'd died after a fire just before her fourteenth birthday, and Nathaniel Alexander II. Five generations followed, ending with her own name—Sarah Elizabeth Prophet. It felt strange seeing her name in print on the cover of a brochure. She'd never really given her heritage much thought, but now it struck her that she was the last of the Prophets.

Sadie flipped the brochure over and the picture of Mrs. Northrup jumped out at her. One hand rested on the porch rail while the other was extended in a welcoming gesture. Anyone who didn't know better would think that she was the owner of Prophet House. Sadie placed the brochure on the table and frowned. "She obviously doesn't want us here."

Dean set his jaw. "That's not our problem. This house belongs to us. We have every right to move in." He pulled down the ropes and dropped them in a pile next to the door. "If she wants these back, she can come get them."

"This table is huge!" Meg exclaimed from the dining room. There were seven claw-footed chairs down each side, with even larger armchairs on each end. "Nathaniel and Sarah must've been used to lots of company."

"There's a smaller table in the kitchen, if memory serves," Dean offered.

Sadie stepped into the parlor, where the painting of the first Sarah Prophet hung over the fireplace. She was indeed a beautiful woman. Her dark hair was partially pulled up, some of it falling in soft curls around her delicate face. But her eyes were her most captivating feature. They were the most vivid blue Sadie had ever seen. The color reminded her of the sky on a clear fall day. Sadie could also see kindness in her eyes. No wonder Nathaniel had fallen in love with her.

A large upright piano sat against the wall opposite the fireplace. Sadie pressed one of the yellowed keys and it produced a clear, if slightly flat, tone.

Dean stepped into the room. "Sounds like it needs to be tuned." He studied the image of Sarah Prophet." The old biddy was right. You do look like her."

Sarah raised her eyebrows. "What's an old biddy?"

"Someone like Mrs. Northrup." He grumbled.

A painting of a young boy hung over the piano. He was wearing the clothes of a gentleman, a waistcoat and breeches, but looked to be no more than twelve years old. His shock of red hair was pulled back and his blue eyes, much like Sarah's, seemed to be looking at something off in the distance.

"This must be their son," Sadie observed. "He looks kind

of like you, Dad."

Dean turned and eyed the painting. "You think so? I never thought much about it, but I guess there is a resemblance."

There was a faint rectangular outline on the wall next to the portrait of the young man. "Did there used to be another painting here?" Sadie asked.

Dean frowned. "It looks like there should be, but I don't recall ever seeing one."

Sadie turned her attention back to the image of Nathaniel II. "Did all the Nathaniels have red hair?"

"My grandfather had dark hair like yours. But all the others had red hair."

Sadie nudged him with her elbow. "Like yours."

"Yeah." He grinned. "That's why your mom fell in love with me. My gorgeous red locks. Isn't that right, babe?"

Meg had returned to the foyer. "Whatever you say, Dean." She grabbed the handrail and started up the steps. "I need my other bag from the trunk."

Dean winked at Sadie. "That's my cue." He made another trip to the car and set two more bags down in the foyer at Sadie's feet. "One of these is yours. Why don't you go find your room?"

Sadie's eyes traveled up the freshly polished wooden stairs. She thought of the face she'd glimpsed in the window. "Can't you go with me? What if there's somebody up there?"

"Sadie, Mrs. Northrup said there's no one else here. It's windy and the window was open. You probably saw the curtains move. That's all."

"I'm sure it was a person!"

"Her mom was slowly making her way up, one step at a time, gripping the rail and favoring her injured leg.

Dean started up after her. "Do you want some help, Meg?"

Her mother looked back and smiled. "No thanks. I've got this."

Dean stopped on the second step and whispered to Sadie, "I keep forgetting…The doctor said to let her do things on her own. It means a lot to her. If she needs help, she'll ask."

Meg reached the landing on the second floor, grinning from ear to ear. "That wasn't so bad! Honestly, I barely felt it!"

He gave her a thumbs-up. "Can you come back and help me with the rest of this luggage?"

Meg laughed. "Nice try."

He turned his attention to Sadie. "She gets first choice on bedrooms, but after that, you can have any room you want."

"Okay, but if there really is somebody in the house—"

"I'm sure you'll be fine." He popped up the handle on her suitcase and handed it to her. "If you see a ghost, just holler."

"Real funny." Sadie threw her backpack over her shoulder. "I can have any room Mom doesn't want?"

"Yep. Most are on the second floor, but there's one on the third floor and a maid's quarters down here. And to answer your next question, no, we don't have a maid."

"Figures." Sadie dragged her overstuffed suitcase up the stairs. At the landing was another set of stairs leading to the third floor. Curious, Sadie left her bags and continued up. To the left of the third floor landing was a roomy bathroom with a claw-footed tub. A large window above the sink looked out over a dense forest of pine trees, bordered by a wide creek. For some reason, an image of someone watching from the trees popped into her head. She shook it off and surveyed the rest of the room. There was no linen closet, but an antique chest of drawers against the wall had ample room to store towels and other bathroom necessities. Next to the chest was a wooden bench that looked as if it had probably been there for the whole two hundred years. Sadie sat on it, but jumped up when it wobbled and creaked in protest.

Stepping back into the hall, Sadie opened the door directly in front of the landing. It led to a large unfinished attic with crates and boxes scattered about the cavernous space. The light from a window near the ceiling revealed a host of cobwebs. Sadie figured there were spiders and probably bats in there too. She shut the door and shuddered.

The sun shone in through a window at the end of the hallway and cast a beam directly on an open door down the hall on the right. No matter what Mrs. Northrup said, Sadie was sure she'd seen someone watching them from the third floor. Since that room would most certainly face the front of the house, whoever had been peering out at them could still be there.

Her mother appeared just below her on the second-floor landing.

Sadie tried to keep her voice low. "Mom, where's Dad?"

"He's on the phone. Why are you whispering?"

Sadie sighed. "Never mind."

Her eyes traveled back to the door as her mom disappeared into the second-floor hallway. Sadie remained where she was, listening for a noise from the open room. After several minutes, she felt a little foolish. Maybe Mrs. Northrup had been right after all. Maybe Sadie had been thinking about ghosts and her eyes had played a trick on her.

She took a deep breath and crept toward the door, listening intently for any sound from within. All was quiet, so she cautiously peaked inside. The room looked empty.

Relieved, Sadie stepped in, then gasped. A young girl was standing at the window. She was wearing an odd sort of blue dress that was cinched above the waist and hung loosely almost to her ankles. Her feet were bare. She didn't seem to notice Sadie's arrival and continued to peer out, her hand on the curtain.

"Who are you?!" Sadie hadn't meant to shout but seeing someone there after all had given her a jolt of adrenaline.

The girl spun around, her eyes wide with alarm. A gust of wind blew in from the open window and caught her hair, whipping it around her head in a kind of pale red halo. When she pushed it back, her face was white as a sheet.

Sadie regained a little of her composure. "You were the one in the window, watching us when we got here!"

The girl's eyes darted around the room as if looking for an escape route. She looked back at Sadie solemnly. "I—I didn't think anyone could see me."

"It's okay. You just surprised me. Mrs. Northrup said the house was empty."

The girl shifted her weight nervously. "I'm sorry. Please don't tell her."

"Why not?"

"I'm not supposed to be here."

"It doesn't matter. Mrs. Northrup isn't in charge anymore. We live here now."

The girl brightened a little. "You do?"

Sadie nodded, stepping toward her. "What were you doing in here?"

A hint of a smile crossed the girl's lips. "I come here often. I love this room."

Sadie took in her surroundings. A massive four-poster bed dominated the sizeable room. When she grasped one of the towering posts, her fingers barely made it a quarter of the way around. Next to the bed sat an old chest with a brass lamp in the shape of a lantern on top. On the other side of the bed was a rolltop desk and a sitting area with two ornately carved wooden chairs with upholstered backs and cushions. They sat atop a thickly woven, oval rug facing a fireplace. Over the heavy wooden mantle was a portrait of the captain. Sadie studied the painting of her great-great-great grandfather. His red hair was pulled back, revealing chiseled features and fiercely intense eyes the color of honey, with flecks of green and gold. A plaque underneath the portrait read: *Captain Nathaniel Alexander Prophet, 1779-1827.*

Sadie was in awe. "Was this the captain's room?"

The girl's face broke into a broad smile. "It was. He and Sarah slept in that very bed. It hasn't been moved since it was built there. Truth be told, I don't think a dozen men could budge it."

Sadie wrinkled her nose. "I hope it's not the same mattress."

The girl giggled. "No. It's not the original one that was stuffed with cotton and goose down." She pointed to an antique telescope, perched next to glass doors that opened onto a balcony. "This was his spyglass. He used it to watch for Spanish ships."

"Maybe he thought they'd come back for the treasure."

The girl's mouth dropped open. "You know about the treasure?"

Sadie nodded. "Everyone knows. Especially in my

family."

"Oh." The news seemed to surprise the girl. "Are you one of the Prophets?" She looked away quickly, chewing her lip. "Of course you are. That was silly of me."

Sadie's eyes traveled around the rest of the room. There were windows on either side of the glass doors. The opposite side of the room was occupied by a rich wooden wardrobe that ran the entire length of the wall.

Sadie cleared her throat. "You seem to know a lot about this place. What else can you tell me?"

The girl collected herself. "There's no other house like it. The captain had a keen mind. He designed it himself and added many things that were uncommon for his day. For example, this wardrobe was built into the room using wood from the cherry trees that grow on the back of the property. It was quite the talk of the town. And these doors and windows were specially made by his own design. When you pull the lever to close one, the other side closes as well."

"You must've taken the tour tons of times," Sadie observed.

"Oh, no," she said emphatically. "I sneak in. Mrs. Northrup doesn't like me."

"We have that in common. She doesn't like me either." Sadie smiled. "I'm Sadie."

"I'm Bess." The girl smiled back. "You must think me odd."

"No, of course not. Well, maybe your dress?"

Bess laughed. "It's quite old-fashioned, isn't it? But it suits the occasion, don't you think?"

"What occasion? Oh! Are you gonna be in the reenactment?"

Bess shook her head. "No one has asked me."

"Then where'd you get the dress?" Bess smiled. "My mother made it. She's quite skilled at sewing."

"You should play Elizabeth in the reenactment. Most of the Prophets had red hair, and you already have a perfect dress. I can ask Mrs. Northrup for you."

"Oh, no! She'll be angry if she knows you've been

talking to me. Like I said before, she doesn't like me…and I'm not supposed to be here. Promise you won't tell?"

Sadie nodded. "Don't worry. Your secret's safe with me."

"Thank you, Sadie."

"Why do you come here if you're scared of Mrs. Northrup?"

Bess sighed. "I just love it so much. I can't make myself stay away. Besides, I'm good at hiding. She doesn't see me… most of the time."

"You must really be into history."

Bess nodded vigorously. "Oh, yes!"

"You'll get along great with my dad. He teaches history at the university. Well… not for much longer. He's there this summer, but he'll be teaching at the high school here in the fall. What grade are you in?"

Bess frowned. "I don't go to school."

Sadie was taken aback. "What… never? How old are you?"

"I'll be fourteen in November. My mother teaches me."

"Oh. You're homeschooled." *That explains a lot*, popped into Sadie's head, but thankfully she didn't blurt it out. "I'd go crazy if my parents decided to homeschool me."

Bess hung her head. "It's not so bad. My mother isn't well. She needs me at home. But it would be nice to be around others my age. I'd like to have friends."

Sadie thought of Emma and Zoey and couldn't imagine what her life in Davenport would have been like without them. She felt a rush of sympathy for Bess. "You can hang out with me any time. I don't have any friends here either."

Bess beamed. "I'd love that! Thank you, Sadie."

The sound of footsteps drifted up the stairs from the second floor. Bess jumped into the wardrobe and pulled the door shut.

"You don't have to hide," Sadie whispered. But there was no response.

"Sadie, you up here?" It was her dad.

She stuck her head out the door. "I found the room I

want."

Dean stepped in and whistled. "I wouldn't mind having this one myself. I don't think your mom could handle the extra stairs though."

"I've already claimed it anyway." Sadie grinned. "And I don't mind the stairs."

"Are you sure?" He pushed open the glass doors and stepped out onto the balcony. "This is pretty high up." The driveway was below, their car still parked in the circle with the trunk open. He stepped away from the rail. "You have shutters for these doors and windows. That probably comes in handy during a storm. I'd hate to have to replace all this old glass." He pulled one of the doors closed and, just as Bess had pointed out, the other side closed too. He opened it again and the other swung open as well. "That's pretty cool."

"Stop playing with my doors, Dad." Sadie rolled her eyes.

He opened one side of the window to the right of the doors, and the opposite pane opened. "I wonder if they all do this."

Sadie shrugged. "Maybe you should go see."

He tousled her hair. "You're not trying to get rid of your old man, are you?" He walked back out onto the balcony. "I don't know about this. What about the ghost in the window?" He looked back at her and winked.

"I—uh..." Sadie hesitated. Bess clearly didn't want anyone else to know she was there. "I guess I don't mind sharing the room with a ghost. It'll give me somebody to talk to."

Her dad chuckled. "Suit yourself." He opened one of the wardrobe doors and Sadie held her breath. "You'll have lots of storage," he said, shutting the door.

She let the air out of her lungs, relieved. "Yeah. Maybe I'll have a neat room for a change."

"Right. I'll believe that when I see it, squirt."

Sadie sighed. "Dad, really?"

"Sorry. How about if I only call you squirt at home and promise not to in front of your friends?"

Sadie thought of Bess hiding in the closet and felt her

cheeks turn red. He didn't seem to notice.

"I wanted to talk to you before your mom comes up here." He put his hand on her shoulder. "This past year's been rough on her."

Sadie's stomach knotted up. "I know." It had been a hard year for all of them.

"I know you were upset when we decided to move to Everleigh, but your mom needed a change. I want her to be happy here. She deserves that after all she's been through. I'm counting on you to help make that happen."

Sadie swallowed the lump in her throat. "I will, Dad. I promise."

He put his arms around her. "That's my girl."

Sadie's mom stuck her head in the door. "Whew! That's a lot of stairs!"

Dean walked over and gave her a kiss on the cheek. "I knew you could make it, babe."

Her cheeks flushed with pleasure. "Oh, Sadie! This is incredible!"

Sadie nodded enthusiastically. "I've decided I want this room."

Her mom raised her eyebrows. "Really? Isn't it a little…"

"What?"

She smiled. "Nothing. It's a little over the top—literally. But it suits you." Her mom glanced around the room. "I have to give credit to crabby Mrs. Northrup. The old furniture does add to the ambiance."

"Ambiance?" Dean winked at Sadie. "Once an English teacher, always an English teacher, I guess. Just say it's cool."

"Fine. It's cool." Meg shot him an amused look. "The moving van just dropped off our boxes. The kitchen boxes are already in there and the others are at the bottom of the stairs for you to bring up."

"Aren't some of them Sadie's?"

"Fine. Sadie can bring up hers as long as they're not too heavy. That only leaves about twenty for you. Our room is the big one on the second floor. It's the closest one to the landing.

You'll see. A few of my things are on the bed." She disappeared down the hall.

"I guess that settles it." His smile faded. "Do me a favor and don't go out on the balcony, okay?"

"Why not?"

"Just humor your old man. It's a long way down."

"Didn't you say you used to go up to the widow's walk when you were a kid?"

"Maybe I'm smarter now. The rail seems strong, but this is an old house. I wouldn't trust it. Just be careful."

"I will."

"Thanks, squirt." He turned and bowed. "Your bedchamber, captain."

Sadie giggled. "Very well, good man. You may go."

As he trotted down the stairs, he called back to her, "Sea captains still have to carry their own boxes."

Sadie groaned. "I'll get them later."

She waited until he was out of earshot before she opened the wardrobe door. There was no sign of Bess. She stepped inside the tight space and looked around. Empty. A chill ran up Sadie's spine as she closed the door and plopped down on the bed.

"This is so weird…" Sadie muttered.

"What's weird?"

Sadie jerked around. "Bess! Where were you?"

Bess gave her a sly smile and pointed at the wardrobe. "There. Where do you think?"

"I looked in there!"

"I'll show you." She motioned for Sadie to follow her into the wardrobe and down to the far end. "Look." Bess pointed at a panel in the back wall. When she gave it a nudge, it sprang open.

Sadie was intrigued. "Where does it go?"

"To the attic."

"How is that possible? The attic is on the other side of the hall."

"The house juts out under the window. You can see it from outside. It leaves a small space to crawl through behind the wall."

"There's a door to the attic. I saw it myself. Why would anyone need to crawl through the wall?"

"It's a secret escape," Bess whispered. "In case the Spanish come back for the treasure." She squeezed through the opening and motioned for Sadie to follow. The narrow chute was about two feet wide and only a little taller.

"I'm glad I'm not claustrophobic," Sadie muttered.

They popped out the other side, into the spacious attic.

"Is that in the brochure somewhere?" Sadie asked.

"What?"

"You know. The thing about the Spanish and the treasure."

Bess pursed her lips. "No. But surely they'd want it back."

Sadie nearly ran into a ladder that descended from a trap door in the ceiling. "Is that to the widow's walk?"

Bess nodded.

"Let's go up there!"

Bess shook her head emphatically. "Someone might see me."

Sadie was disappointed. "So what? I told you. Mrs. Northrup is gone. Don't you want to see what it's like?"

"I know what it's like."

"Then come with me!"

Bess looked as though she was about to cry. "I don't like going up there."

"It's okay." Sadie figured she must be scared of heights. "Wait here. I'll be back down in a minute." She climbed the ladder and pushed on the trapdoor. It opened easily.

The widow's walk was a covered round space about six feet across with wood railing that was painted a crisp white like the rest of the house. The view from so high up was stunning. In the distance, the ocean stretched to the horizon. She could imagine Sarah Prophet clutching the rail, waiting for a glimpse of her husband's ship. When Sadie leaned forward over the railing and looked down, her stomach lurched. If she fell from that height, she wondered exactly how many seconds would pass before the inevitable *splat*.

"Bess! I can't believe how high up this is! Are you sure you don't want to see?"

She could imagine Bess vigorously shaking her head. Sadie sighed. *Why couldn't my first friend here be someone a little more like Emma or Zoey?* She thought of the two close friends she'd left behind. They would've argued over who got to climb the ladder first. Once, when they were in the third grade, Zoey climbed a giant oak tree next to the cafeteria at school. She went so high up that the branches thinned out and she nearly fell when she tried to descend. Principal Seymour had to call the fire department, who arrived ten minutes later with their siren blaring. It took four firemen and a hook and ladder truck to get her down.

Emma and Zoey had promised to visit, but Sadie knew things would never be the same. School would start back in the fall and she wouldn't be there to hear Emma go on and on about some new guy she had a crush on. Sadie wouldn't plop her tray down next to Zoey at lunch, or watch milk squirt out of her nose when she laughed too hard at Emma's imitation of Principal Seymour's nasally announcements.

Sadie felt a tear run down her cheek and wiped it away with the back of her hand. What was the point of torturing herself? If she was stuck here, she'd have to make the best of it. On the bright side, she hadn't even been in Everleigh one day and she'd already made a friend. A slightly odd friend, but a friend nonetheless.

Feeling more optimistic, Sadie stepped away from the rail and took in the rest of the view. The town of Everleigh lay off to the right—quaint rows of colorful houses surrounding a charming town, complete with a bandstand in the center of a park.

Sadie called down to Bess, "You can really see the ocean and the town!"

There was no response.

Sadie climbed down the ladder. "Are you sure you don't want to come up for just a minute?" Her gaze darted around the attic. Bess was gone.

CHAPTER 3

Sadie squeezed through the panel into the wardrobe and stepped into her room. Still no Bess. She dropped to the floor and looked under the bed, but no one was there. Baffled, she plopped down on the floor with her back against the solid foot post. Clearly Bess had managed to slip out of the house without Sadie's parents seeing her. Otherwise, Sadie would've heard something by now.

The wide plank floorboards creaked a bit as she shifted her weight. She ran her hand over the smoothly worn wood and noticed what appeared to be a scuff mark. It seemed oddly out of place. Sadie felt the rough patch and encountered a small chip in the edge of the plank. Curious, she leaned in for a closer look. It was a notch in the shape of a crescent moon, perfectly cut out. She hooked her finger inside and pulled. The floorboard moved a little. She pulled harder and it came up about an inch but stopped there and wouldn't budge.

Sadie's mom called up the stairs, "Sadie, don't forget these boxes!"

The floorboard would have to wait. She pushed it into place again and padded down the stairs to begin the arduous task of carrying her belongings up to the third floor.

Halfway through the process, she was interrupted by a sharp knock at the front door. Maybe it was Mrs. Northrup, there to pick up the velvet ropes or to demand her key back. The thought of encountering her again made a new knot form in

Sadie's stomach.

Her mom was in the kitchen. "Sadie, can you get that?"

"I'm carrying boxes!"

"I'm on the floor cleaning cabinets. Whoever it is will be gone by the time I can get there."

"Where's Dad?"

"For goodness' sake, just answer the door!"

Sadie dropped the box she was holding on the floor and opened the front door.

A boy about her age shoved three pizza boxes at her. "My mom said to bring these over."

Sadie had no choice but to take them. "Uh… thanks. Who's your mom?"

"Amelia Northrup. She's the—"

"I know," Sadie interrupted. "She's the president of the historical society who thinks I look eleven."

He raised his eyebrows. "How old are you?"

Sadie was irritated by the question. What business was it of his how old she was? "Thirteen. How old are *you*?"

He flashed her a dimpled smile. "Thirteen. We're practically twins." A strand of light brown hair fell down his forehead, partially covering one of his blue eyes.

Sadie caught herself staring and felt blood rush to her cheeks.

Dean Prophet appeared at the top of the stairs. "What's this? Pizza?"

The boy straightened his shoulders. "Yes, sir. My mom thought you might not have time to think about food."

"Your mom?"

Sadie rolled her eyes. "Mrs. Northrup."

Her dad rubbed his chin. "Really? That was very, um… thoughtful of her." He shook his head as he descended the stairs. "I'm kind of surprised. She didn't seem too happy we're here."

The boy grinned. "She's not. But don't worry. They're not poisoned."

"Good to know." Dean took the pizzas from Sadie. "Come join us, uh…"

"Henry," the boy offered.

"Join us, Henry."

"Thanks, but I have some other deliveries. My mom has a shop in town, and she offers a free delivery service. During the summer, that's me."

Dean looked him over skeptically. "Are you old enough to drive?"

"I wish. I ride my bike or walk."

"Which are you doing now?"

"Walking. It's only a few blocks back to the shop, and the rest of today's deliveries aren't too far from there."

Dean pointed to a box next to the door. "Do you think you can manage this? It's the brochures about the house. I thought your mother might want them back."

Henry nodded. "Sure."

"Sadie can carry the other one." He pointed at a smaller box, also full of brochures.

Sadie's mouth dropped open. "Dad, I still haven't taken all my things up to my room."

"That can wait. We can't expect Henry to carry both of these boxes, can we?"

Sadie glanced at Henry, who seemed equally uncomfortable. He gave her a tentative smile and she felt her cheeks get even redder. They were probably the color of ripe strawberries by now. She picked up the smaller box, trying not to look in Henry's direction.

"We'll save you some pizza." Her dad winked.

Sadie followed Henry out the door and down the driveway. As they neared the road, they passed a small gatehouse that she hadn't noticed when they'd arrived at Prophet House. Curiosity took over, making her almost forget the embarrassing episode before. She set her box on the ground and tried the door. Locked. There was one dingy window, but it was impossible to make out anything inside.

"We can ask my mom if she has a key," Henry offered.

Disappointed, Sadie picked up her box. "Sure."

Neither of them said a word for the next few minutes as she followed him down the main road into town. Henry came across a smashed soda can and kicked it as they walked. On this tree-lined street of neatly maintained clapboard houses, the can seemed oddly out of place. Plus, the sound was fraying her nerves.

When she couldn't stand it any longer, she asked, "Are you planning to kick that all the way to your mother's store?"

"Why not? There's a recycle bin outside her shop." He grinned. "I recycle."

Sadie looked away. "Great."

He held his box in one arm, picked up the can, and dropped it in. "Better?"

She didn't answer.

He was apparently determined to carry on a conversation. "I guess it must suck to move to a new place. I've never done it myself."

Sadie's interest was piqued. "Really? You've never moved?"

He shook his head. "Nope. I've lived here all my life."

"Do you know a girl named Bess? She's about our age."

"No. Did she just move here too?"

Sadie frowned. "I don't think so. She was in our house when we got there. Your mother said no one was inside, but I saw her in the captain's room. She knew all about Prophet House. She showed me a secret way to get to the attic from my room."

"That's weird. My mom would never let some kid go exploring on her own."

"Bess said your mother doesn't like her, so she sneaks in."

"Really?" He laughed. "My mom would pop a vein if she knew that."

"I was thinking we could ask her about Bess though."

"Probably not a good idea. Take my word for it."

Sadie frowned. "Why? I don't have to say she was in the house when we got there."

"Then how would you say you met her? Believe me, my mom will ask. She has a way of extracting information from people. And then Bess's parents would get an earful. My mom thinks she owns Prophet House. It won't matter if you're okay with Bess sneaking in, because she won't be."

Sadie was disappointed. Everleigh was a small town, and Mrs. Northrup seemed like the person who'd know everyone in it. But she hated the thought of getting Bess into trouble. She stared at the road as they walked along, wondering how Bess had managed to slip in without being noticed by Henry's mother. It was apparently something she'd done other times as well. And how did she get out today without being seen by Sadie's parents? Of course, there was always the possibility…She shook off the thought. Bess was a little odd, but she was definitely not a ghost.

"What's on your mind?"

Sadie jerked back to the present. "What?"

"You look deep in thought."

She felt her cheeks go red again. "I wasn't thinking about anything specific."

He shrugged. "Fine. Don't tell me."

Sadie had no desire to share her musings about Bess. Still, she didn't want to hurt Henry's feelings. It would be nice to have a normal friend to talk to—one who wasn't afraid to be seen and didn't disappear the second you weren't looking. On the other hand, she didn't know Henry at all… and his mother was Mrs. Northrup.

Two boys rode past them on bicycles. One of them swerved and might have run them down if he hadn't turned at the last minute. He and the other boy laughed as they peddled away.

"What was that about?" Sadie asked.

It was Henry's turn to seem embarrassed. "Nothing. They're just a couple of guys from my lacrosse team being jerks."

"Oh." *I hope they're not friends of his,* Sadie thought. "How much farther is it to your mom's store?"

"We're coming into town now. It's around the corner."

The houses gave way to quaint old buildings lining both sides of the street. Most had plaques designating them as historic, giving the dates they were constructed and what their original purposes were. Now they housed shops that sold food, gardening supplies, clothing, and knickknacks.

A pharmacy occupied a brick building with a plaque next to the door that read "Apothecary." In the center of town sat the lovely park with the bandstand that Sadie has seen from the widow's walk. Across the street from the park sat the town hall, housed in what used to be the village meeting house.

Sadie took it all in. "This is amazing!"

In spite of her reservations about moving to Everleigh, she had to admit it was pretty cool to think about her ancestors living here so many years ago. Maybe they'd be pleased to know that their descendants were finally calling Prophet House home again.

"What's it like where you're from?" Henry asked.

"Nothing like this," Sadie said. "It's bigger and most of the buildings are modern. We lived close to the university. My dad's a history professor there—the one everybody wants to get." Sadie smiled. "I loved hanging out with him when I wasn't in school. He'd take me over to the dining hall and buy me hamburgers and ice cream."

"Sounds like a cool dad."

"Yeah. He'll be teaching at the high school here in the fall." Talking about her dad made her miss the life she was leaving behind. She'd loved visiting him on campus after school most days. Sometimes she'd sit across from him in the library, doing her homework while he researched a topic for one of his classes. If she didn't have papers to grade, her mom would join them, and they'd get dinner together before heading home. Of course, that was before her mother's accident. Sadie cleared her throat. "Are we almost there?"

Henry stopped walking.

"This is it."

A sign bearing the name *Amelia's Treasures* hung over a wooden door with a stained-glass window in the center. Sure enough, there was a green recycling bin in front. Henry pulled the smashed can out of the box of brochures and dropped it in. He seemed very pleased with himself.

As they entered the store, a wire attached to the top of the door set off a row of tinkling wind chimes. The quaint, knickknack-filled shop appeared empty, but they could hear

Henry's mother arguing with someone.

"It won't be like before. I told him his family has to cooperate with the town or we won't keep up the property. He promised they'd keep everything exactly the same."

Sadie felt a knot beginning to form in the pit of her stomach. "Is she talking about Prophet House?"

Henry frowned. "Maybe we should come back later."

A man's voice drifted out of the back of the store. "You assured me that the family had no interest in the place!"

"William, that was three years ago. I had no way of knowing—"

"I'm used to having total access to the house and the grounds," he interrupted. "If the family is there, that ends. Why should I pour money into what is essentially a very old house occupied by its owners?"

Mrs. Northrup's voice took on a desperate tone. "They've agreed to four events a year. At least wait until the reenactment before you decide! You might change your mind after you meet the family. Their daughter is the spitting image of Sarah Prophet."

The man lowered his voice and Sadie couldn't make out what he said next.

"Let's go," Henry said awkwardly.

Sadie swallowed the lump in her throat. "Why are they talking about my family?"

Mrs. Northrup suddenly appeared from the back of the store. Her face was flushed.

"Henry! I didn't hear the chimes. Why didn't you tell me you were here?" Her eyes darted to Sadie and her cheeks turned even redder. The man that she'd apparently been talking to came up behind her, wearing a stern expression.

Henry shuffled his feet. "Mom, this is Sadie."

"Yes, I know. We've met." Mrs. Northrup looked as if she'd just taken a bite out of a lemon. "This is Mr. Endicott, Miss Prophet, our generous town benefactor."

Mr. Endicott studied Sadie for a moment, then extended his hand. "It's nice to meet you, young lady. How are you settling in?"

Sadie was still holding the box of brochures. She glanced at Henry, who was also holding his box. Uncertain what to do, she thrust her box at Mrs. Northrup. "My dad wanted to give these back. We won't need them."

Mrs. Northrup took the box and deposited it on the counter next to an old-fashioned cash register. "I'll just save these for later."

Mr. Endicott's hand was still extended so Sadie reluctantly gave it a cursory shake. His palm was sweaty, and she jerked her hand back, realizing with alarm that she'd probably grimaced a little as well.

Mrs. Northrup smiled, but it looked forced. "At the very least, we'll need the brochures when the house is open four times a year. And who knows, your family may decide not to stay in Everleigh."

Sadie swallowed the lump in her throat. "W—why wouldn't we stay?"

Mrs. Northrup sniffed. "Oh, it's just a feeling. Prophet House has a way of running people off. Take your grandfather, for instance."

"Sadie felt anger welling up inside. "What about my grandfather?"

"Well, he—"

Mr. Endicott broke in. "He nearly ruined a rare and priceless historic property when he gutted three rooms in order to install modern conveniences."

Mrs. Northrup nodded her head vigorously. "At least he came to his senses before doing any more damage to the property. Honestly, I was shocked when he suddenly moved out, but you don't look a gift horse in the mouth…"

Henry dropped his box on the floor. "Jeez, Mom!"

Mrs. Northrup waved as if brushing away a fly.

Sadie set her jaw, thinking of her mom and how much they'd needed the move. "Prophet House belongs to my family. I don't think we'll be leaving any time soon."

Mr. Endicott's expression turned stony. "We'll see."

Mrs. Northrup fidgeted with the collar of her dress. "Well, then. We'll have to make the best of it, won't we?" She turned her attention to a greeting card display and began furiously straightening the cards. "I haven't finished the favors for the Olsens' baby shower, Henry. You'll have to wait until tomorrow to deliver them." She seemed to be making an effort to collect herself. "Why don't you two run along. Mr. Endicott and I have a lot to talk about."

"Fine. I'll walk Sadie home." Henry turned on his heel and stomped out.

Sadie followed him out, and as the door chimed shut behind her, rounded on him. "Why did she say Prophet House runs people off? And who is Mr. Endicott?"

Henry stepped back. "He's the rich guy who gives the town money every year."

"I know what a benefactor is, Henry. My mom's an English teacher."

Henry raised his eyebrows. "Then why did you ask who he was?"

"I meant, what does he have to do with my family? He acted like he hates us."

"He showed up about three years ago after the other benefactor, Mr. Warren, died. My mom liked Mr. Warren, but she used to complain that he barely gave enough money to keep Prophet House running and that the foundation needed repairs that the town couldn't afford. Mr. Endicott didn't just fix the foundation—he also had the whole house painted and all the rotten wood replaced. It's all my mom could talk about for weeks. But because he spent so much on Prophet House, he thought he should get a key, pretty much demanded one. My mom liked the house looking so good, but she hated him coming and going whenever he wanted to."

Sadie sighed. "And now he can't do that anymore. So he hates us."

Henry nodded. "Looks that way."

"Perfect." Sadie stared down at the road. Someone had dropped a shiny penny. She leaned over and picked it up. "What'll happen if he stops sending money?"

"I guess they'll have to figure something out…" Henry's voice sounded strained. He looked down at his feet. "So, what now?"

Sadie needed time to digest what had just happened. She dropped the penny in her pocket. "I have to go home. There are about ten boxes I have to unpack." She started walking.

Henry caught up to her. "I'll walk back with you."

She shook her head. "That's okay. I remember the way."

He looked disappointed. "I guess I'll see you around then."

Sadie felt a pang of guilt. It wasn't his fault that his mother and Mr. Endicott were so awful. Henry seemed nice. And having another friend would be good. Who knew if she'd ever see Bess again?

"Hey, Henry. Maybe you could come over tomorrow and show me around Everleigh?"

His face lit up. "Sure. I can do that."

Sadie was surprised by how pleased she was. "Okay. I'll see you tomorrow."

He tipped an imaginary hat and trotted back toward his mother's store.

Okay, he's a little different too, but I like him, Sadie thought. *Even if his mother is Mrs. Northrup.*

As she walked back to Prophet House, Sadie thought about her ancestors who had lived there. She'd heard stories of Nathaniel Prophet all of her life. He had been an unwilling cabin boy on a Spanish ship, *The Isabela*, that had wrecked off of the coast in 1790 with only eleven-year-old Nathaniel and one other crewman surviving. The ship had carried twelve wooden chests filled with Spanish gold coins. Rumor had it that the two survivors had dragged the chests ashore and hidden them. No one had ever proven that Nathaniel had taken the treasure, but as soon as he'd turned of age, he'd managed to build his own grand ship and secure a full crew to sail it, all while having no active profession. And the treasure had never been found.

Sadie replayed the scene in Mrs. Northrup's shop over and over in her head. There was no way her family would be able to keep up Prophet House on their own. So, what would happen if the town couldn't either? Would they be forced to move back to Davenport?

She let that scenario roll around in her brain. She'd be back with her two best friends… back in her old room with the window seat that overlooked Baker Street. Two blocks down was the entrance to the university, where her dad would teach, like he'd done for the last fourteen years. She and Emma and Zoey would meet at the Baker Street Café for chocolate croissants, like they did every Saturday morning and sometimes before school if Emma hadn't overslept. They'd walk to school together and have sleepovers at each other's houses. It would be just like it was before… And that was the problem.

Her mother had nearly died in the accident. Over the past year, Sadie had watched her descend into a bottomless pit of grief and despair. This move was supposed to make things better. And now, before they'd had a chance at this new life, the possibility of losing Prophet House hinged on the opinion of one person—Mr. Endicott.

Sadie pulled the penny from her pocket and turned it over in her hand. It glittered in the sun, much like gold.

If only the treasure were real. That would solve everything. But two centuries had passed and not one of the gold coins had ever turned up. Like her mother said, it was only a legend.

CHAPTER 4

Lost in thought, Sadie turned onto the gravel driveway and tripped over a ladder lying in her path.

An older man stepped out of the gate house. His thick gray hair was pulled back and held with a piece of string.

Sadie smiled as she straightened up. "Hi."

He seemed taken aback, but quickly recovered. "You all right, miss?"

Sadie brushed the dirt off of her jeans. "I'm fine."

"Owen was supposed to move that ladder. I don't know where he got to."

"That's okay. I'm not hurt."

"I'm mighty glad to hear that, miss." He smiled kindly. "You must be the current Sarah Elizabeth Prophet."

"Everybody calls me Sadie."

"Well, Miss Sadie, I'm tickled to meet you. Everybody calls me Bones."

"It's nice to meet you, Mr. Bones."

He raised his bushy eyebrows. "*Mister* Bones. I like that." He took a rag from his pocket and wiped his forehead. "I would've moved the ladder myself if I'd seen it, but I'm afraid these old eyes aren't what they used to be. Owen should have his ears boxed for leaving it in the middle of the driveway."

"You don't have to do that. I'm sure it was a mistake."

"We'll see. Sometimes that young fella's more trouble than he's worth. Can't seem to keep his mind on his work." He chuckled. "Or maybe he knows what he's supposed to do and just doesn't want to do it."

"I know how he feels. You should see all the boxes that I haven't even started unpacking."

"Well, you best get to it. I'll see you around, Miss Sadie."

"See you around, Mr. Bones."

Sadie was nearly to the house when she glanced at the third-floor window and felt her heart quicken. She could have sworn she saw a dark figure duck behind the curtain. It was too tall to be Bess, so it had to be her dad. She smiled, feeling a little silly. Her encounter with Bess when she first arrived had apparently made her jumpy.

She opened the front door and stepped inside. There was a note on the table in the foyer.

Sadie,

Dad had to leave for Davenport unexpectedly to meet with the head of his department. He left me the car and took a taxi. He was sorry you weren't here to say goodbye, but he'll be home next weekend.

The pizza is in the fridge. I'm heading out to the store to pick up a few things. While I'm gone, please get started unpacking the boxes in your room.

Mom

Sadie's stomach knotted up. She was alone, and she was pretty sure someone was upstairs. Maybe Bess had sneaked back into the house. But the figure in the window had seemed much taller than the delicate girl.

Sadie picked up the phone to dial 9-1-1, but hesitated. She'd only caught a fleeting glimpse of whoever it was. If she was wrong and it turned out to be Bess, Sadie would probably never see her again if the police showed up. She placed the phone back on its base and grabbed a heavy pewter candlestick from the table instead.

She crept up the stairs and paused at the second-floor landing, listening. A creaking sound drifted down from the floor above. It sounded as if someone had stepped on a loose board.

Sadie stood perfectly still and waited. There it was again. Definitely footsteps. Clutching the candlestick, she stole silently up the stairs to the third floor. Her heart was pounding so hard, she wondered if the intruder would be able to hear it.

Crouching on the last step, she leaned forward and peered down the hall toward her room. The door was closed, but she was positive she'd left it open. She tiptoed down the hall, raised the candlestick, and froze with her hand on the knob.

Sadie tried to slow her breathing as she wrestled with the temptation to turn around. But she figured that with the adrenalin rush she was currently experiencing, she could probably outrun whoever was in there.

She turned the knob and pushed open the door. A tall young man with scraggly blond hair stood at the window. He was wearing a faded baseball cap turned backwards. As the door opened, the hinges squeaked and he spun around with a scowl. He raised the hammer he was holding as if he were about to bring it down on her if she got any closer. Sadie screamed and jumped backwards into the hall. The man strode into the center of the room, still wielding the hammer.

"What's the matter with you, girl?" he demanded, his voice almost a growl. "You just about got your head bashed in, sneaking up on me like that!"

"Wh–who are you?"

His eyes narrowed. "Who's asking?"

Sadie took another step back. "I live here! And just so you know, I called the police!"

He had no way of knowing that was a lie. The hammer fell from his hand and his eyes darted to the hallway behind her, as if he expected an armed policeman to charge in at any minute. "Why'd you call the cops?" His voice was shrill. "I'm just fixing the shutters. Mrs. Northrup said they've been banging against the house."

Sadie lowered the candlestick. "You're Owen?"

All the color had drained from his face as he stared at her with one blue eye and one brown. The effect was unsettling.

"Yeah. I'm Owen."

Sadie held the candlestick behind her back. "I'm sorry. I

thought…I mean, no one said anything about you working *in* the house."

"Figures." He grunted, shifting his weight nervously. "Shouldn't you be calling the cops back or something? Don't want them showing up for no good reason."

"Oh… sure. I'll do that now." She turned to leave, but spun around again. "Are you finished with the shutters?"

"Yeah."

He slunk past her and down the stairs. Sadie followed and breathed a sigh of relief as she locked the front door after him.

As soon as she was sure he was gone, Sadie padded up the stairs to her room and collapsed on the grand four-poster. Her mom had replaced the bed linens with her own and the familiar feel was comforting. She stared at the wood plank ceiling that curved up into a peak, like an overturned ship. A feeling of melancholy washed over her. The first Sarah Prophet had lain in this very bed and looked up at this ceiling night after night, waiting for her sea captain to return. How lonely she must have been.

Attempting to shake off that dismal image, Sadie closed her eyes and imagined that she was back in her old room with its tranquil blue walls and crisp white trim. It would almost be time for the train to pass by. The engineer always blew the whistle when he came to the crossroads about mile from her house. She barely noticed it anymore, as it blended with other sounds that she'd become accustomed to—the background noise of life in a bustling college town. But lying on the grand four-poster in her great-great-great grandparents' room, the near silence was crushing, and she longed to hear the whistle again.

Sadie sat up and rubbed her eyes. There must be something she could do to get her mind off of home. The untouched boxes were stacked against the wall next to the door, but she had no desire to tackle them at the moment. She rolled off of the bed onto the floor and crawled to the loose plank, determined to pry it open this time. It popped up about an inch again and refused to budge any further. Frustrated, Sadie glanced around the room and noticed Owen's hammer, still on the floor where he'd dropped it.

One side of the claw end fit perfectly into the crescent-moon-shaped slot. She pressed down on the handle, and this time the floorboard popped up, revealing a musty compartment about six inches deep. Inside was a book with faded gold letters on the tattered cover that read: *Sarah Elizabeth Prophet.*

Sadie carefully lifted the fragile book out of the cavity in the floor. Tiny fragments of the cover had flaked off, giving it a mottled appearance, but the name was clear. It must have belonged to Sarah Prophet, or perhaps her daughter, Elizabeth. Either way, the book had to be nearly two hundred years old.

As Sadie carefully opened the cover, something fell out onto the floor. She picked it up and held it in the palm of her hand, barely able to breath. The circular piece of gold was engraved with the image of man on one side and a shield and crown on the other. And there was a date stamped at the bottom––1788. "Oh my God," she muttered, awe-struck. "This is a piece of Nathaniel's gold! The treasure is real…"

CHAPTER 5

The coin was heavy in her hand as she stared at it, utterly mesmerized. "This is amazing," she whispered.

From behind her, a voice asked, "What's amazing?"

Sadie clinched her fist to hide the coin and jerked around. "Bess! Are you trying to scare me to death?! First Owen, now you!"

Bess wrinkled her nose. "I don't like Owen. Why was he here?"

Sadie's heart pounded. "It doesn't matter! Where'd you come from?"

Bess pointed toward the wardrobe.

"That's not what I meant. How'd you get in the house?"

Bess smiled. "Do you want me to show you?"

Sadie was still reeling from her discovery, but wasn't ready to share it with anyone. "Okay, show me." Laying the book on the bed, she shoved the coin under her pillow and followed Bess into the wardrobe and through the panel into the attic. "You know, there's a perfectly good door in the hall that takes you to the same place."

"It squeaks when you open it."

"So you'd rather crawl through a hole in the wall?"

Bess nodded. "Yes."

"Okay, we're in the attic. Now what?"

Bess walked to the far side of the room and motioned for Sadie to follow. She pointed at a nearly invisible crack in the wall. When she gave it a nudge, a narrow doorway opened into a cramped stairwell barely large enough for the two of them.

"This goes to the cellar," Bess whispered, as if to keep anyone else from hearing.

"You don't have to whisper. We're the only ones here."

Bess shook her head. "You can never be sure of that."

"What does that mean?" Sadie thought of the coin under her pillow and considered going back for it.

Bess ignored the question and stepped inside. "Keep one hand on the wall. It's dark when I shut the door."

Sadie reluctantly followed. Sure enough, without the light from the open door to the attic, the tiny space was pitch black. She placed her hand against the wall and slowly descended the steps. She could hear Bess in front of her, seemingly getting farther and farther ahead.

"Slow down!" Sadie called.

"Oh. Sorry," Bess said quietly. "I'm used to these stairs and forgot you aren't."

"Is this how you left earlier? When I was on the roof?"

"Yes."

"You know, eventually you'll have to start coming to the front door like a normal person," Sadie pointed out.

"This is better."

"Have you done this with other people?"

"No."

"Not any other kids?"

"No." Her voice sounded strained. "Careful here. There's a broken step."

Sadie stumbled and almost fell. "Thanks for the heads-up, but maybe tell me a little sooner next time."

"Sorry." Bess slowed down to let Sadie regain her footing.

"Don't you know any other kids at all? What about Henry?"

"Mrs. Northrup's son?"

"Yeah. Have you ever met him?"

"I haven't. But I've seen him here many times." Bess lowered her voice as if sharing a secret. "He's so handsome!"

"Seriously, Bess? Handsome?"

"What's wrong?"

"Nothing. It's just that most girls our age don't say a boy is *handsome*."

Bess giggled. "Well, I think he's handsome, and I don't mind saying so."

Sadie stumbled again as she tried to navigate the tight stairs without a trace of light, but Bess seemed to have no trouble. Sadie wondered how many times she'd done this. She was about to ask when another door sprang open and they stepped into a huge cellar that appeared to run the width of the house.

After giving her eyes a minute to adjust, Sadie looked around in awe. A long row of narrow windows near the ceiling let in ample natural light, revealing antique furniture and farm equipment organized in neat rows that occupied most of the space. Shelves containing flowerpots, gardening tools, and knickknacks lined the wall underneath the windows. And on the far side of the cellar sat a fancy antique carriage, completely assembled and ready to be pulled by two horses. "This is incredible! But how would they ever get the carriage outside?"

Bess pointed to the exit. "There are double doors and steps that lead outside."

"They have to roll that thing up steps?"

Bess nodded. "They do it every year for the reenactment. It takes quite a few strong men."

"I'd like to see that." Sadie looked back at the door leading to the stairs. "Are there any other secret passageways?"

Bess smiled. "Prophet House has many secrets. I can show you—"

From upstairs, they heard a door close.

"Sadie, I'm back." It was her mom.

Sadie whispered. "It sounds like she's right above us."

"She is," Bess answered softly. She pointed up. "The grand foyer is right there."

"I should tell her we're down here."

Bess shook her head. "I have to go."

"Why can't you stick around? I want you to meet my mom." Sadie tried to take Bess's hand, but she stepped away.

"I can't. My mother will be looking for me."

"I can come to your house then. Where is it?"

"It's… not far. You can't come with me though."

"Why not?"

"It's not a good time. I'll come back later. I promise."

Sadie heard her mom shuffling around overhead. "I could use some help with these bags!" she called out.

Not anxious to take the narrow and somewhat rickety stairs back up to the attic, Sadie shoved the passageway door closed. When she turned around, Bess was gone. One side of the cellar door was open, exposing gradual steps that led to ground level. Sadie followed them up into what appeared to be an old, abandoned garden. It was surrounded by a stone wall, barely visible through a mass of creeping vines. A dilapidated iron gate at the far end was slightly off its hinges, leaving a gap large enough for someone Bess's size to slip though. Once again, her new friend had disappeared.

Sadie surveyed the overgrown enclosure. Dried up beds, choked with weeds, and the broken remains of ancient-looking clay pots were all that was left of what had probably been a lovely, secluded garden. The grounds of Prophet House were meticulously maintained, so why was this one spot allowed to fall into such wretched disrepair?

She pushed through the gate and climbed a hill to the side of the house. Looking back, Sadie realized she never would have known about the abandoned garden if Bess hadn't taken her to the cellar. The giant magnolia trees and thick shrubbery on the property blocked any view of it.

She walked toward the front of the house and passed Owen trimming some bushes along the path that wound through the flower beds. He nodded to her but didn't smile. In the yard, he didn't look nearly as scary. But his intense gaze with those mismatched eyes still unsettled her.

Sadie walked through the front door as her mother was attempting to carry a large bag of groceries into the kitchen. "I don't know why I parked in front when there's a perfectly good back door at the kitchen. The driveway goes all the way past the back of the house. I'm just not used to this place yet."

Sadie sprinted after her and reached for the bag. "I can carry that for you, Mom."

"No, Sadie. I have this one. But there are two more in the car."

Sadie ran out to the car and came in with both of the bags. Her mom pulled several canned goods from one of the bags and put them away in the pantry. Sadie noticed with an ache in the pit of her stomach that her mother was favoring her leg.

"Is it hurting much today?"

Meg shook her head. "It's not too bad." Her eyes met Sadie's. "I'll be all right. You don't need to worry."

"I know."

Her mother smiled. "Did you get some pizza?"

"I guess I forgot."

"Goodness, you must be starving! Did you just get back from town?"

Sadie was reluctant to tell her mom about finding Owen in her room. There was no need to worry her, especially since he was probably harmless. And Bess clearly didn't want anyone to know she was coming over. Until Sadie figured out why, she decided not to mention her either. There was also the disturbing conversation she'd overheard between Henry's mom and Mr. Endicott. She felt guilty keeping so many secrets from her mother, but couldn't see any way around it. Her dad's words echoed in her head… *"I want her to be happy here. She deserves that after all she's been through. I'm counting on you to help make that happen."*

"Sadie, did you hear me?"

"Oh! Sorry. Pizza sounds great."

Her mom gave her a quizzical look. "What were you thinking about just now?"

Sadie took a deep breath. "I found a book in my room. A diary, I think."

"You did? Who did it belong to?"

"It says *Sarah Elizabeth Prophet* on the cover." Sadie started to tell her mother about the coin too, but something held her back. What was the point of getting her interested if the entire treasure turned out to be just one coin? It was a weak excuse, but the only explanation she could come up with for why she didn't want to talk about it—yet.

"That's quite a discovery, Sadie! I'm surprised Mrs. Northrup didn't mention it."

Sadie's throat was suddenly dry. She took a glass from the cupboard and filled it with water. "It was hidden under a loose floorboard," she blurted out before she could stop herself, having intended not to mention that either. Another secret. How many more would spill out unintentionally? She took a swig of water.

Sadie's mom raised her eyebrows. "Really? I wonder what else is hidden in this house."

Sadie choked, spitting most of the water out in the sink.

"Good heavens! You're acting awfully strange. What's going on with you?"

"Nothing," Sadie sputtered. "It went down the wrong way, that's all."

Meg put her hands on her hips. "Hmph. Anything else you want to tell me?"

Sadie regained her composure. "Actually, yes. I found an old garden around the back of the house. You need to see it." She gave her mom the brightest smile she could muster.

Her mother eyed her suspiciously. "There are gardens everywhere on this property. What's special about this one?"

"It looks like no one's done anything with it for a hundred years. It's a mess."

Meg sighed. "Owen can take a look, I suppose. But honestly, he already has so much to do."

"You've met Owen?" Sadie asked.

"Yes. He came to fix the loose shutter in your room. I'm surprised you didn't run into him."

Now Sadie was genuinely embarrassed that she'd thought he was up to no good. Still… there was something about him that seemed off, like he was hiding something.

"What'd you think of him, Mom?"

Meg poured a bag of apples into a bowl and set the bowl in the middle of the kitchen table. "He's a little rough around the edges, but seemed perfectly nice," she said pleasantly.

Sadie couldn't imagine using the word "nice" to describe Owen. "I thought he was kind of strange."

"Strange or not, I want you to be polite to him." Meg took the pizza out of a cabinet and placed it on a plate.

"Shouldn't you have refrigerated that?"

Her mom smiled. "Remember when your dad said some of the things aren't really that old?"

"Sure, I guess."

She waved Sadie over and opened the cabinet door. "It's a modern refrigerator. It just looks like a large ice box on the outside."

"What's an ice box?"

Her mom gave her an exasperated look. "Look it up."

"Yeah. I'll get right on that."

Meg popped the pizza into the microwave and set the timer.

Sadie raised her eyebrows in mock surprise. "They had microwaves two hundred years ago? They must have or Mrs. Northrup wouldn't have allowed that past the front door."

"Of course we can have a microwave. We just have to hide it in the pantry when we have people in here."

Sadie rolled her eyes. "Of course. What about the stove? It looks two hundred years old. How are we supposed to cook anything?"

Her mom opened the oven door to reveal another modern appliance. She lifted a cover from the top and there were four gas burners that looked as if they'd never been used. "Your grandfather had it installed. It was part of the remodel when he added the bathrooms. He had it all specially made to appease the historical society. Your dad and I thought it was silly at the time, but after meeting Mrs. Northrup, I think I understand."

Sadie took the pizza out of the microwave and sat at the table while her mom sat across from her, sipping iced tea. "So, Mom, getting back to the garden I was telling you about… I was thinking *you* might want to do something with it. You know, plant a vegetable garden like you had in Davenport."

Meg's face lit up. "I'd love to grow my own tomatoes and herbs again. You said it's at the back of the house?"

Sadie nodded.

"It would get plenty of afternoon sun. Maybe I'll take a look tomorrow."

Sadie smiled. "You should, Mom." Her thoughts turned back to the gold coin. She was anxious to look around her room some more. She took a bite of pizza and glanced up to find her mother watching her. Afraid she'd let something else slip out, Sadie shoveled in bite after bite until she thought she'd explode.

Meg watched her intently. "You must've been hungry."

Sadie examined the half-eaten slice of pizza on her plate. The thought of taking another bite made her stomach lurch. "I'm done, Mom." She groaned, pushing her chair back. "I think I'll go to my room."

"Don't forget about the boxes that are sitting on your floor, waiting to be unpacked," her mom called after her. "And be sure your windows are closed. There's a storm coming."

CHAPTER 6

A gust of wind caught Sadie as she opened the door of her bedroom. The curtains billowed in as if reaching for her, then settled into place before another blast hurled them at her again. When she opened the glass doors and looked out at the ominous clouds over the ocean, a drop of rain hit her in the face. The first crack of lightning followed seconds later. Thunder rattled the glass as Sadie struggled to close the doors and windows against the sudden onslaught of the wind.

Thick clouds spread over Everleigh, blotting out the late afternoon sun and casting them into an early twilight. Sadie ran her hands around the brass lamp until she felt a switch and flipped it on, instantly bathing the area around the massive four-poster in warm light. Relieved, she climbed onto the bed and listened to the raging storm. It was oddly relaxing.

She found the coin still safely stowed under her pillow. It was cool in her hand. She imagined what it would feel like to reach into a chest filled with them and a plan began to grow in her brain. If Nathaniel had taken the coins from the Spanish ship, surely what remained would still be at Prophet House, tucked away in a hidden spot. That spot had eluded the later generations of Prophets for nearly two hundred years, but something told her this time would be different, that the coin in the book was a sign that she was meant to find it. She would do what no one else had been able to do. She would find Nathaniel's treasure. And that would solve everything…

She shoved the coin back under her pillow, lay down,

and closed her eyes. The boxes would have to wait.

Another bolt of lightning cracked, followed by a loud rumble of thunder. Shadows danced around the room, making Sadie rethink her original opinion that the house didn't look haunted. On the contrary, the storm seemed like an ideal backdrop for a ghost to make an appearance.

Sadie let that thought linger in her head until the lamp suddenly went out. She flipped the switch on and off, but nothing happened.

Barely five minutes later, there was a tap at her door. "Sadie?"

"Mom?"

"I brought you a box of candles."

Sadie sat up. "Really? You just happened to have a box of candles handy?"

Her mom carefully made her way over to the bed and lit a short, fat candle with a match. "I picked some up today when the woman in Norman's Produce said there was a storm coming and we could lose power."

"You know, Dad bought a bunch of flashlights."

"I know, but candles seem more fitting, don't you think? Besides, they don't have batteries that run out." Her mom placed the candle on the chest, climbed onto the bed and sighed. "This storm is worse than I expected." Her voice sounded strained. "I wish your dad was here."

"Me too." Sadie's eyes filled with tears. It was bad enough she'd had to leave the home she'd lived in all her life. Having her dad away too made it even worse. "Have you heard from him?"

"He called once to say he had something to tell me, but it would have to wait until the morning because he and Professor Phillips would be meeting tonight."

"He didn't say what it was?"

"No."

"That's weird."

Her mom pulled a tissue from her sweater pocket and dabbed her eyes. "He'll be home this weekend. Are you okay up here on your own?"

"Of course. Are you okay on the second floor by yourself? I can stay down there with you if you want me to."

"I'll be fine. I have three baskets of clothes to put away. That'll keep my mind off the storm."

She kissed Sadie on the forehead. "Holler if you need me. I'm getting pretty good with the stairs."

"I will. You do the same."

Her mother pulled another candle from her pocket and lit it. She paused at the door. "Folding clothes by candlelight in a two-hundred-year-old house. Who would've ever thought…"

Sadie lay down again, pulling the covers up to her chin. "That's what you get for marrying a history professor."

Meg smiled. "I guess so."

Once her mom was gone, Sadie let her gaze wander around the room. The bed felt cozy, but she couldn't seem to relax. In the waning light, the telescope and stand had transformed, and now slightly resembled the praying mantis she'd found on the porch at home last summer. The flickering light from the candle gave the eerie impression that it was actually moving. This must be what it was like in Nathaniel's time. There would've been no electric lights to flick on. Only candles that cast eerie shadows and caused ordinary objects to take on a sinister life of their own.

A brilliant flash of lightning illuminated the room for a split second, followed by an enormous rumble of thunder that rattled the panes of glass in the balcony doors. The temperature in the room had dropped considerably in the last few minutes. Sadie shook off her jeans and grabbed a pair of sweatpants from one of the boxes on her floor. After pulling them on, she climbed back into bed and slid down under the covers.

The windows rattled again as another blast of thunder and a gust of wind shook the house. It sounded as if the storm was directly overhead. Sadie shivered, wondering how much of a beating Prophet House could take. After almost two hundred years, what if it was one bad storm away from collapsing into the sandy soil?

Another crack of lightning flashed, and a huge gust of wind flung open the glass doors. A tall, dark figure stood on the balcony. Sadie gasped and sat bolt upright in bed, her heart beating wildly.

"Who—who's there!" she called, but her voice was nearly drowned out by the storm.

In a panic, Sadie slithered to the floor and crawled under the bed. Another crack of lightning lit up the room again and she thought she could make out a pair of boots. She tried to scream, but nothing came out. Her mother had closed the door when she'd left the room earlier. Sadie tried to calculate how much time it would take for her to crawl out from under the bed, fling open the door, and make it down the hall to the landing. But if she made it to the landing, what then? She looked toward the balcony again, but it was too dark to see anything.

Suddenly, there was another flash. The lightning reflected off of a pool of water on the floor in front of the open doors, but now there appeared to be no one on the balcony. Sadie twisted around, trying to see if the figure was lurking in the room somewhere, but all she could make out were shadows. He could be anywhere. If she tried to run now, he might grab her before she could make it to the door.

She lay under the four-poster, her heart pounding out of her chest, waiting for another flash of lightning. When it came, she frantically looked around again, but there didn't appear to be anyone there. Sadie crawled out from under the bed and grabbed the candle from atop the chest, her shaking hands causing the light from it to dance around. Leaning against a bedpost, she waited for another flash of lightning. When it came, her eyes swept the room. There was no trace of the figure she'd seen on the balcony. How could that be? Had she imagined the specter, boots and all? That was the only explanation that made sense. Still, she was shivering so hard her teeth chattered.

Exhausted from the adrenaline rush, she sat on her bed, trying to recover for several minutes before dragging herself down the hall to the bathroom for towels. After closing the balcony doors and mopping up the water, she returned the candle to the chest and climbed back into bed. She couldn't seem to stop shivering, so she burrowed deeper under the covers. When she did, her foot encountered a hard object near the end of the bed. She flung back the covers and looked. The faded gold letters on the frayed cover stood out in the candlelight. — *Sarah Elizabeth Prophet.* With everything else going on, she'd forgotten about the book!

The glow from the candle illuminated the first page just enough to make out the faded script, but the cursive was nearly impossible to decipher. It took Sadie at least fifteen minutes to read the short passage. As she slowly made out each word, a distinct feeling of foreboding washed over her…

Papa went away today, making my heart ache. I am frightened by the storm, but I mustn't add to Mama's suffering by telling her so. I will try to be brave for her sake even though I am fearful that something bad will happen. If only Papa were here. I hope he is safe.

Sadie stared at the page. How odd that this Sarah Elizabeth would have written something that so closely mirrored Sadie's life nearly two centuries later. Sadie thought of the silhouette she'd seen earlier on her balcony. She'd been excited about the possibility of seeing ghostly apparitions before moving to Prophet House. But now, she wasn't feeling nearly so brave. In all likelihood, the figure on her balcony had been nothing more than shadows playing tricks on her mind. But it had looked real…

Another bolt of lightning cracked barely a second before thunder shook the panes of glass in the doors and windows again. Sadie closed the book and pulled the covers around her head.

Sometime later that night, her mom shook her awake. "Sadie?"

The candle still flickered on the chest by her bed. Sadie sat up and rubbed her eyes. "What time is it?"

"After midnight. The storm passed, but we still have no power."

Sadie groaned. "Great. I guess there's nothing to do but sleep." She lay back down and pulled the covers up to her chin.

"We could eat cold pizza and play cards in the kitchen."

Meg prodded. "I have plenty of candles. You know, we never actually had dinner. It'll be fun."

Sadie yawned. "You're not tired?"

Her mom shook her head. "I can't sleep."

"Ugh! Fine." Sadie climbed out from under the covers and followed her mom down the stairs.

Meg pulled what was left of the pizza out of the refrigerator and plopped a deck of cards on the table. She shuffled the deck while Sadie took a bite of cold pepperoni.

"This is surprisingly good," Sadie mumbled.

Her mother nodded but stopped shuffling. "I had the weirdest dream earlier. I dreamed I heard someone walking in the hall, but when I looked, no one was there. I walked back and forth, looking in all the rooms, but didn't find anyone. Then I noticed wet footprints going up the stairs to the third floor." She shuddered. "I woke up in a cold sweat. I tried to go back to sleep, but it was no use. So here we are."

Sadie felt the bite of pizza she'd just swallowed work its way back up her esophagus. She swallowed… hard.

Her mom frowned. "Are you all right?"

"I'm fine."

So her mother had dreamed that someone was in the house at basically the same time that Sadie had seen a figure on the balcony! She swallowed the lump that had formed in her throat again and looked at the pizza on her plate. It was no longer the least bit appealing.

CHAPTER 7

Sunlight streaming in through the glass doors and windows woke Sadie early the next morning. She wished she had remembered to close the shutters when she'd finally gone to bed at nearly three o'clock. She thought about closing them now and sleeping the rest of the day, but that would mean leaving the comfort of her bed. She pulled the covers over her face and groaned.

A noise from the wardrobe caught her attention.

Sadie mumbled, "Come out, Bess. I know you're there."

From the other end of the wardrobe, she heard a giggle. Then Bess popped out of the door nearest the windows. "Good morning!"

Sadie pushed the covers away and rubbed her eyes. The lamp next to her bed was on, so obviously the power had been restored. "Why are you here so early?"

"I thought we could hang out today, like you said," Bess said cheerfully.

Sadie sat up. The candle on the chest next to her bed had melted down to about two inches, but the flame was still burning. She leaned over and blew it out. "We can for a while. But I have to work on these boxes and I told Henry he could show me around today."

Bess looked at the floor. "Oh."

"Why don't you come with us? It'd be fun."

Bess shook her head emphatically. "I can't. Mama doesn't like me going into town."

"Why not?"

Bess shifted her weight uncomfortably. "I'll stay until you have to leave. I can show you some other secret places in the house if you like."

"Can you at least say hello to Henry? I know he'd like to meet you."

Bess shook her head again. "I'd be so embarrassed. He'd be put off."

"*Put off*?" Sadie gave her a wry smile. "Okay. But I wish you'd change your mind and come with us. Would it help if I asked your mom?"

Bess hung her head. "No, it wouldn't." She was wearing the same dress again. Maybe her mother couldn't afford clothes for her and Bess was too embarrassed to meet Henry.

"I have an idea. We're about the same size. Do you want to try on some of my clothes? I wouldn't mind lending you some."

Bess frowned. "I like wearing this when I'm at Prophet House."

Sadie was sorry she'd asked, especially since Bess seemed bothered by the offer. "I'm sorry. I didn't mean to hurt your feelings."

"Oh no. It's all right." Bess smiled. "What should we do until Henry gets here?"

"You could show me some of those secret places you were talking about?"

"I'll show you one in this very room!" Bess knelt on the floor at the end of the bed and lightly tapped a floorboard. It sprang open instantly. Her mouth flew open in alarm. "Where is it?"

Sadie pulled the book from under the covers. "Are you looking for this?"

Bess snatched it out of Sadie's hand. "How did you find it?"

"I was sitting on the floor and noticed the notch. I had a hard time getting it to open."

Sadie climbed off the bed and reached for the book, but Bess wasn't ready to give it up and hugged it to her chest. "Did you find anything else?" she asked.

Sadie hesitated, then extracted the coin from its hiding place. "Just this."

Bess peered at the coin but didn't seem surprised at all. "That's King Charles the third."

Sadie studied the image. "It is? How do you know?"

"It has his name on it." She giggled.

Sadie frowned. "Oh. I couldn't make it out." She laid the coin on the chest by her bed, suddenly worried she'd revealed too much. "I haven't told anyone else about this."

"Your secret is safe with me," Bess declared solemnly.

Sadie smiled. "Show me how you got the floorboard to come up."

"You have to tap it in just the right place." Bess pushed the board down and tapped the opposite end, making it spring open again.

"That's so much easier!"

Bess laughed. "How did you do it?"

"I used a hammer. I'm glad I didn't break it."

"I am too." Bess reached into the compartment under the floorboard and pulled out a small box.

"Where was that? I didn't notice it before!"

"There's another loose board. See? It swivels. The box was underneath." Bess opened the lid and removed a gold locket. There was an elegantly swirled "E" etched into the oval face.

Sadie was in awe. "That must have belonged to Elizabeth."

Bess nodded. "It's yours now." She placed it gently in Sadie's hand.

Sadie examined the locket carefully. There was an indention along the edge. She used her fingernail to pry it open and found a small lock of red hair inside. "Who could this have belonged to? Do you think it was Elizabeth's?"

Bess leaned in for a closer look. "Hmm. Would she have kept her own hair in a locket?"

"Probably not. Maybe it belonged to a boyfriend."

Bess covered her mouth with her hand. "You mean a suitor?" she whispered breathlessly.

Sadie laughed. "Sometimes I wonder if *you're* from this century."

Bess giggled. "Well, I think that's what they called them back then."

Sadie gently lifted the lock of hair and underneath was a tiny gold key. "This is interesting. I wonder what it's for?"

"It must be something important for her to wear it around her neck."

Sadie nodded. "I guess so." She glanced around the room. "Maybe the desk..." She tried the key in the lock, but it was too small.

"You'll just have to keep looking. But I have a feeling you'll find it sooner or later."

"Maybe it has something to do with the treasure." Sadie imagined finding more coins and felt a rush of excitement.

Bess looked doubtful. "I don't think so."

"Why not?"

"Would the treasure be secured with such a small lock?"

Sadie sighed, disappointed. "Oh yeah. You're probably right." She replaced the key and the lock of hair, snapped the locket closed, and put it over her head. "It's kind of heavy."

"After you've worn it a while, I think you'll barely notice."

"How'd you find the hole in the floor?"

Bess smiled. "I was playing with a puppy and happened to step in just right spot to make the floorboard come up."

"There was a dog here?"

"Oh!" Bess seemed flustered. "He shouldn't have been in the house, but he followed me, and I couldn't resist letting him come inside."

"He's your dog?"

"Sort of. He belonged to a friend, but I was his favorite person." She smiled wistfully. "My friend even said so."

Sadie had always wanted a dog, but her parents had both worked and they'd felt it wouldn't be fair to get one and then leave it all day while they were at work and school. And then, after the accident, her mother had needed help with even the simplest tasks. There'd been no time to even consider getting a pet.

"Maybe you can bring him over some time. I love dogs!"

Bess's face fell. "I can't. He's… gone."

Sadie was alarmed. "Did something happen to him?"

Beth shook her head. "No. The man who owned him went away."

"Thank goodness! I would've hated to hear that something happened to a puppy at Prophet House." Anxious to push that thought aside, she peered into the hole in the floor. "Is there anything else down there?" she asked, hoping for more coins.

"Just the locket and this." Bess handed the book back to Sadie.

Sadie ran her fingers over the gold letters on the cover. "I've only read the first entry. It's hard to make out the handwriting. Honestly, what she wrote was a little creepy. It reminded me of my own life right now."

Bess cocked her head. "Did it?"

Sadie pulled a dried flower from the middle of the book. It crumbled in her hand and bits floated to the floor. "I wonder what kind of flower this was."

"They were her favorite," Bess whispered.

"How do you know?"

"Why else would she have saved it?" Bess pointed out.

"There are so many flowers here. I have no idea what they all are."

"Elizabeth loved flowers. She had her own garden, but her mother refused to allow anyone to tend it after she died."

Sadie was taken aback. "How do you know that?"

Bess fidgeted with a strand of hair. "I heard someone say so."

"Who?"

Bess shrugged. "I don't remember now."

Sadie was disappointed that Bess didn't have more information, but a realization struck her. "I bet I know where it is!"

Bess had a curious expression on her face. "You do?"

"Yes! The abandoned garden behind the cellar! That has

to be it."

Bess smiled. "Yes. That must be it." She glanced down at the book. "You should read one page each day. It would be like you were living Elizabeth's life with her."

"I wish her writing wasn't so hard to read. It takes me a long time to get through it."

"Sadie!" her mom called from the first floor. "Henry's here."

Bess smiled. "I'll be going now, but I'll come back later, and we can explore some more."

In her usual fashion, Bess slipped into the wardrobe and pulled the door closed without another word. Sadie wished again that her new friend wasn't so peculiar. But in spite of her quirkiness, she had to admit that Bess was growing on her.

Sadie pulled on shorts and a lavender top, then brushed her hair until it fell in soft waves over her shoulders. When she got downstairs, Henry was sitting at the kitchen table with a plate of waffles in front of him. Sadie pulled a waffle from the toaster and ate it dry.

Meg put her hands on her hips. "How you do that is beyond me."

Sadie shrugged. "Syrup makes it soggy."

She plopped down in a chair and waited for Henry to finish. When his plate was finally clean, he looked at the toaster, clearly thinking about round two.

Sadie jumped up. "Maybe we should get going?"

"Oh yeah, sure." Henry pushed back his chair. "Thanks for the waffles, Mrs. Prophet."

"My pleasure, Henry." Meg smiled. She handed Sadie the key to the front door. "I may run out later, so you'll need this."

"How will you lock up?"

"I found a second key in one of the kitchen drawers."

"Okay." Sadie dropped the key in the pocket of her shorts. "I'll be back later."

Her mother nodded. "Have fun at the meeting."

Sadie turned around. "What meeting?"

"The reenactment meeting. Don't you remember?

Henry's mother told us about it yesterday as she was leaving. Henry says she's assigning roles today. And, according to her, it's *imperative* that we all participate."

Sadie could tell that her mom was trying to sound enthusiastic, but it was an act. She hated being forced into things.

"Aren't you coming too then?"

"She said I didn't need to. She'll bring my costume over later."

Sadie frowned. "If she's bringing your costume by later, can't I skip it and let her bring mine too?"

"No. Your attendance is required." Meg gave her an apologetic look.

"That doesn't make sense," Sadie huffed.

"Whether it makes sense or not, you're still going." She put the toaster in a cabinet and gave Sadie a quick hug. "Let me know how it goes."

As soon as they were out the door, Sadie plopped down on one of the stone steps and refused to budge. "Why didn't you say something about the meeting when we were together yesterday?"

Henry sat down beside her. "I didn't think about it. Besides, your mom said you already knew."

"And I have to go? What if I don't?"

"My mom will freak out. Trust me. You don't want to see that." He shifted his weight uncomfortably. "She's pretty worried. She's hoping that if Mr. Endicott sees you all in the reenactment… you know, the real Prophet family…"

It hit Sadie again just how much was riding on Mr. Endicott's opinion. She stood up. "Fine. I'll go to the meeting. She'll probably want me to play Elizabeth. I guess that won't be so bad."

Henry brightened considerably. "Great! And you'll get to meet some of the kids you'll be in school with. My best friend and his sister are always in the reenactment. You'll like them."

As they ambled along the main road into town, it didn't take long for the idea of playing the daughter of Nathaniel and Sarah to grow on her. It might actually be fun. Her dad could be Nathaniel and her mother would be perfect as Sarah. After all, they were "real Prophets."

"What are you smiling about?" Henry asked.

Sadie felt her cheeks flush. "Nothing." She tried to think of something else to say to fill the awkward silence, and the shadowy figure on her balcony popped into her head. "Henry, have you ever seen anything weird at Prophet House?"

He frowned. "Like what?"

Sadie wasn't sure how to ask him if he'd ever seen a ghost. "I don't know. Maybe someone or something that you weren't sure was real?"

"Oh." He seemed amused. "You mean ghosts? Nope. It just seems like a regular old house to me. Why? Did you see something?"

"Not really. At least, I don't think so."

He kicked a bit of sand from the side of the road onto her shoe. "Want to go to the beach after the meeting?"

"You have the attention span of a four-year-old." She shook off the sand. "Aren't you curious why I asked?"

Henry shrugged. "You said you didn't see anything."

Sadie shot him an exasperated look. "Never mind." A little sand had gotten into her shoe, so she shook it out. "There is something I want to do after the meeting though. I'd like to see some of the neighborhoods around here—houses that aren't in town."

He raised his eyebrows. "You want to look at houses? I don't think I'm ready for that kind of commitment."

Sadie punched him lightly in the ribs. "Real funny. I'm not kidding. I want to see if I can find out where Bess lives. It can't be that far from here. Otherwise, she wouldn't be able to come and go so often."

"Why do you care where she lives?"

Sadie shrugged. She wasn't sure how to answer that, because she didn't know why she couldn't get it off her mind. On the one hand, it was none of her business where Bess lived. But Sadie couldn't shake the feeling that there was something off about the girl, something more than just being a little odd. Maybe she was in trouble and needed help. Or maybe, she was–
–"

"Are you trying to chew your lip off?" Henry asked.

Sadie snapped out of her reverie. "What?" She reached up and touched her lower lip to make sure it wasn't bleeding. "I didn't know I was…"

"You do that a lot."

Sadie shrugged. "My dad chews his lip when he's thinking too."

"So it's a family trait?" He grinned.

Sadie looked down at the road. "I guess."

"It's okay." He nudged her shoulder. "Look, if you want to know where Bess lives, why don't you just ask her?"

"I did… once. She wouldn't say anything except that it's not far. I think she might be ashamed of it or something."

Henry furrowed his brow. "There's an old housing development down the road on the other side of the woods that's pretty run-down. It's off of highway 70, but it's easy to get to and only about a fifteen-minute walk from your house."

Sadie brightened. "Great! Let's go after the meeting."

Henry flashed a dimpled smile and gave her a thumbs up. Bess's remark about him being handsome popped into Sadie's head and she looked away before he could notice she was blushing again.

CHAPTER 8

The reenactment meeting was being held at the middle school ball field. By the time they arrived, there were at least fifty people there. Several kids about their age were sitting on the bleachers. When Sadie walked up, they stopped their conversations and stared at her.

Henry spoke up. “Hey, guys.”

Sadie smiled awkwardly.

A tall boy with a wide grin was sitting on the bottom step. Henry pointed him out. “This is Cody.” Two other boys were on the top step taking turns shoving each other and trying not to fall backwards off the bleachers. Henry laughed. “That’s Seth and James. They’re on the Lacrosse team with me.”

Sadie recognized them as the boys who had nearly run them down on their bicycles the previous day.

Henry pointed to a pleasant looking girl with black hair that was pulled into a long braid down her back. She had a book in her lap but looked up when they approached. “That’s Cody’s sister, Melanie…”

Melanie smiled warmly and started to say something—but was interrupted by another girl who jumped up and made her way down the bleachers. “Henry, we’ve been waiting for you!” When she got to the last step, she pretended to need help down. Henry took her hand and helped her.

The girl pushed her pale blond hair out of her face and smiled, but it didn’t look genuine. “I’m Henry’s friend, Stevie. It’s short for Stephanie.”

Sadie cleared her throat. "I'm Sadie. It's short for Sarah." Her voice broke on the last syllable and Stevie snickered.

"Hmm… Aren't there the same number of letters though? So, is it really shorter?" Stevie smirked at her own joke.

Henry rolled his eyes. "Cut it out, Stevie."

"If she's planning to hang out with us, she needs to be able to take a joke. Don't you think so, Sadie-not-short-for-Sarah?"

Sadie wished Zoey was there. She'd have probably flattened Stevie by now. Sadie's eyes narrowed. "Of course I can take a joke, Steve."

Stevie gritted her teeth and glared at Sadie. "It's Stevie."

"Oh. My mistake."

Stevie waved as if brushing away Sadie's comment and turned her attention back to Henry. "You missed your mom handing out parts. I'm playing Elizabeth in the reenactment this year, so we'll have plenty of time to hang out." She looked at Sadie and gave her another fake smile. "I'm afraid your part will be in the house the whole time."

Sadie frowned. "My part?"

Stevie chattered on. "Since you're one of the Prophets, they might have asked you to play Elizabeth if your hair wasn't dark brown. You're too short too." Stevie straightened her back. She was a good four inches taller than Sadie. "All the Prophets were tall." She shook her head in mock sympathy. "You don't look like her at all."

Sadie could feel the anger building up as blood rushed to her cheeks. "According to some people, I look like my great-great-great grandmother, Sarah Prophet."

Stevie snickered. "Maybe you should play my mother then."

Henry looked between the two girls as if expecting them to come to blows any minute. "We better go see my mom. We…uh… can't stay long. I promised I'd help Sadie… do some stuff." He grabbed Sadie's hand and practically dragged her away.

Sadie looked back at a smug Stevie. "Just so you know, most of the Prophets had red hair, not blond. So you don't look like Elizabeth either!" As soon as they were out of earshot, Sadie turned on him. "She's one of the friends you wanted me to meet? Stev*ie?*"

Henry held up his hands. "She can be hard to take, but I've never seen her act that snotty! I swear."

"That girl is not going to play my great-great-aunt!"

"Isn't it three greats? No, wait…I think it's four…" He made a goofy face.

"You're not funny, Henry."

Since his feeble attempt to lighten the mood hadn't worked, he abandoned the effort and sighed. "Look. We'll talk to my mom. It's probably a mistake."

Mrs. Northrup was flipping through her notebook when they walked up. "I'm missing a page!" She seemed almost frantic and pointed to a cluster of people standing about twenty feet away, murmuring amongst themselves. "That whole group over there wants their assignments and I can't find where I wrote them down!"

"Mom, did you tell Stevie she could be Elizabeth Prophet?"

"What? Oh, yes, I did. Her father has been pestering me for over a month."

"What about Sadie?"

She glanced at Sadie as if seeing her for the first time. "Oh. Hello, Miss Prophet." She flipped through her notes and found Sadie's name. "The only part left for a girl your age is Elizabeth's maid."

Sadie's mouth dropped open. "*Her maid*?" She glanced over at Stevie, who was watching them, a wicked grin on her face.

Mrs. Northrup took out a whistle and blew it. Most of the people present stopped talking. "I'm so sorry, but I seem to be missing some assignments. If those of you who have not been given a role will stop by my shop later today, I'll tell you which part you have."

There was a general murmur in the crowd as Mrs. Northrup took off to find the missing page.

Sadie stood in stunned silence. Henry's mother didn't

want her to play her own ancestor, Elizabeth Prophet. She wanted her to be a maid! Stevie's maid!

Henry looked like he wanted to fall into a hole. "We'll talk to my mom again. I promise."

Sadie glanced over at Stevie again. She was chatting happily with several other kids. She noticed Sadie staring at her and whispered something to her entourage. Some of them looked her way and smirked.

Sadie gritted her teeth. "I'm not playing her maid for a whole week. And I'm not that short. I'm almost 5'2"."

"Don't pay any attention to her. She's just trying to get a rise out of you." Henry shoved his hands in his pockets. "I'm sorry about the maid thing."

"I'm not doing it. I don't care if your mother doesn't like it. She can find someone else." She caught a glimpse of Mr. Endicott through the crowd. He looked utterly out of place in his dark suit and tie. She nudged Henry and pointed. "I don't care if he doesn't like it either."

Henry turned and looked. "That's weird. He never comes to these meetings."

Sadie ignored his comment. "Seriously. What's the point of being a *real Prophet* if I don't even get to play my own ancestor in the reenactment?"

Realizing that he'd been noticed, Mr. Endicott strode over. "You must be excited about the reenactment, Miss Prophet." His mouth curled up on the edges just enough to be considered a smile, but the rest of his face remained expressionless. "So… you and your parents are still planning to live at Prophet House?"

"Yes, we are."

A bead of perspiration trickled down his forehead. It was at least eighty degrees outside. Sadie wondered why he didn't take off his coat.

He watched her without blinking, even after the bead of sweat rolled into his eye. "Any idea how long you plan to stay?"

Sadie felt like she was being interrogated. She set her jaw. "Maybe forever."

"I see." He finally blinked, but his expression didn't

change. “In that case, I’ll be anxious to meet your parents.” He studied her for a moment. “I believe Henry’s mother was right. You look a great deal like the original Sarah Prophet.”

“That’s what I hear.”

A man with a broad smile bounded over, grabbed Mr. Endicott’s hand, and shook it vigorously. “William! It’s wonderful to see you again.” He glanced at Henry and Sadie. “Am I interrupting something?”

“Mr. Endicott extracted his hand and wiped it on his jacket. “I was just telling Miss Prophet that I’m anxious to meet her mother and father.”

“Oh yes indeed!” The other man exclaimed. “We’re all eager to meet them!”

Sadie didn’t mean to speak up, but she couldn’t help herself. “We just got our parts. Apparently, I’m playing a maid in my ancestor’s house and Henry’s playing…” She looked at Henry pointedly.

“I’m Nathaniel the second,” he mumbled.

Sadie’s mouth dropped open. “You are?”

Henry nodded.

Mr. Endicott flashed the other man a disapproving look. “Now who do you suppose is playing the Prophets’ daughter?”

“I—I, uh…” The man cleared his throat. “I believe it’s… Well, Mrs. Northrup and I thought a local girl…”

Mr. Endicott gave him a disdainful look. “That’s what I thought.”

Henry backed away from the two men and motioned for Sadie to follow. “We were just leaving. I guess we’ll see you later, Mr. Endicott.”

Mr. Endicott didn’t acknowledge the comment, as he continued to stare down the other man.

Once they were out of earshot, Sadie asked, “Who was that guy with Mr. Endicott?”

“Mr. Winslow, the mayor. He’s also Stevie’s dad.”

Sadie huffed. “That explains a lot.”

They didn’t speak on the walk back through town. When they turned onto the road to Prophet House, Henry broke the silence.

"I'm sorry Stevie was such a jerk. She only got the part because of her dad. We'll tell my mom you won't be in the reenactment if you're not Elizabeth."

"That makes *me* sound like the jerk." She kicked a pebble to the side of the road. "I should just skip the whole thing."

Henry frowned. "I wouldn't if I were you. Mr. Endicott expects to see your whole family. I think you need to be there. Otherwise, he might—"

"Stop paying to keep our house up?" Sadie interrupted. "Maybe it wouldn't be such a bad thing if we had to move back to Davenport." It was her anger talking. If they moved back, Sadie's life would go back to normal, but so would her mother's. And that would be awful.

"You want to leave?"

Sadie sighed. "No, I don't. I'll be in the reenactment. And I don't have to be Elizabeth. The truth is, Bess should play Elizabeth. She's perfect for the part. Most of the Prophets had red hair like hers. And she already has the dress. Plus, she's nice and knows a lot about my family."

Henry stopped walking. "Sure, but you'd have to get my mom to agree. Then someone would have to tell Stevie. I wouldn't want to be anywhere around when that happened." He stopped walking. "Stevie's whole family is pretty much the same—totally stuck on themselves. But Stevie's the worst."

"She was jealous."

"Yeah. She always has to be the center of attention. You're Sadie Prophet. She can't stand that everyone knows who you are."

Sadie shook her head. "That's not why Stevie's jealous."

"What do you mean?"

"Can you really be that dense? She's jealous because she likes you. You know, *likes* you."

Henry stared at her. "Eww! She acts like she's better than everybody else because her dad's the mayor and her parents own the biggest boat in the harbor. They take trips to Europe every summer, then bore everyone else with the details for weeks afterwards. All Stevie talks about is how much money they have.

I can't stand being around her for more than a minute."

"And you thought I'd be friends with her? Thanks a lot."

"Of course not. I wanted you to meet the others—Cody, Seth, and James. And Melanie's really nice too."

"Are Seth and James the guys who tried to run us down?"

"They were just trying to get your attention. They're not like that usually. And I think you'll like Cody and Melanie."

"Oh… they did seem okay. None of them talked to me though."

"Stevie didn't give them a chance. Believe me, none of us like hanging out with her."

"Okay, Henry." She smiled. "I'm still not playing her maid, but I'm over the rest of it. Let's go do that 'stuff' you were talking about."

"Remind me what stuff we're doing again?"

"I want to find out where Bess lives."

"What's your plan if we find her?"

Sadie shrugged. "I don't have a plan. I just want her to know I'm her friend. I don't care what her house is like. And maybe I can talk her into being in the reenactment with us. That might actually make it tolerable."

"Ouch. You know, I'll be there."

Sadie giggled. "Sorry. As long as you ditch Stevie, I'll hang out with you too."

"Thanks." He grinned.

"You said there was an old housing development close by."

He nodded. "Yeah. It's not far."

"Okay. Lead on, Nathaniel the second."

CHAPTER 9

They continued past Prophet House and walked less than a quarter of a mile until they came to a dirt road that veered off to the left, past an old abandoned farmhouse and field.

"This used to be the Ewings' farm, but they moved to Canada or somewhere like that to be close to their grandkids. At least that's what my mom said."

Sadie had too much on her mind to care who the Ewings were or why they'd moved, but she nodded anyway. When Henry looked back at her, a strand of hair fell down his forehead over one eye like before. She had to admit it was kind of adorable. *I guess you're right, Bess. He is handsome.*

"What are you smiling about?"

Sadie felt blood rush to her cheeks. "N–nothing…"

Just past the farm, they took a well-worn path into a stretch of dense woods. It wasn't long before they came out the other side into a neighborhood of old houses in various states of disrepair. The closest was a weather-beaten wooden structure with peeling yellow paint and faded blue shutters.

An old man was standing over a wooden work bench in the carport. Years in the sun had showered his deeply lined face with freckles. When they approached, he looked up and smiled. "What can I do for you youngsters?"

"We're looking for Bess. Do you know her?" Sadie asked.

"Sure, I do." He waved them over.

"We're trying to find her. Can you tell us where she

lives?"

"Bessie…" He shook his head. "I haven't thought about her in a while. Used to come around here all the time, looking for handouts."

Sadie frowned. "Handouts?"

"Yes, ma'am. That girl was always hungry."

Sadie was mortified. "She didn't have anything to eat at her house?"

When he smiled, there was a gap where his two front teeth had been. "Lord yes, she was fed plenty good at home. But you know how it is. They're always ready for scraps."

Sadie looked quizzically at Henry.

Henry spoke up, "Where is she now? Can you show us the house?"

"Oh, she ain't at the house no more." He pointed a gnarled finger. "She's in that field over there."

Sadie and Henry exchanged looks. Maybe the old guy's mind had taken a turn.

But Sadie was still determined to get more information from him. "Maybe you could show us where she used to live. You know… before the field."

"It wouldn't matter, kids. She died over a year ago. Hit by a car right out there on Highway 70."

Sadie's knees felt as if they were about to give way, so she lowered herself onto a stack of wood next to the work bench. *Oh my God...Bess* is *a ghost!* She looked at Henry. His mouth was hanging open. "Are you s—sure it was B—Bess who was hit by a car?" Sadie stuttered.

"Oh, I'm dead sure." He chuckled at his own play on words. "Don't fret too much about it, girl. She lived a good long life. I think she was close to eighteen years old when she died.

"Eighteen? I thought she was—"

He rambled on. "Marnie, that's her momma, threw her a grand wake and we roasted wieners in her honor. That dog sure did love wieners. She could put away a dozen at a time."

Sadie jumped to her feet, almost dizzy from relief. "You're talking about a *dog*?"

"Of course. Bessie was the sweetest little golden

retriever you ever met. Everybody around here was crazy about her."

Henry bent double, holding his stomach and laughing so hard he could barely breathe.

"It's not funny!" Sadie scolded.

The old man raised his sparse eyebrows. "You kids know something I don't?"

Sadie tried not to give in to the urge to join Henry. "We're—"

Henry choked out, "We're looking for a *girl* named Bess."

"A girl?" The old guy scratched his white beard thoughtfully. "Oh well, that's different."

Sadie shot Henry a threatening look and he pulled himself together. She turned her attention back to the old man. "She's about my age. Do you know her?"

"Nope. Don't know a girl named Bess, and I know everybody around here and most of the folks in town, if I do say so myself. Sorry, kids."

Tears stung Sadie's eyes. Embarrassed, she brushed them away.

The old man looked at her kindly. "Don't be sad, little girl. You'll find your friend."

Feeling awkward about her overreaction, Sadie thanked him, then marched back down the road and into the woods without looking back. Sufficiently recovered, Henry followed her at a safe distance.

"Slow down, Sadie!"

She spun around. "That whole thing was pointless. You've lived here all your life and you don't know her. That man, who apparently knows *everybody*, doesn't know her. She doesn't go to school. I don't know her last name or where she lives. I don't know anything about her. I'm starting to wonder if I've made her up. Maybe I'm nuts."

"Yeah, that's it. You're nuts." He grinned.

Sadie shot him a withering look and started walking again.

He caught up to her and put his hand on her arm. "Look,

I know you didn't make her up. Maybe she's new around here too. You're just not asking the right questions. Next time she shows up, don't let her leave and call me. I bet I can get some answers."

"How am I supposed to do that? Once she decides she's going, you can't stop her."

"Fake a seizure or something."

"Fake a seizure? That's your idea?"

Henry's eyes rolled up, and he collapsed on the ground.

Sadie stood over him with her hands on her hips. "That's the best you can do?"

Henry rubbed the back of his head. "This ground is hard."

She snickered. "Serves you right."

He sat up. "Somebody around here has a cat."

"How do you know?"

"Don't ask."

Sadie wrinkled her nose. "Eww!"

Somewhere behind them, a twig snapped. Sadie looked back just in time to see a dark figure disappear behind a tree.

She grabbed Henry's arm and pulled him to his feet. "Someone's following us!"

Henry turned around and shrugged. "Lots of people cut through the woods."

"Then why did he duck behind a tree so I wouldn't see him?"

Henry looked back again. There was no sign of movement. "I don't see anybody."

A shiver shot up Sadie's spine and the back of her neck prickled. "Let's get out of here. I have a weird feeling." She headed down the path again with Henry behind her.

There was a rustling noise behind them. Henry looked over his shoulder and stopped suddenly. "I think you're right. I saw someone through the trees, and whoever it was didn't want us to see him."

They took off running and didn't stop until they were out of the woods and almost back to the house.

Henry grabbed Sadie's arm. "Why would someone be

following you?"

Sadie tried to catch her breath. "How should I know? Maybe they're following you, not me."

"I've lived here my whole life. I've been through the woods a ton of times. This has never happened before."

"Okay then, maybe it was some random creeper and we just happened to be in the wrong place at the wrong time." It was better than admitting that someone was skulking around after her. That was a frightening thought.

"You think I'm a wuss now, don't you? Running away like that."

Sadie met his blue eyes and felt her face flush. Even though she barely knew him, she was developing a huge crush on Henry Northrup. She wondered what he would say if he knew. Or worse, what would his mother say?

"Well?" He was waiting for some sort of response from her.

Sadie looked away. "I don't think you're a wuss. What if he was a murderous psycho? Besides, I ran too."

He grinned. "Next time we go on a Bess hunt, we'll take along some protection. I'm pretty dangerous with a lacrosse stick."

She giggled, hoping he hadn't noticed her flushed cheeks. "Great. That'll make me feel perfectly safe."

"Do you want to go into town now? We can look for her later."

Sadie glanced up the driveway. Her mom's car was gone again. "Why don't we go to my house instead? I want to show you something Bess showed me."

"Sure. What is it?"

She looked over her shoulder, but didn't see anyone. Relieved, she headed toward the house. "How do you feel about secret passageways?"

CHAPTER 10

Sadie pulled the key from her pocket and opened the front door. "Let's see if my mom left a note."

There were fresh chocolate chip cookies on the kitchen counter, along with a note that said her mother was running some errands and would be back soon.

Henry helped himself to a cookie. "Your mom's nice."

Sadie laughed. "She *is* nice, but she's also scared of your mom. I think she wants us to be friends."

Henry shoved the last of the cookie into his mouth and grabbed another one. "How about you? Do you want us to be friends?"

Sadie nearly choked on her cookie and instantly felt her cheeks go bright red again. This was getting to be a habit around him.

Henry patted her on the back. "Don't die or anything. I was just asking."

Sadie regained some semblance of composure. "Get over yourself, Henry."

He clutched his chest. "Ouch."

"Ugh! We can be friends, okay?" She wished he'd wipe that grin off his face. "Do you want to see the secret passageway or not?"

He took a third cookie and bit off half of it. "Sure, let's see it."

When they reached the third-floor landing, Sadie grabbed Henry's arm. "Do you hear that?" she whispered. A thumping noise was coming from the direction of her room. It sounded like footsteps.

He nodded. "Maybe your mom is back."

"It's Bess," Sadie said softly.

She motioned for him to follow her as she tiptoed down the hall. Holding her finger to her lips, Sadie slowly pushed open the door to her room.

The glass doors to the balcony were open, but no one was there.

"You can come out now," Sadie said loudly.

Silence.

She walked over to the wardrobe. "Cut it out, Bess. I know you're in there. I want you to meet Henry."

Sadie peeked inside, but there were only her clothes and a few boxes. She crawled through the panel into the attic, but other than the boxes and chests that had been there before, it was empty. This whole thing with Bess showing up and disappearing was getting irritating. As soon as Sadie caught up to her, she intended to put a stop to all the sneaking around.

She crawled back into the wardrobe and rummaged through a pile of clothes on the floor. Since Everleigh was on the coast and storms were common, Sadie's dad had bought a dozen flashlights and made a point that every room should have one. Sadie had stuck hers somewhere in the wardrobe. She found it under a stack of sweaters that she hadn't gotten around to putting away yet. She motioned for Henry to follow her.

"Bess is probably going down the stairs to the cellar."

"Why wouldn't she have answered you?" he asked, eyeing the narrow opening. "You really want me to crawl through there?"

"It's not that bad."

"There has to be another way. A door would be nice."

Sadie was getting impatient. "Come on. Are you claustrophobic or something?"

"I didn't think I was…" he said nervously.

Sadie crouched at the opening and reached out her hand. "Here. I'll help you."

Henry held his breath and scrambled through after her,

letting out a sigh of relief when he tumbled out onto the attic floor. "Okay, now I bet you think I'm a wuss," he muttered.

"Yeah, now I do." She grabbed his arm and pulled him to his feet. The attic was in disarray. The boxes and trunks had all been moved and some were standing open as if someone had rummaged through them.

"Someone's been in here looking for something." Sadie whispered. "It wasn't like this before."

"Maybe it was your mom."

Sadie shook her head. "She's allergic to dust. She'd never come up here."

"Who then?"

"It must have been Bess. I heard her when we were on the stairs a minute ago. We have to hurry."

"You don't know for sure that it was her," Henry pointed out.

"Of course it was her. Who else would it be? One of the ghosts?"

As they made their way to the other side of the attic, he spotted the door to their left and pointed. "Unless I'm wrong, that's a door."

"So?"

"So why did we have to crawl through the hole?"

Sadie rolled her eyes. "Are you gonna be this big a wuss all the time?"

Henry grumbled something Sadie couldn't make out as she felt around the panels on the far side of the attic, looking for the crack that marked the opening to the stairs.

"I know it's here somewhere..."

"What are you looking for? Another hole to crawl through?"

Sadie ignored him and continued to run her hands along the wall until she found it. She gave the panel a nudge and the door creaked open.

"Whoa! Where does this go?" Henry asked.

"The cellar."

Navigating the narrow stairs was much easier with the flashlight. Sadie practically sprinted down them, with Henry close behind. She forgot to tell him about the broken step, and when they came to it Henry stumbled and fell into her, practically causing them both to careen the rest of the way down.

"I think I broke my foot!" he moaned as he hobbled behind her.

"Shh! I just heard something."

At the bottom of the stairs, the door was standing open. Sadie heard a shuffling sound, as if someone was trapsing across the dirt floor. She practically sprang through the door into the cellar, her eyes darting around the cavernous space. Once again, no one was there. "Where'd she go?" Sadie murmured.

Henry rubbed his sore foot. "Why would she run off?"

"I don't know. Why can't she just be a normal friend?" Everything seemed to crash in on her at once. Her mom's accident, moving from the home she'd lived in most of her life, leaving her friends…Sadie felt like crying.

"Hey." Henry put his arm around her shoulder. "Don't let her get to you."

Henry's kind gesture pushed her over the edge and she burst into tears. Utterly humiliated at making such a spectacle of herself, she tried to walk away.

"Wait. Tell me what's wrong."

She wiped her face on the hem of her shirt. "I miss my old friends. I could really count on them, you know? We moved here because my mom…"

"What?'

Sadie sat on an overturned bucket and put her face in her hands. Since there were no other empty buckets, Henry rolled a wheelbarrow over and tried to get comfortable inside.

Sadie took a ragged breath. If she wanted him as a friend, she might as well treat him like one. She looked up tearfully. "My mom had a bad car wreck near our old house a little over a year ago. We weren't sure she was gonna make it. She had to learn to walk again. But the worst part was… she was three months pregnant. My parents figured they weren't having any more kids after me. When they found out about the baby, they were so happy. We all were."

Sadie wondered what their lives would have been like

with a little baby to cuddle. Her little brother or sister would have been nearly four months old now. "I would've loved being a big sister…" She said quietly. Fresh tears stung her eyes. "Mom had a miscarriage because of the accident. She didn't find out until two weeks later when she finally woke up. It was awful when they told her…" Sadie pictured her mother's face when the doctor broke the news and felt a pain in the pit of her stomach. "Every time we left the house, we had to pass the place where it happened. It got to the point where Mom wouldn't go anywhere. Dad thought that if we moved here and started over, she'd be better. She'd be happy again."

"I'm really sorry," Henry said softly.

Sadie wiped her dripping nose on her sleeve. "I should probably change shirts."

"It's okay." He smiled. "Feeling better?"

"Yeah. A little, I guess. Sorry to unload on you like that."

He smiled. "Any time."

This was the first time she'd talked about the accident, or the aftermath, with anyone since her mother came home from the hospital. She felt as if a weight had been lifted off her chest. She wiped her eyes and sniffed. "You're okay, Henry."

"You're not so bad yourself. I wouldn't climb through a tiny hole in the wall for just anyone."

There was a sudden noise to their left that sounded like something heavy hitting the floor. Sadie jumped up in time to see Owen picking up a muddy shovel. His face was bright red, as if alarmed over being discovered. "What are you two doing down here?" he demanded.

"N—nothing," Sadie stuttered. "What are you doing here?"

"Came to get the shovel." He stepped toward them.

"What do you need a shovel for?" Sadie blurted out.

Owen stared at her, an odd look on his face. "I got some things to dig up, miss."

Sadie pressed him. "What things?"

Owen took another step toward them, holding the shovel so that the blade was pointed toward them. "Stumps mostly."

"We were just leaving," Henry said quickly. He tried to

jump out of the wheelbarrow, but it flipped over, and he somehow ended up underneath it.

Sadie grabbed his arm and helped him up. "Henry, are you all right?"

"I'll live," he groaned.

"You're bleeding!"

"Crap. You're right." His elbow was covered in blood and it was running down his arm.

Owen pointed toward the cellar door. "You kids better go take care of that."

Sadie pulled Henry out the door, her heart pounding. "Did you see his face?" she whispered breathlessly once they were outside. "It's obvious we caught him doing something he shouldn't be doing. Why does he need a shovel all the time?"

Henry pulled off his T-shirt and wrapped it around the wound. "Caretakers use shovels sometimes. Duh."

"Well maybe he didn't want to tell us what he's digging up because…" Sadie stopped herself. She wasn't sure if she should say anything to Henry about looking for the treasure yet. He still didn't know she'd found the coin. "Nothing. He's just acting weird. That's all."

"So are you." Henry groaned. "Can we just deal with the fact that I'm trying not to bleed to death?"

"You'll be fine. My mom keeps a first aid kit under the sink in the kitchen."

Henry grimaced. "I might need more than a Band-Aid."

"Wait 'til you see all the stuff in there. We could outfit a trauma unit."

Once upstairs, Sadie removed a large plastic bin from the cabinet and pulled out rolls of gauze and tape. Henry stuck his arm in the sink and gritted his teeth while Sadie washed the cut with soap and water.

"You don't need stitches. It's not that deep." She applied a gauze bandage, wrapped his arm, and taped it securely in place. "There. I think you'll live now."

Henry admired her handiwork and whistled. "How'd you learn to do that?"

Sadie shrugged. "I used to change my mom's bandages

all the time after the accident."

He pulled his T-shirt back over his head but there were steaks of blood all down the front of it.

"I can't walk through town like this. I'll make the local news."

"Hold on." Sadie ran upstairs and came back with one of her dad's T-shirts.

Henry tossed the bloody one into the trash can by the back door before putting on her dad's. "I have long sleeve shirts at home. I just need to change before my mom sees me." He held up his arm. "I'd rather not have to explain this."

"What's the big deal?"

Henry grunted. "You don't know my mom. She freaks out if I get hurt. Once I skinned my knee in a lacrosse game and when she saw I was bleeding, she ran onto the field to make sure I was okay. It was horrible. The rest of the team still teases me about it."

"Yikes." Sadie grimaced.

"Come on. There's a back way to get to my house."

They headed into town but took a different route that wouldn't take them past his mother's store. Once they turned onto Henry's street, they ducked between two houses and jogged through the backyards. The Northrups' house had a screened porch on the back with a door that squeaked loudly when they opened it. Henry cringed and waited a moment, then pulled a key from his pocket and opened the back door into the kitchen. There didn't seem to be anyone home.

"My room's down the hall. We can—"

They heard someone unlock the front door. His mother called out, "Henry, are you home?"

Henry held a finger to his lips. Neither of them moved a muscle until they heard Mrs. Northrup's high heels clicking across the entry hall. They crouched behind the table and waited for her to pass the door to the kitchen.

"What now?" Henry mouthed.

"Wait here!" Sadie whispered. She sprinted lightly out the back, ran around the house, and rang the front doorbell.

Mrs. Northrup answered the door wearing her familiar

pinched expression. "Well, Miss Prophet. This is an unexpected pleasure."

"I just came by to see if… um…" Out of the corner of her eye, Sadie caught a glimpse of Henry sneaking down the hall. If his mother had turned around, she'd have seen him. Sadie tried to picture exactly how that scenario would play out and had an alarming urge to laugh out loud.

Mrs. Northrup cocked her head. "Are you all right, Miss Prophet?"

Sadie cleared her throat. "Oh yeah. I'm fine."

Mrs. Northrup's eyes narrowed. "Are you here to see Henry?"

"No!" Sadie answered a little too emphatically. "You know, we have all those ropes and stands still at the house. Do you want me to bring them by?"

Mrs. Northrup eyed her suspiciously. "I'm sure they'd be too much for you to carry by yourself."

"Henry can help me," Sadie blurted out before she could stop herself.

Mrs. Northrup frowned. "Henry's not home."

"Oh. Right."

Her expression softened. "I have most of the costumes for the reenactment here. Would you like to get yours now? It may need to be taken up. Stevie Winslow had the role last year and she's a little taller than you are."

Sadie resisted the urge to say something snippy. "Um… I can get it later. I'm kind of in a hurry. It was nice seeing you, Mrs. Northrup."

Mrs. Northrup stared after her, a quizzical look on her face. Sadie walked nearly a block down the road, then pretended to get something out of her shoe while discreetly glancing back toward Henry's house. When she was sure his mother had closed the door, she made her way back and found Henry climbing out a window. He was wearing a long-sleeve T-shirt to cover his bandaged elbow.

"That was close!" he whispered.

"Your mother hates me." Sadie sighed. "I can tell."

"She doesn't hate you. She just loves Prophet House and

wants the town to have it."

"It belongs to my family."

"I know. But try to see it from her perspective. She's been working there for years, planting flowers, printing brochures, giving tours. She dragged us around to every antique store within two hundred miles, looking for things to stick in that house. It's been a big part of her life."

"I guess I didn't think of it that way," Sadie said, feeling an unexpected pang for Mrs. Northrup. "I'm sorry."

"Just give her a chance, okay?"

Sadie smiled. "Okay."

"Great! That's settled. How does ice cream sound?"

"We never had lunch."

"The ice cream place sells hot dogs too. I grabbed some money when we were at my house."

"You have money?"

"I get paid when I make deliveries for my mom."

"In that case, ice cream and hot dogs sound good."

Everleigh had only one ice cream shop, called What's the Scoop? According to the plaque on the door, it was housed in an old print shop built in the early 1800s. And apparently, it was the place to be on a summer afternoon. People were milling around on the sidewalk, waiting to get in. It took thirty minutes to get their hot dogs and even longer to get two scoops of rocky road in a waffle cone. They found an open bench along the edge of the park and sat down.

From behind them came a girl's voice. "What part did you get, Sadie?" It was Melanie.

Sadie grimaced, "Elizabeth's maid."

"No! That's awful. You should be Elizabeth, not Stevie! She was gloating when you left the meeting. It was pretty sickening. I bet she got the part because of her dad."

"Obviously," Henry chimed in. "Where's Cody?"

Melanie rolled her eyes. "In line for his second ice cream." She wedged herself in between Sadie and Henry, her eyes sparkling with excitement. "Guess what!"

Henry wriggled free and plopped down on the grass in front of the bench. "What, Mel?"

“I’m gonna be the printer’s apprentice this year.” She beamed. “It’s always been a boy, but I pointed out that making it a boy every year was discrimination.” She giggled. “Sorry, Henry, but your mother’s face turned bright red! Then she sputtered about Everleigh being all about fairness, blah, blah blah. It was awesome! So now I’m the apprentice.” Melanie smiled smugly. “I get to work the old printer.”

“That’s so great! Maybe you can talk to her about my part too.” Sadie laughed.

“Sure! It’s ridiculous that you don’t have a better part. It’s your family!”

Cody walked up, shoving the last of his ice cream cone in his mouth. “Did Melanie tell you she took my part?” he mumbled, trying to swallow.

“Whatever you got is better than my part,” Sadie moaned. “I’m supposed to follow Stevie around all day. I’m her maid.”

Cody’s mouth fell open. “Really? That sucks.”

“Yeah. Melanie’s gonna get me out of it though.”

Melanie grinned. “I’m on it, sister.”

Sadie took the last bite of her ice cream cone. “I think I’d better be heading home. I still have to unpack.” She rubbed her stomach. “I hope my mom isn’t cooking a big meal tonight. I couldn’t hold another bite.”

Henry shook his head. “Not me. I can always eat.”

Sadie gave him a wry smile. “No kidding.”

After saying their goodbyes to Melanie and Cody, Henry walked with her to the edge of town. “Do you want to do something tomorrow?” he asked.

“Sure. We can explore my house. Bess said there are all kinds of secret places.”

She was thinking about the coin, safely hidden under her pillow. If there were other secret compartments scattered all over the house, they could contain coins as well.

“Sounds good! I’ll come over after my deliveries.”

Sadie watched him jog back toward his house.

The breeze from the ocean rustled her hair and brought with it the subtle scent of magnolias in bloom. As she ambled down the row of quaint clapboard houses, she passed an elderly woman watering her flowers while a little dog ran back and forth through the spray. When Sadie paused to watch him, the woman looked up and waved. Sadie smiled and waved back before continuing her walk home.

It dawned on her that the first Sarah and Nathaniel had walked this same road into town almost two hundred years ago. They'd listened to the same sound of the waves breaking against the shore, heard seagulls overhead, and breathed in the delicate scent of magnolias. It wasn't hard to imagine how it was back then since so little had changed. *Okay, I admit it*, she thought. *Everleigh is growing on me…*

Flowers bloomed along the edge of the main road back to Prophet House. Sadie picked a handful of pink and white blossoms to make a centerpiece for the kitchen table. As she neared the bend in the road, about a block from the house, she had a sudden uneasy feeling that someone was behind her. She turned around quickly, expecting to see Henry, but no one was there. Attempting to ignore the knot forming in her stomach, she kept walking. A couple of minutes later, she heard a twig snap in the wooded area to her left, just before her driveway. Sadie peered into the trees and thought she detected movement. It was probably nothing, she told herself. But the hairs stood up on the back of her neck.

"Is someone there?" Sadie called out. There was no answer, but now there was the distinct sound of someone moving through the woods.

She felt her heart beat speed up and tried to shake off the panic threatening to take hold of her. *This is ridiculous! I'm turning into Bess!*

The sound grew louder. Someone was trudging through the trees and underbrush, and that person was getting closer. The rational side of her brain pointed out that whoever was traipsing around the woods had every right to be there. Maybe it was a nature lover, or someone out looking for a lost dog. There was no reason to think she was being followed again.

The sound grew louder and louder. Any second, she should be able to see who was there. She held her breath and stared, waiting for the person to emerge. And then suddenly, the noise stopped, leaving her with nothing but the eerie feeling that she was being watched.

Sadie dropped the flowers and took off running, not stopping until she reached the porch at Prophet House. She leaned her head against the door and tried to catch her breath.

"Everything all right, miss?"

Sadie spun around. Owen was standing by the steps, a pair of shears in his hand.

Sadie looked past him but didn't see anyone. "Where'd you come from, Owen?" she asked suspiciously.

"Right here behind the bushes. I was trimming them up so I could fix that piece of siding." He pointed at a broken board on the ground behind the shrubbery.

"Oh." Sadie's hands were shaking when she pulled out the key to open the front door. She looked back at Owen and her gaze traveled down to his boots. They were covered in twigs and dirt. "Your boots are dirty."

He shifted his weight uncomfortably. "Yep. I was pulling weeds in the flower beds before."

"Oh. I thought maybe…"

"Maybe what?" He changed the shears to his right hand and took hold of the rail with his left.

Sadie swallowed the lump in her throat. "Nothing."

He raised one foot and used the shears to knock some of the debris off his boot. Then he repeated the process with his other boot, leaving a mess on the stone step. When he'd finished, he looked up. "I'll clean that up later."

Sadie backed toward the door without responding.

Owen's eyes narrowed. "What's the matter, miss? You see a ghost or something?

Sadie felt the hairs stand up on the back of her neck. "Maybe I did…"

She flew inside and locked the door.

CHAPTER 11

Her mom was in the kitchen, an alarmed look on her face. "Why was there blood in the sink?"

"Henry fell and cut his elbow. I cleaned it up and put a bandage on it."

"Oh…" She sounded relieved. "I didn't know what to think!"

"Sorry. I should've left you a note."

"Yes, you should've. I was scared half to death."

"Be glad you didn't look in the trashcan," Sadie murmured under her breath.

"What?"

"Nothing."

"Is Henry okay?"

Sadie nodded. "He's fine."

Meg reached for the phone. "I should call his mother."

"No! I mean. He already told her, I'm sure. Anyway, it was an accident."

"I still think—"

The phone rang, cutting her off.

Sadie grabbed it before her mother had a chance to. "Hello?"

"Hey, squirt!"

"Dad!" Relief washed over her. "I can't wait for you to come home! I have so much to tell you!" There was silence on the other end. "Dad?"

"Yeah, I'm here." He hesitated. "I'm afraid I have some bad news. Don Phillips is leaving."

Sadie frowned. "Who?"

"The other senior history professor in my department."

"Oh yeah." A feeling of dread crept up on her. Something was wrong. She could hear it in his voice. "That's too bad, but what does it have to do with you?"

"He was taking a bunch of students to Italy this summer for a study abroad program. I've been asked to go in his place."

Sadie felt as if she'd been punched in the gut. "You can't!"

"Sadie—"

"Why don't they send someone else?"

"There isn't another professor who speaks Italian." His voice softened. "These are my students too, and they need the credit to graduate. I have to go."

Sadie's mom dropped into one of the kitchen chairs. "What's going on?" she asked anxiously.

"Dad says he's not coming home."

"Let me talk to your mother," Dean said firmly.

"First tell me when you'll be back," Sadie demanded.

"Not until the end of the summer."

"That's almost three months! We need you here! Doesn't Professor Phillips know that?"

"It's barely two and a half months. And of course he knows. This isn't his fault. His teenage son is sick and facing months of treatment. Don is needed at home. What would you have me do?"

"But we need you here with us! There are things going on…" Sadie looked at her mom. She'd made no attempt to take the phone, and her face was as white as a sheet.

"What things?" Her dad sounded alarmed.

Sadie wasn't sure she should say anything yet about Owen, or the fact that Prophet House might be losing its benefactor because of them. If he was really leaving, all it would do was make him worry the whole time. Besides, her mom didn't know yet and this seemed like a terrible time to spring it on her. They probably had until the reenactment anyway.

"Sadie, what things?"

She had to say something. "Stevie got my part," she

blurted out.

"Who's Stevie? What part?"

"I should be playing Elizabeth in the reenactment, but Mrs. Northrup gave the part to this awful girl named Stevie because her dad's the mayor."

"That's what you're upset about?" Sadie could hear the relief in his voice. "Just try to make the best of it. Sometimes things work out the way they're supposed to."

"Grandma always says that, and it never makes me feel any better." Sadie bit her lip to keep from crying. "I wish you didn't have to go."

"I do too, honey. But once I get back, I won't have to leave again. I promise." He sounded weary. "Is there anything else you want to tell me?"

Sadie wanted to tell him everything, but heard herself saying, "Not really, Dad."

"All right. I'm going to miss you and your mom so much, but I'll call as often as I can. I'm counting on you to hold down the fort until I get back."

Tears stung her eyes. "Sure, Dad."

"I love you, squirt."

"I love you too."

Sadie handed the phone to her mother and ran out the front door, relieved that Owen was nowhere in sight. She let the tears come as she trudged down the long driveway, dragging her feet. How would they manage all summer without her dad?

Mr. Bones was at the mailbox, hammering the nail that held it to the post back into place.

"Why the long face, Miss Sadie?"

She wiped her eyes. "My dad's gonna be gone all summer."

"I'm sorry to hear that. Would you like to talk about it?"

"Not really." She took her foot and pushed some of the rocks from the driveway into a little pile.

"Were you planning to build something with those?"

Sadie sniffed. "I miss him already. I can't believe I won't see him for almost three months."

"Let me tell you something. That time will fly by. You

wait and see. The trick is to stay busy. A young person like you needs some friends to take your mind off your troubles."

"I have Henry… and I guess I have Bess."

"Two good friends are more than most folks have. Take my word for it."

"Yeah…Melanie's nice too."

"Well there you go. Sounds like you'll have plenty of friends to keep you occupied."

Sadie shrugged.

He smiled. "I tell you what. If you need anything at all, you come see me. I've been here a long time and know pretty much all there is to know about this place. Maybe more'n anybody else."

"Thanks, Mr. Bones."

"My pleasure, Miss Sadie."

She turned to head back, then hesitated. "Mr. Bones, do you know Bess?"

"Sure, I do. Sweet kid."

Sadie's mouth dropped open. "Really? You know who I'm talking about?"

"Of course. Little red-haired girl. She's been coming around here for ages. Used to follow me around all the time, asking all sorts o' questions."

"I, uh…"

"What?"

"Nothing. You'll laugh."

He set his hammer down and leaned on the mailbox. "I promise I won't."

"I was starting to think she might not be real… like maybe she was a ghost or something. I know it's silly, but it crossed my mind a couple of times, especially after I saw someone on my balcony."

Mr. Bones frowned. "Are you in the captain's room?"

"Yeah. Why?"

"Listen to me, Miss Sadie. Prophet House has a way of messing with your head a little, if you know what I mean. It's best not to go looking for things that don't make sense."

"I wasn't looking. It was during the storm. I thought I

saw a man on my balcony, but when I looked again, there was no one there."

"I'd say it was your imagination then."

"I guess."

"Well, Bess is a sweet girl." Mr. Bones said. "Her momma's a little too protective, but she has good reason to be. Her husband died a long time ago and they've had it rough."

"What happened to him?"

"He was a sailor."

Sadie's interest was piqued. "Like Nathaniel?"

Mr. Bones nodded. "I figure that's why she's drawn to this place. He was on a boat when a fire broke out in the galley. Most of the men on board either died in the fire or they drowned trying to save themselves."

"That's horrible."

"It is indeed. Look, miss, you be extra nice to Bess."

"I will, Mr. Bones. I promise."

"Good girl." He smiled. "Now let me get back to fixing this post so your momma gets her mail."

"Okay." Sadie smiled. "Later, Mr. Bones."

He waved. "Later, Miss Sadie."

***

Sadie lay in bed early the next morning, staring at the ceiling. Her mind was churning. Why did things have to be so complicated? Once again, the thought of finding the treasure hammered away at her brain. But where should she even begin? Other people had probably combed the house and grounds for the past two hundred years looking for it, with no success. So, what made her think she could do what no one else had done in all that time? She'd been so sure that she was meant to find it. But now that confidence was crumbling.

Sadie was dying to talk to someone. She couldn't burden her mother with the threat of losing Prophet House, especially when her dad wasn't around to deal with it. Henry was the logical choice, but he was making deliveries for his mother this morning. She had no idea how to reach him without going by

Mrs. Northrup's shop and risking another encounter with her. Sadie sighed. She'd just have to wait until Henry showed up later. Of course, there was always the chance that Bess could suddenly show up again, especially since she seemed to be able to come and go as she pleased. She was familiar with Prophet House and might be some help.

A faint noise caught Sadie's attention. It sounded too far away to be coming from the wardrobe. She jumped out of bed and quickly pulled on jeans and a t-shirt, then tiptoed into the hall. There it was again—the sound of footsteps coming from the attic. It had to be Bess! She opened the door in time to hear the panel in the wall closing.

Determined to catch her, Sadie flew into the attic and flung open the door to the cellar stairs. Someone was definitely ahead of her, moving quickly down the staircase. Since she hadn't thought to grab the flashlight, Sadie left the door open so at least a tiny amount of light would spill into the narrow space. By about halfway down, the passageway was nearly pitch dark and she almost fell when she forgot about the broken step. There was no light coming from below, so she smacked solidly into the door when she reached the bottom. Rubbing her sore nose, Sadie pushed it open and stepped into the cellar. No Bess. Frustrated, she plopped onto the overturned bucket again and tried to catch her breath.

From behind her, a familiar voice said angrily, "Why did you show Henry the stairs?"

Sadie let out a scream.

CHAPTER 12

Bess glared at her from the opening to the passageway. "It was supposed to be our secret! You shouldn't have shown him!"

"You're mad at *me*?" Sadie sputtered. "Seriously? Stop sneaking up on me! And how did you get behind me?"

"I came in through the front door *like a normal person*!"

"But I heard you on the stairs! I followed you down!"

Bess looked perplexed. "No. I followed *you* down the stairs."

Sadie's eyes narrowed. "Tell the truth. You were in the attic when I got up weren't you?"

Bess's eyes filled with tears. "No, I wasn't."

Even though the cellar was a comfortable temperature, Sadie couldn't seem to stop shivering. "Somebody was in the attic… and probably in my room. Do you absolutely swear it wasn't you?"

Bess nodded solemnly. "I absolutely swear."

Sadie put her face in her hands. "Then who was it?" She thought about Mr. Bones' words, that Prophet House can mess with your head. Maybe that was happening to her.

Bess frowned. "I have to tell you something. But you mustn't tell anyone that you heard it from me."

Sadie had a feeling she wouldn't like whatever it was Bess was about to tell her. She stood and motioned for Bess to sit. "You take the bucket. I'll sit in the wheelbarrow."

Sadie climbed into the wheelbarrow and winced. A

screw in the bottom dug into her hip, so she shifted her weight to avoid it, with only partial success.

"Are you sure you're all right?" Bess asked, a concerned look on her face.

"I'm fine. Just tell me whatever it is."

Bess took a deep breath. "There's a legend that says the captain stashed a treasure somewhere in Prophet House or on the property. He was one of the only survivors of a Spanish ship that went down off the coast two hundred years ago.

"I know this story. I've heard it all my life."

"Did you know that twelve chests full of gold escudos were never found?"

"What are escudos?"

"You may know them as gold doubloons. They were coins made of solid gold and stamped with the image of King Charles III of Spain."

"Like the one I found in the book!" Sadie's interest was piqued. "But how do you know so much about the coins?"

Bess ignored her question. "Nathaniel and the other crew member who survived disappeared for ten years. When Nathaniel turned up again, he was twenty-one and the captain of his own ship, *The Sea Hawk*. The other man was with him. His name was John Barry. Nathaniel was devoted to Mr. Barry because he'd been like a father to Nathaniel since the shipwreck."

"What happened to Mr. Barry?"

"Mr. Barry disappeared with Nathaniel," Bess said sadly, "and no one knows what happened to them. Nathaniel loved Mr. Barry like a father. And Mr. Barry thought of Nathaniel as his own son. One never sailed without the other. After they left that last time, neither of them were ever seen again."

"So, I guess Nathaniel and Mr. Barry split the treasure."

"Some people think it's just a story. But there are others who believe it. They believe that most of the treasure is still hidden and they'd do anything to get it."

"But if there really was a treasure, surely someone would've found it by now. Or maybe Nathaniel spent it all building this house. Maybe my coin was the last one."

Bess shook her head. "He could've built ten houses like this and the same number of ships with the gold in those chests. You can't imagine how much there was. The captain kept extensive records in his journal."

Sadie leaned forward and whispered. "And you found it?"

Bess nodded.

Sadie sucked in her breath. "Where is it now?"

"That's not important. Besides, he didn't use any of the treasure to build this house." Bess smiled. "No one else knows that."

"Then how do you know?" Sadie asked. "And where is his journal? It belongs to my family. You have to tell me!"

"I—I'm not sure where it is now."

"Did Mrs. Northrup take it?"

Bess fidgeted with a strand of hair, seemingly deep in thought. Sadie noticed for the first time that the skin on her hands had a reddish appearance. When Bess noticed Sadie looking, she pulled her sleeves down over her hands. "I can't remember where I saw it."

Sadie was crestfallen. "You can't remember? Really?"

Bess chewed her lip. "There are so many hidden places in this house. I'm sorry, Sadie."

"You think you can find it again?"

Bess nodded. "I'll try."

Sadie shifted her position in the wheelbarrow again. "Okay. Go on with the story."

"You're not mad at me?"

Sadie sighed. "No. I'm not mad."

Bess seemed relieved. Her voice took on an excited tone. "One of the early times that Nathaniel was out to sea, he came across an English vessel that was sinking with forty-three people on board. He saved every last one—took them aboard his ship. Because of the extra mouths to feed and the extra weight of their cargo, he had to make for the nearest port."

Bess smiled wistfully. "He didn't mind the inconvenience though. Because he'd met the captain's daughter and fallen instantly in love. Her name was Sarah Elizabeth Everleigh. Nathaniel gave the crew of the English ship safe passage and took no payment nor any of their possessions for himself, not one thing. Captain Everleigh was so grateful that he and Nathaniel became fast friends. After a few weeks on land, he gave Nathaniel and Sarah permission to marry. On their wedding day, Captain Everleigh gave them a large chest of English silver as a dowry and told Nathaniel to build Sarah a home she could be proud of. So Nathaniel built Prophet House for her."

Sadie's jaw dropped. "Please tell me how you know all this! Was it in the journal too?"

"Not all of it. But that doesn't matter."

"It does matter! What else did you find? You have to tell me!"

Bess's eyes filled with tears. "I—I will. Just not yet."

"Okay, fine. But I thought you wanted to be friends."

"I do!"

"Well, friends don't keep secrets."

Bess was crying in earnest now. "It's only a secret for a little while longer. I swear."

At the sight of her friend's tears, Sadie's anger melted away. "Okay… I'll wait. But you promise you'll tell me?"

Bess nodded solemnly. "I promise."

Sadie managed to extract herself from the wheelbarrow without ending up underneath it like Henry. "I'm sorry I got so mad. Let's go back to my room. You can finish the story there."

Bess wiped her eyes. "Friends?"

Sadie nodded. "Friends."

They climbed the stairs up to the attic. Bess waited in the captain's room while Sadie ran downstairs and came back with blueberry muffins her mother had picked up at the store.

Sadie offered one to Bess, but she shook her head. "I already ate breakfast, and I don't like blueberries."

Sadie was starving. She stuck half of a muffin in her mouth and mumbled, "Suit yourself."

Bess giggled. "You eat like a sailor."

Sadie grinned, pieces of muffin in her teeth. "Tell me

more of the story." She climbed onto the four-poster and motioned for Bess to join her.

Once Bess was settled, she continued. "It took almost three years to build Prophet House. A year after its completion, Sarah gave birth to a daughter they named Sarah Elizabeth, after her mother.

With his new family, Nathaniel seemed content to stay on land. As the reigning couple of Everleigh, Nathaniel and Sarah enjoyed a lively social life for the next five years. But eventually, Nathaniel became restless and returned to the sea, sailing away for weeks at a time. When Sarah gave birth to their second child, a son, Nathaniel left again, but vowed that this would be his last voyage.

Shortly after his departure, influenza swept through Everleigh, killing nearly half of the town, including Nathaniel and Sarah's beloved daughter, Elizabeth." Bess wiped her eyes. "Sarah was grief-stricken. She waited anxiously for her husband to return. But weeks turned into months, and months to years with no word of him. Sarah raised their son, young Nate, alone in this grand house. Without her husband to lean on, she fell into terrible despair. Even after many years had passed, she still climbed the ladder to the tower every night, hoping to glimpse his ship on the horizon."

Sadie's eyes filled with tears. "It must've been awful for her. I can't imagine what we'd do if my dad never came home." He'd be on the other side of the ocean soon. She thought of poor Sarah and her son, rambling around in his big house, grieving the loss of Elizabeth and never knowing what happened to the captain.

"Are you all right, Sadie?"

Sadie nodded solemnly. "What does this story have to do with who I followed down to the cellar a little while ago?"

"Many people believed the treasure that was aboard *The Isabela* was hidden here at Prophet House. Sarah was tormented by thieves and people who claimed to be long lost relatives. It got so bad that she had to pay some of the townsmen to guard the house. But even some those men tried to rob her. Over the years, others have tried to find the treasure. The house has been broken into so many times. But no one, to this day, has found even one coin, except you. Still, there are those who believe it's here, and they would do anything to find it."

"You think that's what happened today? Someone broke in to find the treasure, but ran when I followed them?"

Bess nodded. "Some of the would-be robbers have been dangerous criminals. Haven't you ever wondered why none of the Prophets who came after Sarah have lived here for long?"

Sadie thought of her grandfather. He'd only stayed three months. She leaned against the headboard and chewed her lip. If Grandpa had let the town have Prophet House because he was frightened of treasure hunters, wouldn't he have said so? Wouldn't he have wanted his son to know it wasn't safe? And why would he have done the renovations if he'd never intended for any of his family to live here?

Bess didn't say anything else for several minutes. She was staring off toward the balcony. When she spoke, her voice was filled with anguish. "He changed the name of his ship. That's why he never came home."

Sadie was alarmed by the sudden change in her. "What do you mean?"

Bess climbed down from the four-poster and walked slowly to the balcony doors, placing her hand on one of the handles. Both doors swung open. She stepped out onto the balcony and stared out at the ocean. "Before Nathaniel and John Barry left that last time, Nathaniel changed the name of his ship from *The Sea Hawk* to *The Elizabeth*," she said softly. "Most of the men left because of it. He had to hire a new crew."

Sadie hopped down and joined her on the balcony. "That doesn't make any sense. Why would they leave?"

Bess's expression was solemn. "It's very bad luck to change the name of a ship. Everyone knows that. But Nathaniel didn't care. He said he wasn't superstitious. But in the end, he was wrong." Bess continued to look out to sea, seemingly lost in thought.

Sadie felt a chill up her spine. "Bess?"

"I–I think I should go."

"Now? You can't lay all this on me and run off! You

have to stop doing that! Besides, I want to talk to you about Owen. I think he might've been following me yesterday, and maybe even before that. Maybe he was the one in the attic. I've had a bad feeling about him from the beginning. What if he's after the treasure?"

Bess chewed her lip. "He may be the one…"

"What do you mean, 'the one?'"

"Promise me you'll be careful, Sadie. It's an enormous treasure. Men have killed for much less."

Sadie tried to swallow the lump in her throat. "You think we're in danger?"

Bess sighed. "I don't know."

"What should I do?"

"Don't ever let your guard down. And find out everything you can about Owen. If he's after the coins…"

"I should tell my mom."

Bess shook her head. "Keep this between us for now."

Sadie's mouth dropped open. "Why?"

"Trust me." Bess fidgeted with her hair.

"But what if I need help?"

"Ask Bones. He'll know what to do."

"Mister Bones?" Something suddenly dawned on Sadie––what Mr. Bones had said when she'd found him at the mailbox the day before. He'd said that Bess used to follow him around asking questions. That's why she knew so much about the Prophets! Mr. Bones had been at Prophet House a long time, and by his own words knew more than anyone else about the place. So that had to mean he also knew about her family! Maybe he even had the captain's journal!

Bess backed away. "I do have to go. Please don't be upset." She stepped inside and stopped at the door to the wardrobe. "I mustn't stay any longer."

"What are you so afraid of?"

"I can't be gone long from my mother…" Bess pulled open the door and disappeared inside.

Sadie stared after her but didn't move. She'd learned the hard way that there was no point in following her. She climbed onto the four-poster, mulling over everything that Bess had told her. It made sense that Mr. Bones would be her source of information. Living on the property, he'd probably soaked up even more knowledge over the years than Mrs. Northrup. Sadie's occasional musings that perhaps Bess was a ghost seemed pretty silly now. Bess was just a lonely girl who was obsessed with Prophet House and the whole Prophet family. But she was also sweet and sincere. Sadie intended to heed her advice and find out all she could about Owen. If he was after the gold, Sadie needed to know.

The diary was sticking out from under a pillow. Sadie opened the book to the second entry and slowly deciphered the script.

I saw someone as I walked home. He did not think I was aware of his presence as he watched me from the trees. I wish I had seen his face, though I have my suspicions that he is someone I know. There have been other times when I knew he was near, following just out of sight. I dare not speak until I am sure, but I fear he means me harm.

CHAPTER 13

Sadie sat in stunned silence. Once again, Elizabeth had related an incident that closely matched Sadie's own experience. How was that possible? Nearly two hundred years separated them. Sadie tried to shake off the uneasy feeling, but it was no use.

Maybe Prophet House was messing with her mind, like Mr. Bones had warned. She lay down and closed her eyes. The doors to the balcony were still open and the birds in the magnolias were chattering away. Off in the distance, she heard a low rumble of thunder moments before a soft breeze blew across her face. She took a deep breath and let it out slowly.

Maybe it was an odd coincidence that the first two entries had been so familiar. Sometimes strange things happened. That's why there's such a thing as déjà vu. She continued to breathe in and out slowly. After several minutes, she felt her body slipping into a relaxed state. It would be easy to drift to sleep, listening to the birds… the wind… the ocean sounds.

"Hey!"

Sadie jerked upright. "Henry! You scared me to death! It's bad enough that Bess sneaks up on me. Don't you start!"

"Sorry. Your mom said I could come up. She said to knock first, but I guess I forgot."

Sadie leaned against the headboard and clutched her chest. "I think I'm having a heart attack. That's the second time today."

Henry grinned. "You look okay to me."

"Oh, thanks. I feel so much better now." She threw a pillow at him and he ducked away, laughing. Henry picked up the pillow and chucked it back at her.

"Why is it the second time?" he asked.

Sadie hopped down from the bed. "Bess was here earlier. She said that thieves have come here looking for the gold Nathaniel took from the Spanish ship two hundred years ago. Have you ever heard of anyone breaking into Prophet House?"

"I've heard my mom talking about it before."

"Great. One more thing to worry about."

Henry sat on the floor and rubbed his chin. "It's been a long time since she mentioned a break in. Maybe everyone's given up."

Sadie plopped down beside him and shook her head. "I don't think so. There was someone here today."

Henry's eyes widen. "Someone broke in?"

"I don't know for sure, but somebody was in the attic and I followed him down the stairs to the cellar. But when I got there, he was gone. Then all of a sudden Bess came up behind me and almost scared me to death."

"Maybe she was the one you heard."

"I thought that at first too, but there's no way she could've gotten behind me on the stairs without running around the house and coming in through the front door. It would've taken too long. It couldn't have been her."

"You should tell your mom."

"What would I say? I thought I heard someone in the attic and in the secret passageway to the cellar that I didn't tell you about, but I never actually saw anyone?"

"Yeah. Exactly that." Henry nodded. "You should also tell her about Bess."

"You mean the strange girl who hides in my wardrobe, tells me things about Prophet House, and comes and goes as she pleases?"

"When you put it like that…"

"Trust me, Henry. My mom would freak out and start asking me all these questions about her until my head exploded."

Henry scratched his head. "She hides in the wardrobe?"

"That's how she shows up every time. She comes through the opening from the attic."

"Wow… that's weird."

"Yep."

"I still think you should tell your mom about her. What if she nuts or something?"

"She isn't. She's a little odd, but she's nice. Her mother homeschools her and she doesn't have any friends. I think she's lonely." Sadie shrugged. "I like her, and it's pretty cool how much she knows about Prophet House. And she agrees that something's not right about Owen."

"Who?"

"The second caretaker... the creepy one."

He raised his eyebrows. "There are two caretakers?"

Sadie shot him an exasperated look. "You should know since your mom's the history club president."

"Historical Society."

"Whatever."

She jumped up. "There's something I could use your help with, Henry."

He looked skeptical. "What?"

"Bess is right. Something's up with Owen. She said I should find out everything I can about him."

"You want to snoop on the creepy caretaker?"

Sadie lowered her voice. "I think he might be the one who was watching us in the woods. I'll explain along the way." She motioned for him to follow. At the landing, she stopped. Telling him to wait, she ran back to her room, took the coin from under the pillow and dropped it in her pocket. From now on, she intended to keep it with her all the time, just in case.

When she returned, Henry was leaning on the top rail, tapping his foot. She grabbed him by the arm and pulled him down the stairs. "Come on! He lives in the cottage behind the house. He's probably out working on the grounds somewhere, so it should be safe to check it out." At the bottom step, she called, "Mom, Henry and I are going outside."

Meg stepped into the hallway. "Do you want another muffin? I have plenty."

Sadie grabbed two, handed one to Henry, and hugged her mother. "Thanks, Mom. We'll take it with us."

Henry shoved nearly the whole muffin in his mouth and mumbled, "Thanks Mrs. Prophet!" as Sadie dragged him out the back door.

The cedar-and-stone cottage was on the other side of the woods behind the house. In front of the cottage was a pristine pond surrounded by yellow and white flowers and filled with the largest goldfish Sadie had ever seen. More flowers bordered a cobblestone walkway leading to a crimson red door. Wind chimes, hanging from the eaves, tinkled delicately in the gentle breeze. All it needed to fit perfectly into a fairy tale was a thatched roof.

Sadie was spellbound. "This is amazing!"

"You've never been back here?"

"No. I can't imagine Owen living in a place like this." Sadie touched one of the chimes. The melodic sound made her think of fairies. "It's like an enchanted garden, don't you think?"

Henry shrugged. "If you say so."

He started to knock on the door, but Sadie grabbed his arm and pulled him back.

"Let's make sure he isn't home first," she whispered.

"Wouldn't knocking on the door accomplish that?"

Sadie ignored the question and crept around the side of the cottage, peering in windows.

"See anyone?" Henry whispered.

"No." She made her way to the back, where there was another door. It was locked. "Anyone home?" she said loudly. No response.

"It seems to be locked up tight. Maybe we should take that as a sign," Henry whispered.

"No, maybe we should see if any of the windows are open."

Henry let out a loud sigh, then he made a trip around the cottage, checking the front door and every window. He returned and shook his head. "No luck."

Sadie stared at the chimney. "Do you think—?"

Henry's eyes widened. "No, I don't!"

"Calm down, it was just a thought." Something else caught her eye. "What's that?" She pointed at a small metal door, about a foot and a half by a foot and a half, near the ground. It had an iron latch.

"It's the wood chute… you chop wood and stick it in there instead of carrying it into the house."

Sadie was impressed. "How do you know that?"

"Do you remember my mother, the president of the historical society? I'm pretty sure you can thank her for the whole enchanted garden theme too."

"That explains it." Sadie laughed. "So, you put the wood in here and you can reach it from inside?"

"Of course. There's another door like this beside the fireplace."

Sadie looked at him pointedly.

His mouth dropped open. "I'm not crawling through that thing! No way!"

"You don't have to. I'll let you in."

She pulled the door open and slithered inside. It was tighter than the passage from the wardrobe to the attic, but at least it wasn't winter, so the chute was devoid of wood. Sadie wriggled forward and pushed on the other metal door. It didn't budge. It occurred to her at that moment that it was probably latched from the inside. She tried to back out, but she'd pulled her knee up under her and couldn't get her leg to straighten out. For a terrifying moment, she imagined being stuck there when Owen got home.

Suddenly, the inside door popped open and there stood Henry. He grabbed under her arms and pulled her out onto the floor.

Sadie took in a deep breath of fresh air. "That was awful!"

"What did I tell you?" Henry helped her to her feet.

"But how'd you get in?"

"I lied before. The front door was open." He gave her a sheepish grin.

"Henry Northrup! I could've gotten stuck in there!"

He held up his hands. "Sorry. But someone has to be the

mature one. We can't break into people's houses and expect that nothing bad will happen."

"We're not breaking into houses. We're just breaking into *one* house. And we didn't actually break in because nothing's broken. Besides, if Owen's stalking me, I have every right to check it out. Mr. Bones lives here too, and he's my friend. I'm sure he won't mind."

"Who's Mr. Bones?"

"Oh my God, Henry! He's the other caretaker."

"Okay, Sherlock. But remind me why we're doing this?"

"I think Owen was the one in the woods. I think he was following me home yesterday too."

"Did you see him?"

"Not exactly. I heard someone in the woods next to my house. Whoever was there was careful not to let me see him. I got freaked out and ran the rest of the way home. As soon as I got to the porch, Owen appeared out of nowhere. His boots were wet and covered with dirt and twigs. He said he'd been watering flowers, but I don't believe him. I think he was the one running through the woods. There's a creek next to our property. I saw it from my bathroom window when we moved in. He would've had to cross it, then wade through a bunch of stuff to get back home without me seeing him."

Henry frowned. "Why would he follow you around? You must have a reason."

"I believe he thinks my family knows where Nathaniel hid it all."

"What are you talking about?"

"I think Owen wants the treasure."

Henry stared at Sadie with his mouth hanging open. "You mean it's real?"

Exasperated, Sadie put her hands on her hips. "Of course the treasure is real. It has to be. I found one of the coins!"

Henry's eyes widened. "You found one? You actually have it?"

Sadie reached into her pocket and pulled out the coin.

Henry whistled.

"Shh!"

“Sorry. Can I hold it?”

Sadie dropped it into his hand and watched with pleasure as he admired it for several minutes before handing it back to her.

Henry shook his head. “I can’t believe it. My mom’s talked about the treasure for years, but… I don’t know. I guess I never really believed it was real.” He put his hands on Sadie’s shoulders and looked her in the eye. “Do you know where the rest of it is?”

“Of course I don’t!”

His face fell. “Then how do you know there’s more?”

“How else can you explain my great-great-great-grandfather becoming such a rich sea captain? He was only a poor cabin boy on that Spanish ship. He barely survived when the ship went down and didn’t have anything but the clothes on his back. No money. No family. How did he turn up ten years later with a huge ship of his own and a crew to man it?”

Henry nodded solemnly. “I guess he had the treasure.”

“Right.” Sadie decided not to share the story about Nathaniel rescuing Sarah and her father, along with the whole crew of their ship. She still had no idea if everything Bess had told her was true or not.

“So, what’s the plan?”

“We make sure we find the gold before Owen does. The only thing is, apparently people have looked for two hundred years without finding a single coin. How are we supposed to do it?”

“Well, you’ve already found one coin, which is more than any of those hunters could do. Henry smiled. “And besides, I think you could do anything you set your mind to.”

Sadie felt blood rush to her cheeks. She looked away, embarrassed. “Okay. We’ll look for the coins after we see what Owen is up to.” He let out a whoop, and Sadie clamped her hand over his mouth. “Be quiet!”

“Sorry,” he whispered.

Sadie studied her surroundings. A leather sofa and two upholstered chairs sat on a woven rug in the center of the room, facing a stone fireplace, much like the one in her room. Over the fireplace was a painting of the red-haired Nathaniel Prophet with another man who looked older. Sadie figured he had to be the other sailor—the one Bess had told her about. Strangely, something about him seemed familiar. In the picture, he was turned slightly, facing Nathaniel, with his hand on Nathaniel's shoulder in a fatherly gesture. His brown hair was pulled back and tied with a piece of twine.

"Who's that with the captain?" Henry asked.

"It must be his friend, John Barry, the other sailor who survived the shipwreck."

In the portrait, Nathaniel had his booted foot firmly planted on a large wooden chest.

Henry whistled. "And I bet that chest is full of gold."

Sadie had been thinking the same thing. She examined the painting more closely. The two men were standing on a long wooden pier with a large ship in the background. She couldn't make out the name but felt sure it was the *Sea Hawk.*

She tore her attention away from the painting and surveyed her surroundings. There was a desk in the corner next to the hearth. Unlike the rest of the tidy room, the desk was strewn with papers, candy wrappers, and even a few dirty plates that looked as if they'd been there a while. Sadie sorted through the mess while Henry searched the other rooms.

"What are we looking for, Sherlock?" he asked, remembering to keep his voice low.

"I don't know exactly." Sadie picked up several receipts, most of them for groceries or takeout food. Two other receipts were from the local gas station, and one was for mail order contacts.

"Anything interesting?"

"Not really. Just ads, bills, and receipts."

Henry opened a door down a short hall. "You should take a look in here."

Sadie followed him into a small room with a twin bed, a chest of drawers, and a side table. On the table was a wallet containing Owen's driver's license and seventeen dollars.

"Look at this, Henry." She handed him the driver's license.

"It's not a great picture, but my mom says all driver's license pictures come out looking like they belong in a book of police suspects."

Sadie took the license back and studied the picture. "Actually, it's not bad. Something isn't right, though."

"Hey, his name is Owen Thomas Owensby," Henry pointed out.

Sadie shook her head. "You'd think his parents would give him a first name that wasn't just a shorter version of his last name."

"I have a cousin named Ronald James Donald. Everybody calls him Ron Don. So our family's bar is set pretty low."

Sadie giggled. "That's just sad." She continued to stare at the photo on his license. "I know what's weird about his driver's license picture! His eyes are the same color!"

"Okay?"

"You don't understand. Owen's eyes are different colors—one blue and one brown. But in this picture, they're both brown."

Henry looked at the picture again. "Maybe he was wearing contacts."

"Right… the receipt."

"What?"

Sadie shook her head. "It doesn't matter."

They looked through Owen's room, and found a newspaper article about Prophet House that was a year old. The headline read: *HISTORIC HOME MAY CONCEAL A RICH SECRET.*

"So he has an article from a year ago. What does that prove?" Henry asked.

Sadie sighed loudly. "It proves he read about the legend of the treasure and came here because of it."

"Maybe. But it's not enough to confront him if you ask me. He might have been working at Prophet House already when this came out. Do you know how long he's been here?"

"You'd have a better idea than I would. Your mom probably hired him," Sadie pointed out.

"I don't pay attention to that kind of stuff. That's my mom's department. We can ask her though."

"Okay. Until then, let's just keep looking."

Sadie followed Henry down the hall to a sparsely furnished second bedroom. The bed was neatly made, a pair of work boots under the end. A small chest sat in the corner. Sadie pulled open one of the drawers and found clothes. The closet contained several shirts and another pair of boots.

Sadie closed the closet door. "This must be Mr. Bones's room. It doesn't look like I would've pictured it."

"It's pretty depressing," Henry admitted. "Maybe he doesn't want a lot of useless stuff sitting around. My uncle's like that."

"It just doesn't make sense that this is all he has. He's lived here forever."

"You could ask him about it next time you see him."

"Don't you think that'd be rude?"

Henry gave her a wry look. "Excuse me for stating the obvious, but that doesn't seem to stop you."

Sadie goosed him in the side. "Don't be a jerk."

"You know I'm right though—"

She put her finger to her lips. "Shh! Did you hear that?"

They both froze. Someone outside was whistling, and the sound was getting closer.

CHAPTER 14

"What now?" Henry whispered frantically.

Sadie dashed over to the window and peeked out. Owen was walking up the path to the cottage, a shovel over his shoulder. She grabbed Henry's hand. "Out the back!"

Just as Owen stepped in the front door, they slipped out the back and took off through the dense woods behind the cottage. About twenty feet into the trees, Sadie caught her foot on a root and landed face-down in the underbrush.

From behind them, Owen called, "Who's back there?"

Henry pulled Sadie to her feet and they kept going, running blindly as branches whipped them in the face. They could hear him trudging through the bramble behind them, but eventually the sound faded until they didn't hear it anymore.

After several minutes, Sadie gasped, "Henry, stop!" She collapsed on the ground and tried to catch her breath.

Henry plopped down beside her. "Let's not do that again. Ever."

"It's not like he was gonna kill us or something! He works for my family!"

"I saw him through the window and you're right. Definitely creepy. Plus, he had a weapon."

She rolled her eyes. "It was a shovel."

"Sadie, have you *ever* seen a horror movie??"

"Oh… right."

They sat on the ground, listening intently for any evidence that Owen was still in pursuit, but all was quiet.

Henry helped her up. “I think we better take the long way around to go back.”

“Fine with me.” Sadie motioned for him to go ahead. She stared at the ground as they trudged along, utterly disappointed. She’d been sure they’d find more incriminating evidence against Owen—something that proved beyond a doubt that he was after the treasure. But all they’d found was a newspaper article that could have been in the cabin before he ever came to Prophet House. Still, she had a nagging feeling that there was more to Owen than he was letting on. Something wasn’t right about him.

They continued on through the trees and underbrush until they came to a narrow path that led to the opposite side of woods. When they stepped out into a clearing, there was nothing but open field around them.

“Okay… where’s the house?” Sadie asked.

Henry pointed to another group of trees at the far end of the field. “Through there.”

Sadie groaned. “Great. More woods.”

They sprinted across the open space, keeping their eyes peeled for Owen the whole way.

When they walked in the back door of Prophet House, Sadie’s mom took one look at them and gasped. “What in the world happened to you two?”

“What do you mean?” Sadie asked.

“You’re filthy!”

“Oh… we…”

Henry jumped in. “We saw a deer in the woods and decided to chase it.”

Sadie’s mom furrowed her brow. “Why on earth would you do that?”

Henry looked to Sadie for help.

“Henry’s never seen one up close.” Sadie offered, realizing too late how ridiculous that was. With all of the woods and undeveloped land around Everleigh, Henry would have never seen deer up close?

Her mom shook her head. “Well, I hope it was worth it. Go wash your face and hands, both of you. Henry, you can use the bathroom down the hall. I just put fresh towels in there this morning. And Sadie… how did you tear a hole in your jeans?"

Sadie glanced down. "I fell in the woods."

"We'll talk about this later. Go upstairs and get cleaned up."

Henry obediently trudged down the hall while Sadie ran up to her bathroom on the third floor. When she shook out her pants, the coin fell out, along with several twigs and a clump of dirt. She came down fifteen minutes later, washed and wearing a clean white top and blue shorts, with the coin safely in the pocket. Henry was at the kitchen table, eating a grilled cheese sandwich.

"I made one for you too." Her mother set a plate down at Sadie's place.

Sadie pulled her chair back and sat down. "Thanks, Mom." She looked over at Henry, who was shoving down his sandwich and trying not to make eye contact with her mother.

Meg stood at the sink, rinsing dishes and loading them into a dishwasher that Sadie hadn't noticed before, as it was built into the lower cabinets. Another sneaky addition by her grandfather.

Meg closed the cabinet doors and sat down across from Sadie. "Owen came by looking for you."

Sadie coughed up the bite she'd just taken. "He did?" She glanced at Henry, who looked like he was having a similar problem swallowing.

"I told him you were upstairs, so he said he'd come back in a little while." She looked at the two of them, munching their sandwiches as if they were chewing wood. "Any idea what he wanted?"

Sadie and Henry shook their heads.

"Hmm. Nothing you want to tell me?"

"No, Mom."

"Well, I certainly hope you've not been giving poor Owen a hard time."

Sadie looked at Henry. He was clearly thinking the same thing—*Poor Owen*? If she only knew…

"I have no idea what he wanted, Mom. And Henry has to go by his mom's store, so I'm going with him. I'll be back by dinner, okay?"

Her mother eyed them both suspiciously. "I suppose so. Don't be too late."

"I won't." Sadie grabbed what was left of her sandwich and practically sprinted out of the house with Henry on her heels. As soon as they were out of earshot, she spun around. "Owen knows we were in his house!"

"I think that's obvious," Henry replied. "What do we do now?"

"Nothing. He didn't actually see us. So if he says anything, we'll just deny it."

"I'm not sure it's that easy."

"It doesn't matter. If he thinks we're on to him, he'll be watching us," Sadie said. "We have to be more careful next time."

"Next time? You're planning to go back?"

"Maybe not to the cottage, but he's not the only one who can follow people around."

"You're crazy. What if he's dangerous?"

Sadie was worried about the same thing. But saving Prophet House for her family overshadowed any fear she had of Owen. She started walking again without answering him.

Henry didn't say anything again until they were almost to town. When he did, his tone was serious. "This isn't a joke, Sadie. You could get hurt."

"I know. I'll be careful. I promise."

He put his arm around her shoulder. "I guess I better hang around… in case you need saving." That same strand of hair fell down over one eye. Sadie caught herself staring and looked away.

"Maybe I'll have to save you." She laughed.

Henry grinned. "Either way, I guess we're in this together."

***

When Sadie returned home at dinnertime, she found her mom sitting at the kitchen table. She didn't notice Sadie come in.

"Hi, Mom."

Her mother turned around. "Oh, Sadie… what time is it?" Her eyes were red-rimmed, and the tissue box was on the table next to her.

"It's about six o'clock." Sadie flipped on the light near the stove. "Can I help you with dinner?"

"I guess the time got away from me. Your dad called. He's in Florence. He hated that he missed you."

"Is he okay?"

"He's fine."

"How long will he be in Florence?"

"They're leaving shortly, driving through the night to Villa San Giovani and taking the ferry to Messina. They plan to be in Catania in the morning"

"I have no idea where any of those places are."

Meg chuckled. "They're in Italy, Sadie."

"Duh. I meant I've never heard of them."

"Catania is an ancient port city at the foot of Mount Etna." Meg said. "He's a little worried about being on the road all night. He's had his hands full with the students, and apparently they get on the bus driver's nerves. He says he's picked up a few new words from him."

Sadie put her arms around her mother. "This summer will fly by," she said, repeating the words Mr. Bones had said to her by the mailbox. "We'll all be together again, and he won't have to deal with annoying college students or listen to any more bus drivers cuss in Italian." Sadie wished she was as sure as she sounded.

Her mom blew her nose on a fresh tissue and smiled. "I know. It's just hard being here without him."

Sadie had an idea. "There's a diner in town. I saw it when I was with Henry. It's called Stella's, I think. Why don't we get dinner there? It's not far."

Her mother's expression brightened. "That sounds great, honey. Let me get a sweater. You should get one too. I've noticed it's pretty chilly here in the evenings."

Sadie ran upstairs and grabbed a hooded sweatshirt from

her wardrobe. As she turned to leave, she noticed Elizabeth's journal on the floor. She was sure she'd left it under her pillow. Frowning, she picked it up and laid it on her bed. One of the wardrobe doors was cracked open.

"Bess? Are you here?"

Sadie stood perfectly still and listened. After a few minutes, she pulled the sweatshirt on and headed downstairs.

Meg was waiting by the front door, her auburn hair freshly brushed and pulled back. She looked lovely in her white slacks, yellow blouse, and pale green sweater with little daisies on it.

"You're so pretty, Mom."

Her mother seemed touched and gave Sadie a hug. "My leg isn't hurting today. Let's walk."

"Are you sure?"

Her mom nodded. "I'm sure."

The walk to Stella's took no more than fifteen minutes. The interior of the diner was warm and welcoming. There were tables covered in red checked table cloths in the middle and cozy booths around the perimeter.

A tall woman with graying hair and a warm smile greeted them from behind the register. "Goodness me! You must be the Prophet ladies!"

Sadie and her mom exchanged looks.

Her mother spoke up. "I'm Meg, and this is my daughter, Sadie."

"I knew it! Amelia described you both perfectly! She said I might be seeing you, with your husband out of town and all." She leaned toward them and lowered her voice as if sharing a secret. "No man to cook for. Well, when the cat's away…" She turned her attention to Sadie. "Aren't you just as pretty as a picture."

"Thanks," Sadie mumbled, embarrassed by all the attention. Most of the other diners had stopped eating to look at them.

"Amelia was right. You're the spitting image of the captain's wife!"

"Amelia?" Sadie's mom asked.

"Amelia Northrup. She's owns a shop here in town. She's also the president of the Everleigh Historical Society and our former mayor."

Meg raised her eyebrows. "I didn't know she used to be the mayor."

"Oh yes! But the historical society took up so much of her time she decided to step down. Of course, now that you're here, I suppose she'll have some free time again. We're all excited to have Prophets living in the house again!"

"We're happy to be here too." Meg smiled at the woman.

"Listen to me going on and on!" She grabbed two menus and motioned for them to follow her. "Take this booth by the windows. You'll have the best view of the marina."

"I didn't know there were this many boats here!" Meg exclaimed. "We may have to get one ourselves."

Sadie perked up. "Really, mom?"

Meg gave a little shrug. "Maybe a little one."

Stella nodded. "There are fifteen or more docked here at any given time, but we've had as many as thirty during reenactment week. Most of the ones there now belong to locals, and I'm sure any one of them would be happy to take you out fishing or sightseeing. We also have a few regular visitors that come and go. They pay to keep a slip open."

She laid the menus on the table. "I'll give you a few minutes to look these over and I'll be back."

"Thank you…" Meg looked at her name tag. "Thank you, Stella."

Stella beamed. "I'll bring you each a tall glass of sweet tea, on the house. We have the best on the east coast, if I do say so myself."

Sadie leaned toward her mother and whispered, "I guess not everybody here is like Henry's mom."

Meg smiled. "Henry seems nice though."

Sadie felt herself blushing, so she picked up her menu and pretended to concentrate on the contents.

Her mother laughed. "Yep. That's what I thought."

They ordered cheeseburgers and fries, with chocolate cream pie for dessert. Stella was beside herself with pleasure and refused to take any form of payment.

As they were leaving, Meg favored her leg a bit.

"Are you okay, Mom? I can go get the car." Sadie grinned.

"Nice try, but there's no need to break any laws. I'm fine. My leg barely hurts anymore. I think your dad was right about moving here. I just wish he was with us. I miss him. We've never been apart like this."

Sadie put her arm around her mother. "I know. I'm sure he misses us too."

They paused briefly to enjoy the view of the ocean. As the sun went down, Everleigh fairly twinkled as the shops lit up.

Meg sighed. "This really is a beautiful place,"

They continued toward home in silence, each with their own thoughts. Sadie's mind was on the treasure. She reached into her pocket and touched the coin. This couldn't be the only one left. There were more somewhere…

As they ascended the stone steps to the porch, Meg put her hand on Sadie's arm. "What do you think Owen wanted today?" she asked.

Sadie swallowed the lump in her throat. "I can't imagine…"

Her mother pulled out her key and stuck it in the lock. "I guess we'll find out eventually."

I hope not, Sadie thought. "I'm really tired. I think I'll go upstairs and get ready for bed."

"Me too," her mom agreed. "I finally got the kitchen organized today. I'm ready to crawl into bed with a book."

Sadie paused on the second-floor landing. "Mom? Do you ever think about the treasure?"

Her mother seemed surprised. "Honestly, not often. I think if the chests of gold were still here, they would've been discovered years ago. Don't you?"

"I guess so. Do you ever worry that someone might come after it though?"

Meg raised her eyebrows. "You mean pirates?"

"You're right. It's silly." Sadie continued up the stairs and called over her shoulder, "Good night, Mom."

After bathing and changing into pajamas, Sadie crawled into bed and opened Elizabeth's diary. After several attempts, she managed to make out the words.

Mama is brokenhearted over Papa's departure. Molly made her favorite raspberry tarts this morning and Mama barely ate a bite. I find her weeping at the lookout so often that I am afraid she will catch her death from the cold sea air. I pray he comes back to us soon.

"I know just how you feel, Elizabeth," Sadie muttered. "My mom is sad too."

She heard a noise coming from the attic and froze. It sounded as though someone had opened the trapdoor to the widow's walk. Sadie jumped out of bed and pressed her ear against the bedroom door. Then she heard the faint sound of footsteps on the roof. Her heart pounding, she crept down the hall and cracked open the attic door. Sure enough, the trapdoor was open. She tiptoed to the foot of the ladder and heard someone weeping.

Terrified that it was the ghost of Sarah Prophet, Sadie considered running. But her feet wouldn't move, even as a sense of foreboding descended on her. The ladder creaked a little as she climbed through the trapdoor. Standing at the rail in her nightgown was her mother, crying softly as she gazed out at the ocean.

"Mom?"

Meg turned, her face filled with anguish. "There's been an accident in Italy."

Sarah's legs nearly gave way. "Is Dad okay?"

Meg turned back to the ocean. "I don't know. The bus they were in went down an embankment. I had a message on my phone when we got home. I think it was from someone at the hospital. I listened to it over and over, but I couldn't make out the name. I tried calling the number back, but the person who answered was speaking Italian. No one at the hotel knows anything. I don't know what to do or who to call."

Sadie flew to her mother's side and threw her arms

around her. "He'll be all right. I know he will."

Her mother's voice sounded far away. "I think I understand how Sarah must have felt—standing up here, watching for Nathaniel. What torture that must have been."

Sadie burst into tears. "He's not like Nathaniel! He's coming back!"

"I'm sorry, Sadie. You're right. He's probably focused on his students right now. I'm sure I'll hear from him as soon as he's able to call."

At Sadie's insistence, her mother went back to her room to lie down. Sadie stayed with her by the phone late into the night, but her dad didn't call. Finally exhausted, Sadie dragged herself back to her room and collapsed on the bed. Elizabeth's diary was on the chest. Sadie thought of the passage she'd just read and the words that now hit even closer to home. She picked up the book and threw it across the room.

CHAPTER 15

Sadie woke just before dawn. Her mother was gently shaking her, relief all over her face.

"I heard from your dad." She climbed onto the bed next to Sadie. "Apparently the bus they were in hydroplaned and went down a twenty-foot drop into a sort of ravine. They were just outside of Rome when it happened. The driver has a broken leg and three broken ribs. A few of the students were banged up pretty badly, but no broken bones or other serious injuries. Your dad has a gash on his arm that took eight stitches. Otherwise, he's okay."

Sadie sat up. "Is he coming home?" she asked hopefully.

Her mom sighed. "No. They've hired another driver. They're taking a week off to recuperate, then they'll go on with the trip." She kissed Sadie on the forehead. "Thanks for helping me last night. I was so worried."

"Me too. We'll get through this, Mom."

"I know we will. In the meantime, let's get this place in order. I want it to be perfect when your dad gets home. I'm planning to start on the garden behind the cellar today. There's a plant store in town next to the grocery. I'll pick up some tomato plants and some herbs—maybe rosemary, basil, and thyme."

Sadie smiled. "Sounds good."

"Oh, I found this on the floor." She laid Elizabeth's diary on Sadie's lap.

Sadie nodded. "I've been reading some of it, but her writing is hard to make out."

Meg flipped open the book. “Hmm. It’s an interesting form of cursive. Granted, her writing is a little difficult, but it doesn’t look impossible.”

“Yeah, well, it’s hard for me.”

“You should keep trying.” She picked the clothes up off the floor where Sadie had discarded them the night before. “Where’s your hamper?”

“It’s in my bathroom.”

“I was just making sure you hadn’t lost it.”

Sadie grinned. “Sorry. It’s just that it’s all the way down the hall. Then I have to open the door. It’s a lot of work.”

“Right. Put your clothes in the hamper next time.” She threw a sock at Sadie and walked out, chuckling all the way down the hall.

After putting on shorts and a light blue T-shirt, Sadie pulled her hair into a ponytail and headed downstairs. Her mom had scrambled eggs and bacon already on the table.

“I hope this doesn’t mean we have to always get up this early.” Sadie groaned.

Her mom smiled. “I want to get started. There are three other bedrooms on the second floor besides your dad’s and mine. Two are finished so they look authentic for the tourists, but they could use a good dusting. The third one has apparently been closed off for years. I don’t know why, but it’s an absolute disaster. It looks like every random thing that didn’t have a place in this house has been thrown in there. I’d like to get it cleaned up and organized. Do you think you can handle that? I have a lot to do getting my room done, cleaning the rest of the house, and starting the garden.” The news that Sadie’s dad was all right had clearly given her mother a shot of energy and a renewed sense of purpose.

“Sure, Mom. I’ll take care of the disaster room.”

Sadie stuffed in the last of her breakfast and padded upstairs to see what she’d gotten herself into. Her mother wasn’t kidding. Sadie could hardly step inside the room for all the furniture, boxes, and random pieces of junk.

The top of an ornately carved headboard stuck out above the rest of the clutter. She decided to focus on creating a path to the bed, then go from there. By noon, she had dragged enough of the junk into the hallway to create a three-foot-wide open space. There were still boxes piled high against the far wall, but she was pleased with her progress so far. She pulled the dusty linens from the bed and piled them next to the door.

Her mom stuck her head in and gasped. "You've really made a dent in this room! The bed is beautiful. It's not like anything else in the house."

Her mother ran her fingers over the elegantly carved flowers on the headboard. "I have a feeling this was their daughter's room. It looks like a young girl, don't you think?"

Sadie nodded. "I wonder why they let it get like this."

"Who knows? She died pretty young. Maybe it's been closed off ever since." Meg started to look through the bed covers on the floor but stopped when the dust made her cough. "I don't know if we'll be able to save any of these."

"They don't look that old. They're just dusty."

"Maybe Mrs. Northrup bought them because they look old fashioned. But why bother if you're not going to have the room open?" Meg lifted a corner of the coverlet but let it drop when she had another coughing fit.

Sadie shrugged. "I was thinking we could throw them in the wash, then it hit me that we might not have a washer and dryer in this house."

Meg wiped her eyes on the hem of her shirt. "We have to do it all by hand from now on."

Sadie's mouth fell open. "Mom! Really?"

Meg shook her head, laughing. "Of course not. There's a brand-new washer and dryer in the closet in the maid's quarters downstairs."

"Thank God."

She looked Sadie over. "You're covered in dust. Why don't you go change and I'll make sandwiches."

"Okay. Henry's coming over soon anyway."

"Oh, is he?" Meg raised her eyebrows.

"Mom, stop. He probably has nothing else to do, that's all."

"Right. I'm sure it's not that he likes you or anything."

She grinned.

Sadie took off upstairs before her mom could see her face turn beet red. Blushing seemed to be her new thing.

Henry arrived as Sadie was swallowing the last of her turkey sandwich. She ushered him outside before her mom could engage him in conversation.

"What's the hurry?" he asked once they were on the porch.

"Nothing. I just want to get started."

"Started?" He raised his eyebrows. "What's on the agenda today, Sherlock?"

"Bess said that there are all kinds of secret places in this house. So, I figure the coins could be in one of them. Plus, I'm cleaning out one of the rooms on the second floor that's been nothing but storage for years. I bet no one has looked in there for the gold."

"Was it the last room on the right?"

"Yeah. Why?"

He shrugged. "Just an old ghost story I heard when I was younger."

Sadie was intrigued. "Tell me."

A truck came lumbering up the driveway.

"Later," Henry said.

Meg stepped out onto the porch as the truck came to a stop and a stout man stepped out.

Sadie's mom waved him over. "This is Mr…."

"Oh just Frank, ma'am."

"All right. This is Frank, from the Everleigh Garden Center. Frank, this is my daughter, Sadie, and her friend, Henry."

"Very nice to meet you young folks." He gave them a big smile, exposing a gold tooth right in front.

"I met Frank at the farmer's market in town. He was nice enough to offer to help me with the garden."

Frank nodded. "I got the tomato plants you wanted, Mrs. Prophet."

Meg smiled. "I'm looking forward to getting my hands dirty again. When can we get started?"

"Why don't I run by about eight in the morning?"

"Don't you have to be at the garden center?"

"I can take tomorrow off to help the lady of Prophet House."

Sadie's mom seemed pleased by her new title. "All right then. The earlier the better."

He unloaded the tomato plants. "Where would you like me to put these?"

"Right here is fine, Frank."

"All right, Mrs. Prophet. I'll see you in the morning." He climbed into his truck and waved as he drove away.

Meg waved back. "What a nice man," she said as she picked up the pallet of tomato plants.

Sadie and Henry exchanged amused looks.

"Lady Prophet." Sadie curtsied. "May I carry your tomatoes?"

"Very funny." Her mom laughed. "If you really want to be useful, you and Henry can finish the junk room."

"Actually, Henry and I were about to go to his house. I can work on it later if that's okay."

"Just don't be too late," Meg called over her shoulder.

Once they were out of earshot, Henry asked, "When did we decide we were going to my house?"

"*We* didn't. I did."

"My mom could be there, you know."

Sadie nodded. "That's what I'm hoping."

Henry stopped walking and stared at her. "Did you get a head injury in the wood chute? I thought you didn't like my mom."

"I have questions about Owen and she's probably the only person who can answer them."

"Oh." Henry seemed pleased.

***

When Henry and Sadie walked in, Mrs. Northrup was pulling a loaf of banana bread from the oven.

"Hi, Mrs. Northrup." Sadie tried to make her voice as

friendly as she could without sounding obviously phony.

Mrs. Northrup seemed slightly taken aback as she set the steaming banana bread on top of the stove. "Hello, Miss Prophet."

"Mom," Henry spoke up, "Sadie has something she wants to talk to you about."

Henry's mother raised her eyebrows. "If it's about Stevie Winslow playing Elizabeth in the reenactment, there's nothing I can do about that now."

Henry shook his head. "It's not about that."

She seemed relieved. "What is it then, Sadie?"

It was the first time Henry's mom had used her name and Sadie found it both pleasing and a little unsettling. "Do you know the caretaker, Owen?"

Mrs. Northrup frowned. "Of course I know him. I hired him. Is there a problem?"

She motioned for Sadie to sit at the kitchen table. Henry took the seat across from her.

"No. I just wondered how long he's been here."

Mrs. Northrup rubbed her chin. "Well, let me see… Cal Simpson had the job before Owen. He left last July. And when I say left, I mean he was here one day and the next he was gone. Didn't even collect his last paycheck. It's hard to find people with a decent work ethic anymore." She huffed. "It was a stroke of luck that Owen showed up two days later. He'd worked as a caretaker at another historic property across the country."

Sadie thought of the newspaper article about Prophet House that they'd found in Owen's room. It couldn't be a coincidence that he'd arrived looking for a job at just the right time. She was more convinced than ever that Owen was here for the treasure.

"Why did he come here then?" Henry asked.

"He said his uncle lives close by. Apparently, that's his only living relative. Being so far away, they hadn't seen each other in years. I figured, any young man who wants to move across the country to be near an aging uncle must be all right." Her familiar pinched expression returned. "Why are you asking about him? Has he done something wrong?"

Sadie shook her head. "Not really. I was just curious. Thanks for telling me about him, Mrs. Northrup."

Her expression softened ever so slightly. "You be sure to tell me if there's a problem. I feel responsible since I hired him. I didn't even check his references, I'm ashamed to say. I was so moved by his story."

"I'm sure he's okay. Don't worry."

Mrs. Northrup pulled three plates out of the cupboard. "You kids might as well try my banana bread and tell me how you like it. I'm thinking of selling it at the bake sale, so be honest."

After eating two slices each and assuring her that it was delicious, Henry walked Sadie home.

"So, what do you think of my mom now?" he asked.

Sadie grinned. "She's not nearly as scary as I thought she was."

Henry smiled. "I guess she cleared things up for you about Owen?"

"Absolutely! Now I'm positive he's after the treasure.

Henry stopped and stared at her. "What about the uncle he came here to be close to?"

"There is no uncle, Henry!" Sadie let out an exasperated sigh. "Think about it. The guy who had Owen's job disappeared without even getting the money he was owed. And then miraculously, Owen showed up with a sob story about his long-lost uncle? Not to mention the fact that we found a newspaper article about Prophet House in his room that was from a year ago. It's obvious! He murdered the other caretaker, then made up the story about his uncle so he could get the job and steal the treasure!"

"Wait." He caught up to her. "You can't go around accusing people of murder without proof. Maybe Mr. Simpson just got fed up, or inherited some money, or thought he saw a ghost and got freaked out. There could be a logical explanation for him leaving like he did. And maybe Owen really did work at another old house across the country. What if you're wrong?"

"What if I'm right?"

Henry frowned. "Then we'd have a bigger problem than

the missing treasure."

Sadie felt a sudden knot in her stomach. "And we better warn Mr. Bones. He could be the next one to disappear!"

***

Sadie rose early the next morning and tiptoed downstairs to the kitchen, so as not to wake her mother. She pulled a piece of paper with Henry's number on it from the pocket of her jeans. He answered on the first ring.

"Hi, Sherlock." He sounded sleepy.

"Are you ready?"

"Give me a few minutes. My alarm just went off."

"I'm leaving a note for my mom, then I'll meet you at the end of my driveway."

"I'll be there in fifteen minutes."

There were fresh pastries in a bowl on the table. Sadie grabbed two chocolate croissants and wrapped them in a napkin. Then she pulled on her sneakers and trotted down the driveway toward the road.

Mr. Bones was clipping the weeds next to the gate house. "Good morning, Miss Sadie. You're up mighty early."

"I'm meeting Henry."

He gave her a knowing look. "Does your momma know what you're up to?"

Sadie blushed. "Of course she does."

He chuckled. "I'm just teasing. He's a good boy. I can tell."

Sadie felt her cheeks getting even redder. "He's okay."

"Don't be embarrassed, Miss Sadie. I was young once, you know." He hoisted the clippers over his shoulder.

"Mr. Bones?"

Yes?"

Sadie was suddenly tongue-tied.

"Is there something you want to talk to me about, Miss Sadie?"

"I was… I mean, I wanted to ask if you…" Sadie squared her shoulders. "Mr. Bones, I think Owen did… uh…did something bad to the other caretaker, the one that was here before him. I wanted to tell you to be careful because he might try to do the same thing to you."

Mr. Bones scratched his beard thoughtfully. "Well, that's a peculiar thing to say. Why would he have hurt the other caretaker?"

"Henry and I think he's after the gold that Nathaniel and Mr. Barry took from the ship."

"That's a little hard to believe, Miss Sadie." Mr. Bones looked at her kindly. "I don't think you should worry about Owen. He doesn't strike me as the dangerous type, and I've seen my share of those."

"Still, promise me you'll be careful," Sadie pleaded.

Mr. Bones smiled. "I'll be careful, miss." He tipped his cap. "I best be getting to the rest of my chores before this morning gets away from me."

"Okay. Remember what I said."

"I will. See you around, Miss Sadie."

Sadie watched him amble away, chuckling under his breath. He didn't believe her.

Henry showed up about five minutes later as she was finishing her croissant. His hair was tousled as if he'd literally crawled out of bed thirty seconds ago. "Remind me why we're up this early."

Sadie handed him a croissant. "I want to start looking for the treasure. And I figured we'd start here, at the gate house."

"Isn't it locked?"

"We'll break in."

"You can't keep doing that!"

"Henry, my family owns this whole property, so that makes it *my* gatehouse."

"Oh. I guess you have a point. But wouldn't it still be easier to ask for a key?"

"Ask who? My mom? She'd want to know why. Besides, she only has the key to the house. Or maybe you're thinking we could ask Owen."

"What about Mr. Bones?"

Sadie shook her head. "I don't feel like chasing him

down right now. I told him about Owen."

"What did he say?"

"He didn't believe me. It was obvious."

Henry stuck the last of the croissant in his mouth and chewed it thoughtfully. "At least you warned him. That's better than nothing."

"I don't think it did any good." She pushed on the gate house window, but it wouldn't budge. "We might have to break it."

Henry walked over to the door and turned the knob. It swung open easily. "Or we could just use the door." He grinned.

Sadie poked him in the side. "Get over yourself. It was locked before."

They looked around the gatehouse for thirty minutes, with no luck. It seemed to be a catch-all for gardening tools, auto parts and old newspapers. As they were about to leave, Sadie stepped on a loose floorboard. Remembering how Bess had made the board pop up in the captain's room, she pushed on the opposite end. Sure enough, it sprang open. When she peered into the hole, the hairs on the back of her neck stood up.

"What is it?" Henry asked.

Sadie reached into the hole under the floorboard and pulled out a wallet. Inside was a driver's license that read, Calvin Julius Simpson. She swallowed the lump in her throat and looked up at Henry. His face was white as a sheet.

CHAPTER 16

As they sat on the grass outside the gatehouse, an Everleigh Garden Center truck turned into the driveway and stopped. Frank stuck his head out of the window to greet them. "You kids sure are up early."

"Hi, Frank." Sadie shoved the wallet behind her back. "Henry's helping me with a project."

"What kind of project?"

"We're… uh…" Sadie looked at Henry for help.

Henry grinned. "I'm helping Sadie learn her way around this place. She has no sense of direction."

Frank chuckled. "Well, that's nothing to be ashamed of, Sadie. I couldn't find my way out of a paper bag when I was your age." He put the truck into gear and revved the engine. "Stay out of trouble, you two."

"We will," Sadie called after him. She turned to Henry. "No sense of direction? Thanks a lot."

He held up his hands in mock surrender. "Hey, I had to come up with something."

Sadie opened the wallet again. Besides the driver's license, there was a credit card and several receipts—two from the garden center and one from Stella's.

"I think this proves it," Sadie said. "Owen did something to the other caretaker. Why else would he hide Mr. Simpson's wallet in the gatehouse?"

"Well… there's one other possibility."

"What?"

"What about Mr. Bones?"

Sadie frowned, disliking Henry's tone. "It isn't Mr. Bones. He's a sweet old man, and he's my friend. I'd know if he was a murderer. It has to be Owen. He's the other caretaker, so he'd have a key to the gate house."

"Okay. What now, Sherlock?"

She fiddled with the coin in her pocket. "Nothing's changed. We're gonna find the gold." She pulled it out and studied it, running her finger over the beaded edge. "We just have to watch our backs while we're searching." She shoved the coin back in her pocket.

"Yeah. I'd rather not run into Owen doing the same thing."

Sadie felt a pang of sadness, even though she'd never met Mr. Simpson. "I wonder where he is."

"Owen?"

"No. Mr. Simpson."

"I don't know. Do you think we should call someone?"

"I wouldn't know who to call. All we have is his wallet. There's no real proof something bad happened to him. Who's gonna believe a couple of kids?"

"I guess."

They walked up the driveway and around to the back of the house. Frank was loading empty pallets into his truck.

"Where's my mom?" Sadie asked.

He hoisted a pallet into the back and leaned over to pick up another one. "She's inside talking to Mrs. Northrup." He grunted, wiping his brow.

Henry's mouth fell open. "My mom is here?" He looked around and spotted her car on the other side of Frank's truck.

Frank nodded. "Man, that woman can talk. She came out here asking me all kinds of questions about your caretaker."

"Owen?" Sadie's breath caught in her throat.

"Yeah. I told her I couldn't express an opinion because I don't know the young fella."

"Oh." Sadie glanced at Henry. He looked as if he wanted to find a hole to crawl into.

She cleared her throat. "We're going inside to get

something to drink. Can we bring you something, Frank?"

He gave her a broad smile. "That's mighty nice of you. But your momma already brought me some lemonade about fifteen minutes ago. I just have a few more of these pallets to load."

"Okay. We'll see you later."

"You sure will." He threw the last of the pallets into the truck.

"I'm glad Frank's here to help my mom," Sadie said as they headed inside.

"He seems really nice." Henry said absently. He was obviously worried about his mother being there.

Sadie stopped without opening the back door. "Do you think she's telling my mom that we came over and asked her about Owen?" she whispered.

Henry frowned. "Maybe."

"Great. This should be fun…" she moaned.

When they entered the kitchen, Meg and Mrs. Northrup were sitting at the table, sipping on lemonade and laughing about something. Henry and Sadie exchanged surprised looks.

"Well, look at you two getting to know each other," Henry's mother said cheerfully.

Henry shoved his hands in his pockets. "Hi, Mom."

"Mrs. Northrup brought over some delicious banana bread." Meg smiled. "Would you kids like some?"

Sadie looked at Henry, and he shook his head.

"We're… uh… figuring out where everything is on the property. Henry's helping me find my way around. We just came in for drinks."

Meg waved her hand. "You know where everything is, Sadie. Help yourselves."

Relieved that there was no mention of Owen, Sadie grabbed two glasses of water and Henry nearly choked himself chugging his down as fast as possible.

Mrs. Northrup looked over, frowning. "Goodness, Henry!"

"Sorry, Mom. I was thirsty."

Sadie grabbed two cookies and wrapped them in a

napkin. "We'll be back later," she said, nudging Henry toward the door.

Once outside, she turned to him. "Can you be more obvious?"

Henry seemed rattled, "Sorry."

Sadie sighed. "I don't think your mother said anything to my mom about us coming over. If she had, my mom would've said something just now."

"Maybe not." He took the bundle of cookies from Sadie and stuck the first one in his mouth, biting off at least half of it. "But if my mom starts questioning Owen, he's gonna know we talked to her."

"I can barely understand you, Henry."

"Oh." He shoved in the rest of the cookie. "I think I need some real food soon. All these sweets are making me feel weird."

"What are you kids up to?" a voice asked behind them.

Sadie nearly jumped out of her skin. She whirled around. It was Owen. "Mrs. Northrup b–brought us banana b–bread!"

"Mrs. Northrup's here?" Owen gripped the rake he was carrying until his knuckles turned white.

Sadie looked at his boots—covered in gunk again. Owen caught her looking, so he took the end of the rake and tried to scrape it off. When he looked up again, Sadie noticed a bruise under his left eye.

"How'd you get hurt?" she asked suspiciously.

Owen's eyes widened. "It's nothing. Just stepped on this rake a while ago and it came back and hit me. That's all." He gripped the rake and took off toward the cottage.

Sadie turned to Henry. "Did you see his black eye? I think somebody hit him."

"Like who?"

"I have no idea. But he was acting weird, don't you think? Like he was scared of your mom."

"Who isn't?"

"Henry, I'm serious."

He wiped his forehead with the back of his hand. "I think it's pretty clear he knows we're up to something. What do we do now?"

Sadie lowered herself onto one of the steps and put her face in her hands. Her stomach sank as she thought of Mr. Simpson's wallet again. "You think he'd actually try to hurt us?'

Henry sat down beside her "To get to the gold that's probably worth a gazillion dollars before us? Yeah. I think he would."

"I guess we can't search the house with your mother here."

"Probably not."

Sadie hopped up. "Come on. Let's see where Owen went."

They sneaked around the house and caught a glimpse of him going into a dense cluster of magnolias. As they neared the trees, they heard voices.

"I didn't know she'd be here! I can't keep her on a leash! Don't get distracted. You know what you have to do." Sadie didn't know who it was, but his voice sounded familiar. "Don't make me come out here again."

Sadie's heart nearly jumped out of her chest. "Who's that?" she whispered.

Henry held his finger to his lips and shook his head.

"Why don't you handle it yourself?" It was Owen's voice.

"Do what I say and get rid of them, or you'll be the next caretaker to disappear," the other man growled.

Henry grabbed Sadie's hand and took off toward the front of the house with her stumbling along behind him. Once they reached the porch, they both collapsed.

"W—who was that talking to Owen?" Sadie stammered.

"I don't know."

"Come on. We have to tell our moms now." Sadie marched through the front door and into the kitchen. "Mom, Owen was just outside arguing with someone! Whoever it was wants us gone from here!"

Meg gasped. "What on earth are you talking about?"

"There's a man outside who wants Owen to get rid of us! Henry and I just heard them talking!"

Meg and Mrs. Northrup jumped up at the same time. Under any other circumstances, it might have been funny.

"Show me where they are!" demanded Mrs. Northrup.

Sadie led them out the kitchen door to the dense grove of magnolias. They pushed their way through, but no one was there.

"Are you sure this is where they were?" Meg asked anxiously.

"Yes I am." Sadie noticed the rake sticking out from under one of the magnolias. "Owen was carrying that before." She picked it up, gripping the handle tightly to keep her hands from shaking.

"I'll get to the bottom of this." Mrs. Northrup stepped out of the trees and hollered, "Owen!"

Owen appeared from the back of the house. "Yes ma'am?"

"Come here, young man!"

Owen hung his head and proceeded to plod in their direction as if heading to the gallows. "What is it, Mrs. Northrup?" he asked without looking up.

"My son and Miss Prophet overheard you arguing with someone."

Owen's eyes darted briefly to Sadie before looking down at his shoes. "Yes, ma'am. I was arguing with the tree guy."

Mrs. Northrup's eyes narrowed. "Would you care to share that conversation?"

Owen shifted his weight nervously. "We got some dead trees on the property that need removing, that's all. He thought I should've done it by now."

Sadie jumped in. "I heard him say you'd disappear like the old caretaker!"

Owen's face lost what little color it had. "He was threatening to get me fired."

Sadie glared at him. "You're lying!"

Meg cleared her throat loudly, then smiled at Owen. "Nobody's getting fired, Owen." She took the rake from Sadie and handed it to him. "The kids just misunderstood what they heard." She gave Sadie a stern look. "Back to the house, Sadie."

"But Mom!"

"Now."

Mrs. Northrup pointed toward the driveway. "Henry Northrup. Get in the car. I'm taking you home."

***

Sadie spent the rest of the day under house arrest. Her mother had ordered her to stay in her room until the rest of her boxes were unpacked and everything in them put neatly away. She imagined that Henry was suffering a similar fate, since neither of their mothers had believed them earlier.

Several hours into her incarceration, Sadie heard Owen's truck lumbering down the driveway. She ran out to the balcony and saw it turn onto the main road towards town. Here she was, stuck in her room, and the person who probably deserved to be behind bars was free to come and go as he pleased!

Frank's truck was parked out front. He smiled and waved as he climbed in and drove off. Her mom had probably filled him in on the "misunderstanding" with "poor Owen" while they were together in the garden.

"It isn't fair…" Sadie murmured.

"What's not fair?"

Sadie spun around. "Bess!"

Bess grinned. "This room looks much better without so many boxes."

Sadie sighed loudly. "My mom is punishing me."

Bess raised her eyebrows. "What did you do?"

Sadie plopped into one of the chairs by the fireplace and moaned. "Henry and I heard Owen and some other guy talking about getting rid of us. When we told our mothers, they didn't believe us."

Bess frowned. "You really heard him say that?"

"Yeah."

"This is very grave, Sadie. You should tell your father. He'll know what to do."

"My dad's in Italy. What can he do?"

Bess chewed her lip. "I know someone else who may be

able to help you."

Sadie leaned forward. "Who?"

Bess smiled. "Just…trust me."

"Sadie!" Meg called from downstairs. "Stella's here with dinner."

Sadie jumped up and ran to her bedroom door. "I'll be down in a minute!" She turned around. "Who do you know—?" Her eyes darted around the room. Bess had disappeared. Sadie stomped her foot. "Why do you keep doing that?!" she demanded. But of course, there was no reply.

Stella seemed giddy over the chance to step inside Prophet House while it was occupied by some "real Prophets." She stood in the foyer chattering away for so long that Meg asked her to stay for dinner. The invitation brought on another tidal wave of enthusiasm from Stella, which thankfully continued for most of the meal. At least it meant that Sadie didn't have to hear more about how she'd jumped to conclusions once again about "poor Owen."

Sadie excused herself and turned in early. She couldn't get Bess's comment off of her mind. Why had she run off again before explaining? And who was the mystery person who could help?

Sadie checked the wardrobe every few minutes, even crawling through the hole to the attic twice and listening for her at the cellar steps. She finally gave up around midnight. Bess wasn't coming back. Sadie would just have to wait until she showed up again. It was frustrating to say the least. She crawled into bed, expecting to be awake all night. But exhaustion took over and she was asleep in less than five minutes.

She awoke to the sound of a floorboard creaking. Someone was in her room! She flicked on the brass lamp. Owen stood over her, wearing dirty clothes and an angry scowl.

"They were all empty! Every last one! So you're gonna tell me where they are!"

Sadie's heart beat wildly. "Wha–what?"

"Don't play dumb with me, girl! Where's the gold that was in those chests?" he demanded.

Sadie sat up, shaking all over. "I don't know where it is!"

Owen grabbed her shoulders and shook her. "Tell me where they are or I'm the last thing you're ever gonna see!" His hands moved up to her neck.

Sadie grabbed the lamp and slammed it against his head, sending him reeling. She sprang out of bed and made a beeline for the wardrobe door while Owen writhed on the floor, clutching his bleeding head. She quickly crawled through the opening to the attic and ran for the other side as he opened the door from the hallway and staggered in.

Sadie felt his hot breath on her neck as she pulled open the narrow door and bolted down the stairs. His footsteps pounded directly behind her until they came to the broken step and she had the satisfaction of hearing him stumble and fall. For a moment she thought she was safe—until she heard him behind her again, groaning and swearing. As she reached the bottom, the cellar door flew open and there stood Bess. She grabbed Sadie's hand and pulled her out of the stairway...

Sadie sat bolt upright in bed, trying to catch her breath. It took a few moments for her to realize she'd had a nightmare––that none of it had really happened. She fumbled for the switch on the lamp, breathing a sigh of relief when it flicked on. She could still see Owen standing over her. The whole thing had seemed so real.

She lay down again and tried to relax enough to go back to sleep, but it was no use. The dream played over and over in her head—Owen… the lamp… the stairs. She finally gave up.

The diary was lying open on the table beside her. Anxious to get her mind on something other than the dream, Sadie picked it up and slowly deciphered the words.

My anguish is nearly unbearable. Why did Papa agree to take that man aboard the ship? I do not trust him and have told Papa as much. Some of the crew think he is cursed and his presence on the ship will bring disaster. I am worried that they may be right. There is something wicked about him. He hides it well in front of Papa, always smiling. But I have seen the dark side of him and so have others. If he sails aboard The Elizabeth, I fear I may never see my beloved Papa again.

Sadie set the book back on the table and lay down, pulling the sheet up around her chin. Elizabeth's words in the diary haunted her. Maybe the man on the boat had been dangerous, like Owen. She wanted to know how it had turned out. She turned the page.

I tried to warn her, but Mama doesn't believe me.

Sadie tried to swallow but her throat had turned bone dry. "My mother doesn't believe me either," she choaked out. She read the words over and over until they blurred on the page.

***

Sadie slept later than normal the next morning. Worn out from her fitful night of tossing and turning, she trudged down the hall to the bathroom and filled the claw-footed tub with hot water. After lowering herself in, she rested her head against the end and closed her eyes. Slowly but surely, the tension in her muscles relaxed, but she couldn't get the last entry in the diary off of her mind. Sadie couldn't help but feel that it was meant for her. And then there was the dream. Maybe it was a premonition of what was to come. She wondered if she'd inherited the ability to sense future events from Grandma Mary.

Her grandmother talked about having premonitions all the time. On the morning of Sadie's mother's accident, Grandma Mary had called twice to be sure everything was all right because she'd had one of her "feelings." Sadie sometimes had feelings about things that were about to happen too. She was having one right now, a sense of dread that caused her to shiver in spite of the warmth of the bath. Something was about to happen at Prophet House. Something frightening.

CHAPTER 17

The water had cooled down, so Sadie climbed out and wrapped herself in a towel. Catching her reflection in the mirror over the sink, she gave a little gasp. Her hair was a damp mess and there were traces of dark circles under her eyes. After brushing out her hair and splashing some cold water on her face, she decided that she looked a little more presentable.

When she walked into the kitchen wearing shorts and a T-shirt ten minutes later, Frank was there with a steaming mug in his hand.

"Morning, Sadie." He smiled. "Your momma sure does make a good cup of coffee."

Sadie smiled back. "I'll take your word for it. I'm not really a coffee drinker."

"Well, you're young yet. Give it some time." He turned the cup up and swallowed the last of it. "I'm heading outside again. You should come out back and see our progress."

"I will later. After breakfast, I'm supposed to work on the junk room some more."

"That's right. Your momma said you'd be working in one of the rooms on the second floor this morning. Have you found anything interesting in there so far?"

Sadie shook her head. "Not really. It seems to have only been used for storage. We threw away a bunch of stuff that had been in there for years."

Frank flashed a gold-toothed smile. "This is an amazing house. You never know what may turn up. You let me know if you find anything worth mentioning."

"I will."

"Oh, by the way, your young man is on the front porch. He got here about an hour ago."

"Henry's here?" Sadie asked. "I wonder why my mom didn't wake me! Where is she?"

"She went back to the garden center. I think she's planning to plant enough vegetables to open her own farmer's market." He chuckled. "She's a good woman, your mother. I bet Mr. Prophet will be happy to see what she's done with the place when he gets home."

"I'm sure he will," Sadie answered hastily.

She hurried from the kitchen and out the front door. Sure enough, Henry was sitting on the top step with his head against the rail post. His eyes were closed. She touched his shoulder and he practically jumped two feet.

"Jeez, Sadie! You almost gave me a heart attack! I was dreaming that Owen was chasing us through the woods with a shovel!"

Sadie plopped down beside him on the step. "I would think you'd be happy I woke you up before he knocked your head off with it."

"Okay, there's that, I guess."

"Besides, that's nothing compared to the dream I had."

He perked up. "Tell me."

"Maybe later." She didn't really feel like rehashing the whole thing. "If you're finished with your nap, want to help me finish cleaning the junk room?"

"Sure."

"After that, we can do the other thing."

His face broke into a wide grin. "Look for huge piles of gold?"

Sadie held her fingers to her lips, then whispered, "Frank's in the kitchen."

Henry clapped his hand over his mouth. "Sorry."

As they started up the steps to the second floor, they heard a car door shut out front. A minute later, Meg walked in. Her face was flushed with excitement.

"I can't wait to show you all the plants I picked up for the garden! With Frank helping me, I'll be able to grow three times the vegetables we had in Davenport!"

"That's great, Mom." Sadie smiled. It was nice to see her mother acting so much like her old self. "Henry's helping me in the junk room."

Meg beamed. "How nice of you, Henry. We'll have sandwiches for lunch later."

Sadie gave her a thumbs-up, then headed up the stairs with Henry behind her.

When she opened the door, he whistled. "You weren't kidding. This is gonna take some work."

"The main thing we need to do now is to get all the boxes of junk against the wall moved out into the hall. After that, it's just a matter of putting the furniture back in place and cleaning up."

Henry tried to pick up one side of the closest box, but immediately let it drop to the floor. "Man, that's heavy! Open the top and see what's in there."

"It's sealed up and I don't have any scissors."

"Well, find some. I may have just found the gold… or the old caretaker."

"Don't be gross, Henry!" Sadie leaned over and tried to lift the box. "I see what you mean though. What could possibly be in there that weighs so much?"

After they dragged the heavy box out of the room and into the hall, Sadie ran to her mother's room and came back with a pair of scissors. They were disappointed when they opened the lid and found it crammed with old books.

They carried eight more boxes into the hall, inspecting each one before determining its ultimate destination. Most were headed to the dump, but her mom would never allow the books to be thrown away. She'd want them to be donated. There was nothing interesting in any of the other boxes. Just yellowed samples of wallpaper, broken knickknacks, and cans of paint that had solidified after years of sitting undisturbed. No treasure maps or any other clues to the location of the elusive chests of gold.

Sadie plopped down on the floor. "What were you starting to tell me before about this room? You called it a ghost story."

Henry set an old can of paint against the wall and sat down. "It's been a long time since I heard this story, but I think Elizabeth Prophet died in this room. She had the flu or something like that. One night, while she was sick in bed, something happened that caused the room to catch on fire. When it started, she got up and tried to put it out herself with a blanket. She was burned pretty bad. But she couldn't stop it. The fire burned through the floor into the parlor below. Most of the town showed up to help put it out. Over the next few days, Elizabeth went downhill. She never got out of bed again, and died exactly one week after the fire, at the same time in the evening that it started.

After that, things started happening. People would hear her crying and sometimes they complained of smelling smoke, even though all the burned boards were torn out and replaced. My mom came in to look around once and she said the room suddenly went cold and she felt someone touch her shoulder. She was scared to ever come back."

Sadie looked around doubtfully. "I haven't had any trouble and I've been in here tons of times."

Henry nodded. "Yeah. It seems fine to me too."

"It's a scary story, though." She suddenly had goosebumps as the feeling that something bad was going to happen crept up on her again. "Maybe we should finish up. I'm starting to get a little creeped out."

Yeah, me too."

When they had the room cleared of the things that weren't staying, they moved the furniture that had been huddled together on the far side of the bed back into place. That proved to be harder than it sounded. Sadie would point at a spot and Henry would dutifully move a table, chair, or lamp there, only to have her change her mind and have him put it somewhere else.

"C'mon, Sadie, we're not going for perfection. Just make a decision and stick with it. I'd like to get out of here."

Sadie shot him a withering look. "I want to get it right.

It's important. Besides, I'm over the whole 'ghost in the room' thing." That wasn't exactly true. The uneasy feeling was still nagging at her, but something stronger had taken its place. For some inexplicable reason, she felt compelled to recreate Elizabeth's room as it had been two hundred years ago. And a voice in her head was helping her—a voice that wasn't her own.

"Well, I'm not over the ghost thing. And why is having the chair over there more right than having it here, or where it was before… or before that?"

"I just have a feeling that none of those spots are where it's supposed to be."

Henry rolled his eyes. "You have a feeling?"

"Yes. I can't explain it. Except, it's like I've been in this room before, but I don't remember where everything is supposed to be until I see it in the right place. Does that make sense?"

"No, it doesn't. But I'm moving it anyway… for the fifth time."

Sadie distinctly heard someone giggle. Then *He's funny…* Her breath caught in her throat. "Did you hear that?"

"Did I hear what?" Henry asked as he dragged the chair about two feet from where it had been before.

"Never mind." She scrutinized the chair's position, then shook her head. "That's not where it goes either."

Henry plopped down on the floor in protest. "It looks fine here! Seriously, what difference does it make?"

"It's important. I want her to be happy. She deserves it."

"Who?"

"Elizabeth."

Henry's eyes widened. "Okay, now *you're* creeping me out."

"Forget it. Just move the chair." She didn't blame him for being creeped out. It was creepy to her too. But there was no denying that Elizabeth Prophet wanted her room the way it had been before. Sadie didn't know how she knew this, she just did.

It took two more moves for Sadie to be satisfied that everything was where it should be. The last piece of furniture was a heavy mahogany chest of drawers at least six inches taller than she was. It took both of them to budge it. When they finally had it positioned on the wall opposite the bed, they collapsed on the floor and Sadie distinctly heard a voice say, "*Thank you…*"

"You're welcome," Sadie whispered.

Henry frowned. "What?"

Sadie smiled. "Nothing."

"Please tell me we're done." Henry moaned. "I really want to get out of here."

Sadie lay on the floor with her hands behind her head. "We still have to actually clean. Everything's covered in dust."

"Sadie! Henry!" Meg hollered from the foyer, "I have sandwiches and warm cookies just out of the oven if anyone's interested."

Henry looked at Sadie hopefully. "There's always tomorrow…"

"Fine," she said, rubbing her stomach. "Besides, I forgot to eat breakfast. I'm starving!" She jumped up and followed Henry downstairs. Sadie's mom had places set for them and glasses of iced tea poured. Frank came in from the garden and planted himself directly across from Sadie.

"Did you kids get a lot done?" he asked as he loaded his plate with mound of potato salad and a turkey sandwich.

"We still need to clean up," Sadie said between bites. "But the rest of the boxes are in the hall and the furniture's back in place."

Her mom seemed pleased. "You've really been working. Why don't you finish tomorrow?"

Henry nodded. "My thoughts exactly."

As they ate lunch, Meg chatted happily with Frank about the garden and Sadie's mind wandered. She couldn't stop thinking about Owen. So far, they hadn't found anything that proved he was after the coins. Still, she had a feeling in the pit of her stomach that the evidence was right in front of them, just waiting to be found. But where?

"Sadie, did you hear what I said?" Meg asked.

Sadie jerked back to the present. "Huh?"

"I asked if you'd mind showing Henry's mother the room you've been working on."

Sadie stared at her blankly. "Henry's mother?"

Meg gave her an exasperated look. "Yes, Sadie. She asked if she could come by to take some pictures. Since you and Henry have worked so hard on Elizabeth's room, I thought it would be nice if we let her take pictures in there too."

Sadie looked at Henry. He was holding his sandwich in mid-air.

"When is this supposed to happen?"

As if in answer, someone knocked on the front door and a second later said, "Hello? Meg? It's Amelia Northrup! Your door was unlocked."

CHAPTER 18

Meg jumped up and disappeared into the hallway that led to the foyer. "Come in, Amelia!"

Frank seemed suddenly flustered and pushed his chair back. "I think I'll head back out to the garden." When the back door closed after him, Sadie noticed the half-eaten sandwich on his plate.

"He sure was in a hurry to get out of here all of a sudden," Sadie commented. "I've never seen him leave food. It's almost like he didn't want to see your mother."

"My mom sometimes has that effect on people."

Sadie pursed her lips and stared at Henry. "Did you know your mother was coming to take pictures today?"

He shoved in the last bite of his sandwich and mumbled. "She might have said something about it."

Sadie frowned. "And?"

Henry sighed. "Fine. She's making a new brochure for the reenactment week and wants everything to be perfect this year, so maybe Mr. Endicott will reconsider." He took a deep breath. "This is the part that might make you mad."

Sadie crossed her arms and waited.

"She's bringing Stevie… in her Elizabeth Prophet costume. She's planning to put her in the brochure."

Sadie jumped up. "No way!"

"Keep your voice down!" he whispered.

Sadie lowered her voice. "It's bad enough that she's playing Elizabeth. Now she has to be in the brochure too?"

Meg stuck her head in the kitchen door. "What's going on?"

Sadie set her jaw. "Nothing, Mom."

"It didn't sound like nothing."

"It's okay. Henry and I were just disagreeing about something. But it's fine now."

"Hmph." Meg pursed her lips. "Anything I need to be aware of?"

Sadie shook her head.

"We'll talk about this later. Right now I need you to get out here and speak to our guests." Meg headed back to rejoin Mrs. Northrup and Stevie.

Sadie peaked down the hall to the foyer. Stevie was standing in the doorway, wearing a long yellow gown with daisies on the bottom and ankle boots. She was clutching a small velvet handbag in one hand and smoothing her tightly wound blond ringlets with the other. Sadie looked back at Henry and pretended to gag.

"*Stop*," Henry mouthed

Sadie was seething. "I hate the thought of Stevie poking around Elizabeth's room," she whispered.

"Maybe you should go with them. At least that way you can make sure she doesn't mess with anything."

Sadie sighed. "Fine. At least you'll be there to keep me from punching Stevie."

Henry didn't budge from the table.

"Aren't you coming?" Sadie asked.

Henry shook his head.

Sadie's eyes narrowed. "Henry Northrup, if I have to put up with Stevie Winslow, so do you."

Henry's shoulders slumped, but he dutifully followed.

The foyer was empty now, but they could hear voices drifting down from the second floor. They found Stevie making herself at home in Elizabeth's room. She was perched in one of the chairs with her feet resting on an upholstered stool. It took all of Sadie's self-control to resist yanking her onto the floor by her lace-up boots.

Meg seemed relieved when she saw Sadie. "There you

are! Mrs. Northrup was just saying what a wonderful job you did on the room."

"I'm sorry it's so dusty," Sadie said. "We haven't gotten around to that yet. If you want, you can come back another day."

Mrs. Northrup waved her hand. "That's not necessary. I don't think it'll show up in the pictures." She clutched her chest. "I must say, seeing it like this is very moving." She dabbed her eyes with a handkerchief she pulled from her purse. "I can picture Elizabeth in here. It's just lovely."

"Thanks. Henry was a big help."

Henry reluctantly stuck his head in the door. "Hi, Mom."

Mrs. Northrup raised her eyebrows. "I wondered where you'd taken off to so early this morning, Henry." She turned her attention to Meg. "I hope he hasn't been a bother."

Meg smiled. "Not at all. We've enjoyed having him around. And I'm sure Sadie appreciated his help with this room."

Stevie glared at Sadie.

Mrs. Northrup snapped a photo, then lowered the camera. "Stevie, dear, I'll be using these pictures in the brochure. From what I've heard, Elizabeth was a pleasant child, not a petulant one."

Stevie forced a smile. "I'm sorry, Mrs. Northrup."

Henry's mother nodded. "That's better."

For the rest of their visit, Sadie managed to avoid eye contact with Stevie. Meg ducked out and left Sadie and Henry to supervise. Mrs. Northrup continued to gush about the room and seemed pleased with the photo session. All in all, it wasn't as painful an experience as Sadie had imagined it would be, especially since Stevie seemed so miserable the whole time.

As they were about to leave, Henry's mother turned to Sadie and smiled.

"Thank you for helping with our photo session today, Sadie. You'll be a wonderful addition to the reenactment team this year. I gave your costume to your mother. Henry can fill you in on your duties. I'm afraid I have to run. I left Jocelyn in charge of the store, and she's a bit of a scatterbrain."

Henry wouldn't look Sadie in the eye.

The second the door was closed, Sadie turned on him.

"What duties?"

Henry shifted his weight uncomfortably. "It's not that bad, really. All we have to do is hand out flyers the last two weeks before the reenactment and help set up for the cast party in the park in a couple of weeks."

"A cast party? Isn't that what you have *after* a production?"

"That's what my mom calls it. Everyone in the reenactment shows up in costume so my mom can make sure they look right for their parts. After that, there's a huge picnic. Everyone in town is invited. It's pretty cool, actually."

Sadie set her jaw. "I have more important things to do! Like finding Nathaniel's treasure so we don't lose Prophet House!" A realization struck her like a brick wall. She didn't want to leave Everleigh—she belonged here. At some point, she'd stopped missing Davenport. This was home now. "I don't ever want to leave here, Henry."

"I don't want you to either. I'll help you. I promise. We can look for the treasure practically every second of every day when we're not helping my mom."

"Fine. I'll help with the cast party and the flyers. But I'm not dressing up unless I'm something other than Stevie's maid."

Henry grinned.

"What's so funny?"

"I switched your costume," he answered smugly.

"What?"

"This morning. Mom had the bags by the door and one had your name on it. So I switched it. You don't have the maid's costume."

"What am I now? The village idiot?"

"You're the preacher's daughter—Rebecca."

"You knew this all day and didn't say anything?"

"I probably should've told you right away, huh?"

"Ugh!"

Henry opened his mouth to say something but clearly thought better of it and snapped it closed again.

Meg appeared at the top of the stairs, wearing a dark wig and a beaming smile. "Amelia wants me to play Sarah in the reenactment! What do you think?"

All of Sadie's anger drained away in the face of her mother's excitement. "I think you look amazing, Mom." She smiled.

"Really?" Meg fiddled with the dark tendrils that framed her face. "I never thought of myself as a brunette, but I think I love it!"

"It looks great. And you have blue eyes like Sarah, so it's perfect."

"I haven't tried on the dress yet, but one of the ladies in town is a seamstress and will do alterations if I need them." Meg's smile broadened. "Amelia has a costume for you too, Sadie. It's in the bag by the door."

Sadie nodded. "Henry was just telling me I'm playing the preacher's daughter."

"Oh that's wonderful! By the way, Amelia said that there used to be shells in the vase on the dining room table. Apparently, it was a tradition started by the first Sarah Prophet. I thought you two might like to go to the beach and get some. We want to be as authentic as possible when visitors come through the house. There's a bucket on the front porch."

"You're really getting into this aren't you, Mom?"

Meg gave them a wry smile. "Okay, I admit it. Now run along, you two. And no broken shells."

Sadie smiled. "No broken shells. Check."

CHAPTER 19

As they walked barefooted down the beach, Sadie picked up shells and dropped them into the bucket without saying a word. She was deep in thought. Every so often she stopped to gaze out at the vast expanse of water. Somewhere out there, what was left of Nathaniel Prophet's ship languished on the ocean floor, lost forever. It was a somber thought.

Henry rolled up his jeans and walked along the edge of the water. He found an unbroken scallop shell and dropped it in with the others. "I'm sorry I didn't tell you right away about the costume."

Sadie held the bucket out and he dropped in another perfectly formed shell.

"I'm not mad, Henry. I don't care about the costume. If it means we get to stay here, I'll play any part your mom wants me to. I don't want to leave Prophet House. But I'm worried about the money. What if we can't find the coins? No one has been able to for almost two hundred years."

Henry put his hand on her shoulder. "I'll help you find the coins. I promise."

It was an empty promise. He had no more of an idea where to look than Sadie did. But she appreciated his offer and gave him a small smile. "Thanks."

The wind had begun to pick up. Henry pointed at a mass of ominous clouds moving in. "Maybe we should turn back."

They'd barely covered the bottom of the bucket when the first drop of rain fell. As it quickly turned into a downpour,

Henry grabbed Sadie's hand and took off for a small hut on the beach. They huddled together inside, waiting for the rain to let up. Henry still held her hand, their fingers laced together. She looked up to find him watching her.

"You aren't cold, are you?" he asked.

Sadie realized she'd been shivering. "I thought summer at the beach was supposed to be hot, even when it rained."

The strand of hair that always fell was in his eyes again. This time, Sadie pushed it back before she had the presence of mind to stop herself.

He grinned. "Thanks."

Sadie felt blood rush to her cheeks and jerked her hand back. After staring at the peeling floor for several minutes, she looked up. He was still grinning from ear to ear.

"Get over yourself, Henry."

"You can mess with my hair any time you want."

"I don't want to mess with your hair! It was annoying me. That's all."

"Whatever you say, Sherlock."

The rain continued to pummel the tiny shack, and every so often, a stream of water poured in directly over Sadie's head.

"What's the point of sitting in here if we're still getting wet?" she asked.

"It's a flat roof with kind of a dip in the middle. The water pools on top and eventually it has to relieve itself. You know, like when you have a full bladder."

Sadie stared at Henry, then burst out laughing. "The roof is peeing on us? Really?"

Henry snickered. "Yep."

Sadie scooted over against the back wall. "I take it you've been in here before when it was raining?"

"Yeah. Why do you think I'm sitting here, instead of where you were?"

Sadie poked him in the side with her elbow. "Thanks a lot."

"My pleasure."

She peeked outside. "Looks like the rain's stopping."

He crawled to the door and looked out. "Yep. Are you

ready to head back?"

Sadie nodded. "I want to finish cleaning Elizabeth's room."

Henry's shoulders slumped. "That's what you want to do for the rest of the afternoon? Clean dust off of old furniture? What about looking for the coins?"

"We can start looking for the treasure tomorrow morning. My mom will be out in the garden for hours. She won't see us snooping around."

Henry grimaced. "Okay. Let's go clean a dusty two-hundred-year-old room on a summer day when we have no school. Nothing I'd rather do."

Sadie poked him in the side again and laughed.

He rubbed his side, pretending to be in pain. "You know, you could break a rib doing that."

Sadie rolled her eyes. "Good grief. Man up."

He grabbed the bucket and took off across the sand with Sadie on his heels. When he reached the wooden walkway over the dunes, he stopped to let her catch up.

As they made their way across the dunes, Sadie had a distinct feeling that they were being watched again. She looked around but didn't see anyone. Still, the hairs were standing up on the back of her neck and she felt sure someone was there.

Sadie's mom was relieved when they walked in the front door. "Thank goodness! I was worried when the storm passed over. I sent Owen out to look for you."

"You sent Owen to the beach?" *That explains who was watching us,* Sadie thought.

"Yes. And he hasn't come back. I hope he's okay."

"I'm sure he's fine." She grabbed Henry's arm and practically dragged him after her. "We're going to Elizabeth's room to finish up."

"Wait! Did you find any shells?" Meg called after them.

"Just a few. They're in the bucket on the porch."

"What are you planning to use to clean the room?"

Sadie stopped at the landing and looked back. Her mom was holding a bucket filled with rags and a bottle of spray cleaner.

Henry sprinted down the stairs and retrieved them. "Thanks, Mrs. Prophet."

"You're welcome, Henry." Meg smiled. "Don't let my daughter work you too hard."

"No problem!"

Henry got started wiping down the dusty furniture while Sadie ran upstairs to change out of her wet clothes. When she walked into her room, Bess was sitting on the bed, looking at the diary.

"Bess!"

Bess hopped off the bed. "Where have you been? Were you out in the storm? You're all wet!"

"I went to the beach with Henry. How long have you been here?"

Bess smiled smugly. "Nearly an hour. Your mother came up once but I hid in the wardrobe." She seemed very pleased with herself.

"I'm glad you're here. You can help Henry and me clean Elizabeth's room."

Bess climbed onto the bed again and shook her head. "I'd rather stay right here."

"Look. Henry told me about the rumors of it being haunted, but that's all they are—rumors. We were in there for hours and nothing weird happened." *Except for the voice in my head...* she thought.

Bess chewed on her lip thoughtfully. "Did you find anything... unexpected?"

Sadie grabbed some dry clothes from the wardrobe. "Like what?" She pulled on shorts and a t-shirt, then threw her damp clothes in the corner by the door. Something hard hit the floor and Sadie realized she'd nearly forgotten the coin. She retrieved it from the pile of wet clothes and shoved it in her pocket, mentally scolding herself for being so careless. As an afterthought, she took the locket from a drawer in the chest and slid the chain over her head.

"You'd know if you saw it."

Sadie looked up. "Huh?"

"For goodness sake, pay attention! This is important."

Sadie frowned. "Just tell me what you're talking about."

Bess cocked her head to the side. "There are secret compartments all over this house, you know. Maybe even in that room."

Sadie perked up. "You mean the treasure might be there?"

Bess shook her head. "It's something else."

"Is it in the floor?"

Bess shook her head again.

Someone knocked on the door and Sadie jerked around.

"Sadie, are you coming?" It was Henry. "I'm not doing this by myself."

"Give me a second, Henry!"

"What's taking so long?" He sounded impatient.

"I'm coming in just a minute."

"Fine. But I'm timing you."

Sadie heard him march down the hall to the stairs. "Can you believe that? You'd think I'd been up here for an hour!" She turned around to an empty room. Bess was gone. "Good grief," she muttered.

Checking in the wardrobe was a waste of time. The panel that covered the crawl space to the attic was open, but there was no sign of Bess.

"Typical," Sadie grumbled.

When she opened the door, Henry was sitting on the top step, tapping his foot.

"Bess was in my room when I got there," Sadie said matter-of-factly.

He turned around. "Really? I didn't see her."

"She disappeared again… of course. I can't figure her out." Sadie started down the stairs, an odd mixture of annoyance and excitement churning in her stomach. "She said there's something hidden in Elizabeth's room."

Henry jumped up. "What?"

"She wouldn't tell me. But she said it's not in the floor. So what does that leave? We've checked all the furniture."

Henry darted past her. "The walls?"

Sadie caught up with him on the second floor. "Exactly."

Henry set the bucket down outside the door. "Now what, Sherlock?"

"You take that side of the room and I'll take this one."

They started around in opposite directions, running their hands along the walls and looking for any signs of an opening. They ended up on either side of the fancy headboard with nothing to show for their effort.

"Looks like she was wrong." Henry sounded disappointed.

"I don't know…" Sadie ran her hand down the wall slightly behind the bedpost and felt something. "Help me move the bed a little!"

They shoved it about three inches toward the door and there it was—an almost imperceptible seam that ran all the way to the floor. They shoved the bed another two feet and could see the outline of a door. Sadie tried to push it open, but nothing happened. She pushed harder, but it still didn't move.

"This is weird. The one in the attic is easy to open."

Henry ran his hand down the crack. "What's this?" He leaned in for a closer look. "It looks like a really small keyhole."

Sadie sucked in her breath. "Oh my God, Henry! She pulled the locket from under her shirt and popped it open.

"Where'd you get that?" Henry asked.

"It was under the floor in my room." She could barely contain her excitement. "This has to work!" She extracted the key from under the lock of hair. It was a perfect fit and made a satisfying click when she turned it. This time, when she pushed on the wall, the panel sprang open.

Inside was what appeared to be a painting wrapped in brown paper and tied with twine. A note was tucked under the knot. The writing was familiar…

"This is Elizabeth's writing." She handed the note to Henry. "See if you can read it."

Henry studied it for a couple of minutes, his expression solemn.

"Henry, what does it say?"

He began to slowly read out loud.

My dear Mama,

This terrible illness has taken over every part of me and I am growing too weak to fight it. Please do not blame yourself. The fire was not your fault. I tried to stop him but I did not have the strength. It is of no consequence now that you and Nate are safe. Truly, the burns on my hands scarcely hurt now. That is a blessing. But my breathing is laboured and I know my life is ending soon. My heart aches for your loss. First Papa and now me. You still have little Nate and he will need you more now than ever. I promise, if it is in my power to do so, I will watch over both of you until we are reunited.

I'll miss you so, my dearest Mama. I love you with all my heart,

Your Bess

Sadie was thunderstruck as the realization hit her. Deep down, she'd known all along. Her hands trembled as she pulled the painting out of the wall and unwrapped it. The edges of the frame were charred, but Sadie barely noticed, because staring back at her was a young girl whose light red hair hung in ringlets around her face. The girl was sitting on the floor leaning against a bed post in the captain's room—the room that was now Sadie's. The two glass doors behind her opened onto the balcony that overlooked the ocean. On the floor next to her were two gold coins. Her hazel eyes sparkled with delight as she cuddled a white puppy that seemed determined to plant a wet kiss on her chin. The girl looked as if she were about to laugh out loud. Sadie knew what that laugh would sound like, because she'd heard it before. At the bottom of the painting, the artist had written: *Portrait of Elizabeth Prophet*. Sadie felt hot tears roll down her cheeks.

Henry put his hand on her shoulder. "Sadie, what's wrong?"

"I know who this is." Her voice quivered. "We have the same eyes. I hadn't noticed before…"

"It's Elizabeth Prophet, right? Nathaniel and Sarah's

daughter?"

"Yes." Sadie nodded solemnly. "But I know her. Henry… this is Bess."

"Bess looks like her?"

Sadie felt like her heart would beat out of her chest. "No. Bess *is* her."

"I don't understand."

"What don't you understand?" she demanded tearfully. "This is Sarah and Nathaniel's daughter, Elizabeth. Only they apparently called her Bess for short. This is also the Bess I know—the one who wears the same dress that she's wearing in this painting. The one who said she doesn't go to school and runs off every time anybody else shows up. The one who was in my room when we first arrived and told me she didn't think anyone could see her! And the one who was sitting on my bed ten minutes ago with the diary…*her* diary!" She shivered as another realization hit her. "Now I know why she didn't want to go up to the widow's walk. She wrote about it in her diary. She found her mother up there crying, night after night. It all makes since now!"

"You're saying that the Bess you've been telling me about—the one who was just upstairs— is the ghost of your great-aunt, or great-great-great-whatever aunt? She's not a live person? She's a ghost? Is that what you're saying?" Henry's voice was shrill, his eyes wide with panic.

"Take a deep breath, Henry. Here…" She pulled a chair over and made him sit down. "There's nothing to freak out about."

"Nothing to freak out about?" he asked incredulously. "You've been hanging out with a ghost all this time! A ghost!"

"I know."

"That's it? You know?"

"I can't explain it. I know I should be hysterical. But I feel… I don't know… peaceful." It was true. She felt utterly calm. "It all makes sense now—why she knows so much about Nathaniel…why she was so weird about meeting anyone else. She only wanted *me* to see her. Maybe I'm the only one who *can* see her. Well… except for Mr. Bones. He's seen her too. So she must only appear to certain people. It's kind of cool if you think about it." She plopped down on the floor next to Henry's chair. "I wonder who it was that started the fire. It had to be the man who'd been following her, but she never said who he was."

Henry stared at her. "I guess we'll never know, but seriously, you're really okay with all of this?"

"Yeah."

He took a deep breath. "What do we do now, Sherlock?"

"There are coins in the painting, just like the one I found. Which must mean there are more in the house somewhere. We have to find them before Owen does." She looked at him soberly. "I can't leave Prophet House. Not now. Not after this."

"You need to tell your mom about Bess, and about Owen."

"Tell her what? One of my friends is the ghost of Elizabeth Prophet? You don't know my mom. She was nervous about ghosts the day we got here. She'd freak out and want to move. And we have no proof that Owen is only working here so he can steal the treasure. I can't just say I have a feeling. We have to actually catch him breaking into the house or something like that."

"How are we supposed to do that?"

"I don't know. We'll just have to keep our eyes open."

"I have a bad feeling that being friends with you will turn out to be hazardous to my health."

"Don't worry," Sadie said. "Bess and I will protect you."

"Great. You and a ghost will protect me. That makes me feel so much better..."

Sadie did her best to rewrap the portrait of Bess, then carefully placed it back in the cubby and pushed the panel into place. Anyone who didn't know what to look for would never know it was there.

"You're leaving it in there?"

"Yeah... for now." Bess hadn't wanted anyone but Sadie to know about her. It felt wrong to violate her trust. She carefully placed the key back in the locket.

Henry watched her, a strange look on his face. "So it's true."

"What?"

"What people have said about Prophet House… It's haunted."

"Yes. It's true."

***

Sadie's mom opened the door to her room early the next morning. "Henry's here. We need to discuss some boundaries. First, you should talk to him about calling first." She chuckled. "I was in my robe at the kitchen table drinking my first cup of coffee."

"Sure, Mom. I need to shower. Can you feed him or something?"

Meg sighed. "I suppose. What should I fix?"

"From my experience so far, he'll eat anything."

Meg retreated downstairs and Sadie ran to the bathroom and showered off quickly. Back in her room, she pulled on shorts and a top, then pulled her damp hair back into a ponytail.

When she stepped into the kitchen, Henry was working on a plate of bacon and eggs.

"Don't they feed you at your house?" Sadie teased.

Henry grinned. "Not enough."

"Where's my mom?"

"She went out to the garden with Frank."

"Great! Are you ready to get started?"

He pushed his chair back. "I'm ready."

"Me too. But to tell you the truth, I don't know where to begin." She chewed her lip thoughtfully. "It has to be somewhere we haven't thought to look."

Henry rubbed his chin. "People have looked for the coins for years. They have to be someplace no one would think of. What about the outhouse?"

Sadie wrinkled her nose. "Really? The outhouse? No one would put treasure in an outhouse, because sooner or later they'd have to go back and fish it out."

Henry made a gagging sound. "Good point."

Sadie thought of the compartment under the floor in the

captain's room. There was no telling how many other secret places there were in Prophet House. "We need to look for other hidden places in the house. And I think we should start in the captain's room. That's where Bess was in the painting and there were two gold coins on the floor."

They headed up to her room and spent an hour crawling around the floor, feeling for loose boards. Nothing. The compartment where she'd found the diary was apparently the only one. Next, they went around the room, searching for seams in the wall. Still no luck.

"I wish Bess was here." Sadie sighed.

"Do you think you'll see her again?" Henry asked nervously.

"I don't know. Part of me hopes so, but the other part of me thinks it would be too different now that I know."

"And you're absolutely sure Bess isn't just some obsessed Prophet House fan who looks and dresses like their Elizabeth?"

Sadie nodded. "I'm absolutely sure."

Henry left after lunch to head to his mother's shop to make deliveries. Sadie's dress for the reenactment was still in a bag at the front door. She carried it upstairs and laid it on her bed. It was an off-white gown with a high waist encircled with a blue ribbon. She had to hand it to Henry's mom. Except for the color, it was remarkably like the dress Bess wore. Mrs. Northrup had obviously made an effort to accurately depict the clothing of Nathaniel and Sarah's time. Maybe dressing up for the reenactment wouldn't be so bad.

CHAPTER 20

For the next two weeks, Henry came over every morning after his deliveries. They inspected all the floors and every wall in the entire house for more hidden compartments. They found seventeen but were disappointed to find them all empty—except for a particularly intimidating spider in the last one.

Sadie ran into Mr. Bones every day. He always seemed to turn up just when she needed someone to talk to. Sadie had nearly told him about finding Bess's portrait in the wall, but ultimately decided against it. She didn't know how the news that Bess was a ghost would affect him, and she wouldn't be able to stand it if he left because of it. Mr. Bones had become her good friend. He made her dad's absence a little more bearable.

Sadie read the diary every night. A few of the entries were about ordinary things, everyday life at Prophet House. But most were more fearful. Bess worried about her papa and John Barry, and had a bad feeling that her family was in danger. She mentioned being followed and believed she knew the identity of the stalker. Apparently, it wasn't the sinister man that she'd warned the captain about, because he was on the ship with Nathaniel the last time they sailed. It was someone else, although she never called him by name.

Sadie hadn't seen Bess since the day she found her on the four-poster with the diary. She was pretty sure she'd heard Bess a few times, but when she'd gone to look, she wasn't there. Maybe now that Sadie knew the truth, she'd never see her again. That thought made her feel like crying. Ghost or not, Sadie missed her friend.

Frank came every day to help her mother in the garden. He built up the beds with garden soil and compost and installed a simple sprinkler system to keep the plants watered. He hauled over pallets of tomato plants, peas, asparagus, spinach, cabbage, lettuce, and squash. The tiny plants were already poking their heads out of the rich soil, and he assured Meg that she would soon be the envy of the Everleigh Garden Club.

But to Sadie, the best thing about the garden was seeing her mother so happy. Sometimes, she almost forgot that they were living there on borrowed time. Mrs. Northrup still hadn't shared the news about Prophet House losing its benefactor with Meg, and Sadie didn't have the heart to tell her. The only thing that could save them for sure was finding the treasure.

With so much of her focus on finding the coins, it didn't occur to Sadie until later in the second week that she had seen very little of Owen. It crossed her mind that he might be avoiding her. She wondered if it had to do with the other man he'd been arguing with in the magnolia grove. The supposed "tree man." His identity was still a mystery. She'd tried to come up with a likely suspect but kept drawing a blank. Mr. Bones said he was keeping an eye on Owen, but Sadie knew he still didn't believe her. He was just being kind, as he always was.

As Sadie got ready for bed the night before the cast picnic in the park, her mother called up the stairs. "Your dad is on the phone!"

Sadie tore downstairs. "Hi, Dad!"

"Hey, squirt. Sorry. I know you don't like me calling you that anymore."

"No, it's okay. I kinda miss it… and I miss you."

"I miss you too."

"How's your arm? Does it hurt?"

"Not much anymore. All things considered, I came out better than I should have. I was sitting right behind the driver, and he was hurt pretty badly."

"I hope he'll be okay."

"I hear he's doing fine. He's out of the hospital and recuperating at home. What's been happening around Prophet

House?"

Sadie swallowed the lump in her throat. She wanted to tell him everything, but what was the point? He was thousands of miles away.

"Tomorrow's the reenactment cast party in the park. I'm going with Henry. We've been hanging out a lot."

"Is that so?"

Sadie could tell he was smiling. She could hear it in his voice. "Yeah. I met a few of his friends and they seem nice. Well…except for Stevie. She's still a jerk."

"A jerk, huh? In what way?"

"She thinks she's God's gift to the world." It was a relief to be able to talk freely about something that had nothing to do with Owen or the treasure or losing Prophet House. "She's completely wrong to play Elizabeth!"

"How do you know? After all, Elizabeth was the daughter of the most important people in a town named after her mother. She might have been stuck on herself too."

"She's not! She's shy and—" Sadie sucked in her breath. "Well…I mean, I think she was probably that way. I can't imagine her being like Stevie."

"Listen, you'll run into people like Stevie your whole life. Might as well make the best of it."

Sadie sighed. "I'll try."

"Anything else you want to talk about?"

Sadie suddenly had the overwhelming urge to burst out crying. Her dad was in Italy, and they were probably going to lose Prophet House unless she and Henry found the gold. And after so much fruitless searching, that was seeming less and less likely. Her eyes filled with tears. "I just wish you were here."

"Me too. I'm counting the days, believe me. Your mom said she has something to tell me when I get home. Any idea what that is?"

Sadie lowered her voice. "Did you ask her?"

"She said it's a surprise. She was pretty mysterious about it, but assured me it was something I'd be happy about."

Sadie was relieved. Apparently, it wasn't anything about Mr. Endicott. Maybe she was talking about the garden. "I don't know what it is. But if it's a surprise I couldn't tell you anyway."

"You're right. Just thought I'd give it a shot. By the way, why are you still up? It's 11 pm there."

"It's summer. But I'm getting ready for bed now."

"Right. We're on summer rules."

Sadie chewed her lip. "Dad, there is something I wanted to ask you."

"Shoot."

"Did Grandpa ever tell you why he only stayed at Prophet House for three months?"

"Of course, Sadie. He was sick. Unfortunately, none of us knew it at the time, not even your grandmother. She'd stayed in Davenport while the renovations were going on and found out when the doctor called to ask why her husband wasn't coming in for treatments. It was quite a shock. She drove to Everleigh and insisted he come home. He barely lived a year after that. I think the stress of the renovations weakened him."

"I remember visiting him in the hospital. He told me he was just a little under the weather. That was the last time I ever talked to him."

Her dad sighed. "He didn't want you to worry."

"Yeah. I thought maybe it was because of …" Sadie caught herself, almost blurting out the news that the house was haunted by the ghost of Elizabeth Prophet.

"Because of what?"

"Uh… because of Mrs. Northrup."

"Oh." He chuckled. "No. Your grandfather wasn't intimidated by her."

"I thought she scared everybody."

"Not the Prophet men." He said in an authoritative voice.

Sadie laughed. "Right."

"Anything else you want to ask me about, squirt?"

"I just wondered… Did Grandpa look for the treasure when he lived here that summer?"

"I don't know. If he did, he obviously didn't find anything. Why?"

"Some people think it's still here."

He sounded skeptical. "Anything's possible, but don't

get your hopes up. I'm pretty sure that place has been searched top to bottom in the last two hundred years."

Sadie reached into her pocket and touched the coin, tempted to go ahead and tell him about it. But before she could get it out, she heard someone speaking Italian in the background.

"I've gotta go, squirt. The sun will be up in about a half an hour and the bus is here. We have a full day planned so we're getting an early start."

"Oh… okay." She let go of the coin. Her sense of impending doom wormed its way into her brain again. She thought of Sarah Prophet, climbing the ladder to the widow's walk, night after night, hoping for Nathaniel's return. Sadie swallowed the lump in her throat. "Be careful, Dad."

"I will. Take care of your mom until I get back."

"I will. I promise."

"I'll call again in a couple of days, I love you, Sadie."

"I love you too."

As she hung up the phone, her lip began to tremble and tears stung her eyes.

She plodded upstairs to her room and collapsed onto the four-poster. Elizabeth's journal was on the chest next to the bed. Sadie opened it and began to slowly decipher the script.

I have been such a fool. Blind to the truth. How can I forgive myself for the vile thoughts that have festered in my mind about him? I could not have been more wrong. He wants only to keep us from harm. But I am afraid that will not be possible. He is no match for the one who wants to finish us.

"Who are you talking about, Bess?" she whispered.

There was no answer.

***

Sadie sat on the front steps and watched Henry stroll up the driveway around ten the next morning. He was dressed in regular clothes.

"I thought we had to wear our costumes today," Sadie said.

"We're supposed to, but I have to move all the tables afterwards and my mom doesn't want me to mess up my reenactment clothes."

"If you're not wearing yours, I'm not wearing mine either. I'm supposed to be helping too."

"Fine with me." He smiled. "We'll be the only normal people there."

Meg was still preparing the food she'd signed up to bring. "Aren't you changing into your costume Sadie?"

"I'm helping Henry with the tables, so we don't have to dress up."

"Hmm." Meg studied them skeptically. "Henry's mom seemed pretty adamant about the costumes."

"It'll be okay, Mrs. Prophet." Henry chimed in.

"All right then. You two go on. I'll see you there later."

As they turned onto the main street into town, Sadie was surprised to see parked cars lining both sides of the road.

"How many people turn out for this thing?" she asked.

Henry shrugged. "Lots."

The park was bustling with people. Tables, laden with food, were set up opposite the bandstand, where a string quartet accompanied an old-fashioned country band. Displays depicting life in the early 1800s were scattered all over. But the most impressive thing to Sadie was that nearly every man, woman, and child were dressed in period clothing, some more authentic looking than others. She felt a little out of place in her shorts and t-shirt. If it weren't for all the cars along the road, it would have appeared that they had stepped back in time.

"I can't believe it. I had no idea it would be like this."

Henry nodded. "Everleigh gets into its history in a big way."

"Obviously."

Mrs. Northrup came up behind them. "Miss Prophet! Why didn't you wear your costume?"

"I figured I'd try it on later, Mrs. Northrup." Sadie said, even more embarrassed now that Henry's mother had pointed out her lack of conformity. "I thought I'd help with the clean up afterwards."

Henry's mom gave them both a stern look. "Henry knows he's supposed to be in costume, but somehow he always manages to avoid it. I'm sorry he passed that attitude along to you."

Henry shot Sadie a side glance and winked. "Sorry, Mom. I didn't want to get my reenactment clothes dirty. Sadie said she'd help with the tables and everything, so we figured she shouldn't wear hers either, just to be safe."

"Hmph. I heard a similar excuse last year." His mother gave him a reproachful look. "Why don't you show your intended around. A couple of your friends are over by the bandstand. *They* wore their costumes, as requested." She marched off, shaking her head and mumbling something inaudible.

Once she was out of earshot, Sadie asked, "What did she mean by that?"

"Clearly she's mad we didn't wear our costumes."

"Not that. Why did she call me your intended?"

"Oh…" Henry's face turned red. "You're playing Rebecca. She was making a joke."

"Sadie put her hands on her hips. "What's the joke?"

Henry cleared his throat. "Rebecca Morgan married Nathaniel Prophet the second."

"Ha! I knew the name sounded familiar! She's in my family tree—in the brochure. At least I'm playing one of my relatives."

"So you don't mind playing my future wife…" He rubbed his chin. "Interesting."

"Good grief, Henry."

"Don't say it. Get over myself, right?"

"Yep."

Sadie looked back and saw Mrs. Northrup across the lawn, standing with Mr. Endicott. The two of them were engaged in what appeared to be a tense conversation. Mr. Endicott wagged his finger in Mrs. Northrup's face angrily.

Sadie nudged Henry's arm. "Look."

"Just ignore him." Henry grunted. "He's a jerk."

Mr. Endicott looked over at Sadie. Even from a distance, his gaze made Sadie's skin crawl.

It was a welcome distraction when Cody and Melanie joined them. Melanie was wearing a brown frock with a white bonnet, and Cody was in brown breeches and a blue waistcoat.

Melanie smiled. "I heard you're playing Rebecca."

Sadie nodded, still trying to recover from the visual daggers Mr. Endicott had hurled at her.

Melanie cocked her head. "What's going on? You two look like you just swallowed a bug."

Henry snickered. "My mom's mad we didn't wear our costumes."

Melanie pursed her lips. "You *never* wear yours, Henry. She gets mad at you every year."

"Right. You'd think she would've given up by now."

Sadie took a deep breath and smiled at Melanie. "I like your outfit."

Melanie held up her hands. "Look." Her fingertips were covered in ink. "I'm embracing my role."

Sadie laughed. "I hope it comes off."

"Sadly, we've already answered that question." She held out her skirt and it had black smudges down the front. "I don't think it shows up that much, but Henry's mother had an absolute fit. I pointed out that at least I wasn't wearing the white apron, but that didn't help." She pointed to a table behind them. "I'm getting some of that chocolate cake. My dress is already messed up, so I might as well enjoy myself."

Henry and Cody disappeared toward the hamburger table while Sadie and Melanie grabbed two pieces of cake.

Melanie took a big bite and some of the chocolate icing fell onto her skirt. She shrugged. "Like I said. It has to go to the cleaners anyway." She tried to brush it off, but it just smeared. "By the way, I'm glad you got out of playing Stevie's maid. Amanda has the part now."

"Who's Amanda?" Sadie asked.

"The girl following Stevie around like a puppy." Melanie pointed toward the band stand. Stevie was perched on the step and there was another girl sitting at her feet. "Take my advice and avoid Stevie today. She's pretty mad that you're playing Henry's future wife."

At that moment, Stevie looked up and locked eyes with Sadie before stomping off through the crowd, Amanda on her heels.

Sadie sighed. "Great. I'll have to avoid her for the whole reenactment."

"We'll hang out," Melanie said brightly.

"That'll be great!" Sadie smiled.

The boys came back with six cheeseburgers and four bags of chips.

Sadie shook her head. "Who's planning to eat all of that?"

Henry shoved a huge bite of his burger into his mouth and mumbled. "Two each for Cody and me. One each for you women folk."

"Very funny." Sadie grabbed a cheeseburger and sat on the ground under a huge oak. The others joined her while the string quartet played a lively tune. As she finished her burger, she looked around at the other food stands nearby. They had everything from cakes and pies to sandwiches and burgers. "At least the food isn't weird. I expected roasted possum or something like that."

Henry and Cody exchanged looks. "Funny you should mention that. We get normal food for the picnic in the park, but during reenactment week, it's the real deal. It gets pretty awful. We usually sneak off to Stella's for burgers at least a couple of times."

Melanie nodded. "Last year we got caught with pizza. I thought Henry's mom was literally gonna explode."

Henry groaned. "Don't remind me."

Sadie leaned forward and whispered. "I'll hide some snacks in my room. We can sneak up there so we don't die of hunger."

Melanie hooked her arm through Sadie's. "Looks like you're my new best friend."

Cody took Sadie's hand. "If you decide not to marry

young Nate, you can marry me, Jeremiah Smith. I'm the carriage maker's son. You'd always have a ride."

Sadie giggled and jerked her hand away. "I'll think about it."

They spent the rest of the afternoon touring the park and admiring the displays that were to be used in the reenactment, finally plopping down under the oak tree again. Meg was busy at one of the pie tables, doling out slices of pie. She seemed to be very popular, as her table had the biggest crowd. Sadie watched her smiling and chatting with the people around her and felt the familiar knot in her stomach that happened every time she thought about leaving Everleigh.

Henry put his hand on her shoulder, jolting her out of her reverie. "What's up. You look kinda sick."

"I do?"

"You were rubbing your stomach."

Melanie and Cody were studying her too.

"Too much cake, I guess. I'm fine now."

Melanie jumped up. "No more sweets for you. Let's go see the horses."

Two Clydesdales, named Big Jake and Rufus, were on loan from a stable about twenty miles down the road. Children took turns having their pictures taken atop the massive horses, who seemed perfectly content with the whole affair. They were also trained to pull practically anything, and patiently pulled a wagon, loaded down with excited youngsters and their parents around the park. Each time they arrived back at the starting point, the children lined up to offer carrots and apples. Their owner, Mr. March, gave each horse an affectionate pat on the neck and they returned the gesture by nuzzling his shoulder with their soft muzzles.

"They're beautiful," Sadie admired.

"Thank you, young lady. They're my pride and joy."

"Do they work on a farm?"

"Not these two. We mostly show them and take them to events like this. They have a pretty easy life."

Sadie stroked Big Jake's forehead and he rubbed his face on her shirt.

Mr. March looked on approvingly. "He likes you."

Sadie laid her cheek against Jake's neck. It was as soft as velvet. "I'd love to have a horse like this."

"You come on down to Chester and visit anytime you want. I'd be happy to see you. Any friend of Jake's is a friend of mine."

"I'll do that."

Melanie approached Rufus and cautiously patted his forehead. He responded by tossing his head, making his blond mane brush her face. Melanie giggled. Henry and Cody stood a good ten feet away and refused to budge. Sadie motioned them over, but they shook their heads in unison.

"Come on. They're sweet horses."

"We'll take your word for it," Cody said.

Sadie gave the two horses one last hug each and joined her friends. "You guys are a couple of cowards."

"I'm okay with that," Henry said. "When you get trampled by a two-thousand-pound horse you'll need someone to take you to the hospital."

As they walked away, Melanie hung back with Sadie and whispered, "I think the horses are beautiful."

Sadie smiled. "Me too. When I go visit them you can come along."

Melanie nodded enthusiastically. "I was gonna wish to win the math Olympiad this coming year, but I think I'll wish for a horse instead. What are you gonna wish for?"

Sadie raised her eyebrows. "I didn't know I had a wish coming."

"It's just something we do at the reenactment every year. We bring a new penny to the old well and throw it in while we're making our wish. It's dumb, I know. But everyone gets into it."

Sadie's mouth dropped open. "There's a well at Prophet House?"

"Of course there is. How do you think they got their water? There's a modern one now, but that's not the one I mean. The wishing well is the old one that's boarded up. They only open it once a year for the reenactment."

Sadie felt like her heart was going to leap out of her

chest. A well would be a perfect place to hide the coins! "Do you know where it is?"

"Yup. Everybody knows. I'll show you when you invite me over." Melanie grinned.

Seth and James showed up just as they were finishing the clean-up, so Henry and Cody stopped to talk to them while Melanie and Sadie headed back in the direction of Prophet House. As they reached the edge of town, Melanie pointed down the street to their left.

"My house is down this road. I'll see you soon, okay?"

"Okay." Sadie smiled. She really liked Melanie.

Henry caught up with her as she turned onto the driveway to Prophet House. "Did you have a good time?"

"Yes! Why didn't you tell me about the old well?"

Henry stopped and stared at her. "Oh my gosh… the well!"

Sadie nodded. "Melanie says you all throw pennies in there every year. But you know what I'm thinking?"

"Pennies might not be the only coins down there?" He grinned.

"Exactly!"

Henry suddenly frowned. "Hey, isn't that Owen?"

As they approached the house, Owen came out the front door. He was perspiring and his hair was even more disheveled than usual. When he saw them, his eyes widened in alarm.

"What were you doing in my house?" Sadie demanded.

"I was uh… taking a look at that shutter I fixed before. Making sure it didn't get loose again."

Sadie glanced around for her mother's car, but she wasn't home yet.

"You shouldn't do that when no one's home. How'd you get in?"

He pulled a key from his pocket and dangled it in the air.

"Where'd you get that?"

Owen's eyes narrowed. "The caretaker always has a key. In case of emergencies."

Sadie set her jaw, trying to appear braver than she felt. "You don't need a key. Leave it in the door."

Owen studied her for a moment without moving. Then he turned and inserted the key in the lock. "I'll be going now, miss."

Sadie nodded.

As he passed them on the steps, he hesitated. "You may want to rethink me having a key, Miss Sadie. You never know when you're gonna need help."

CHAPTER 21

Sadie lay in bed that night trying to figure out what Owen had really been doing in the house while they were away. She suspected that he was looking for the treasure. But she had gone over her room with a fine-tooth comb and hadn't found anything out of place. The other rooms seemed undisturbed as well. If he'd been rummaging around the house looking for the coins, he was good at covering his tracks.

She'd told her mother, but Meg had brushed the whole thing aside, saying that he was probably doing exactly what he said—checking to make sure the shutter hinges were still tight. She even went so far as to say that it was 'very conscientious" of him to follow up on his work.

Sadie held the house key she'd taken from Owen and studied it. It was identical to the other two, except for one thing. This key had a "B" etched into the head instead of a "P."

"Was this your key, Bess?" Sadie muttered. Of course, it could also have belonged to John Barry. He'd been like a father to Nathaniel and had most likely lived with them at Prophet House. He would have needed a key.

She turned it over and over in her hand. Like the other two keys, it was large and heavy, not like a modern house key that any locksmith could easily copy. Only a craftsman could make a key like this. Sadie pulled the locket from under her shirt and ran her fingers over the E. It was a different letter, but the same script.

She laid the key and the locket on the chest next her and

closed her eyes. She'd had a warm bath before climbing into bed and felt wonderfully relaxed. A gentle breeze floated in through the open balcony doors, bringing with it the scent of the ocean. She lay there, listening to the sound of waves gently washing onto the beach. An image formed in her mind of Nathaniel on the balcony, keeping watch while his family slept peacefully inside.

As she drifted off, the faint sound of boots on the wood floor tickled her brain, but not enough to rouse her. "Go to sleep, Sarah Elizabeth. I'm watching over you."

***

Sadie woke the next morning to the sound of rain pelting the house. She buried her face in her pillow and groaned. Another summer storm! She'd wanted to look in the well today with Henry. It crossed her mind that Bess may know if the gold was in there. But Bess hadn't shown herself since Sadie learned the truth about her.

She swung her legs over the side of the bed and dropped to the floor. Padding quietly to the wardrobe, she pressed her ear against the wood and listened. Nothing.

"Bess, please come back," she said softly. "I need you. We're gonna lose the house unless I find the treasure. I've looked everywhere I can think of except the well. Do you know if the coins are in there? Help me, please."

Something banged against the floor and Sadie spun around. Elizabeth's diary had fallen off the chest. Sadie slowly walked over and peered down at the open book. Written on the page were three words, easy to make out.

I don't know

Sadie slid to the floor and stared at the page. Her heart was threatening to pound out of her chest. She swallowed the lump in her throat and gently touched the script. As she pulled her hand away, the ink had smeared a little. It was fresh.

Her eyes darted around the room. "Bess? Are you here?"

There was no answer. She reached down with trembling hands and picked up the book. That's when she saw something else—a footprint next to the bedpost.

"Sadie!" her mother called from the stairway. "Henry's here."

Sadie pulled on jeans and a t-shirt and ran downstairs. Henry was waiting for her in the foyer.

"What's the plan today, Sherlock? Looking for the treasure?" he whispered.

"Come with me!" She grabbed his hand and sprinted upstairs to her room with him stumbling behind, trying to keep up.

"What was that all about?" he asked breathlessly.

"Look." She pointed to the faint print next to the bed. "Do you see it?"

Henry leaned over and examined the spot on the floor. "Looks like part of a footprint."

"It's from a boot."

"How do you know?"

"I know because I saw him on the porch during the storm that night and he was wearing boots. And then last night, he came back."

"Who?"

"I think it was the captain. Nathaniel Prophet."

Henry's eyes widened. "Did you see him?"

"Not exactly. I saw his silhouette on the balcony before, and last night he…"

"He what?"

Sadie lowered her voice. "He said he was watching over me. I thought I dreamed it, but then I saw his boot print!"

Henry looked skeptical. "You were looking for proof that Owen was in your room. Maybe this is that proof and it's just a coincidence that you dreamed about the captain."

"I don't think this is Owen's footprint, and I don't think I was dreaming last night!"

"It's the only thing that makes sense." He rubbed his forehead. "Of course, you have talked to a ghost before, so I guess anything is possible."

"Anything *is* possible," Sadie repeated softly. "The boot print isn't the biggest thing!" She picked up the diary and showed him the page with the three words. "This just happened! When I woke up, I went to the wardrobe and tried to get Bess to answer me. I told her I needed help finding the coins and asked if they were in the well. All of a sudden, the book fell off the chest and opened to this page."

Henry's mouth fell open. "This wasn't here before?"

Sadie shook her head.

"You're sure?"

"I'm sure. The ink was fresh. See?" She held up the finger with the ink on it.

"Okay, I admit it. That's freaky." Henry's eyes darted around the room. "You think she's here now?"

"I don't know. She won't show herself."

"What about the captain?"

She shook her head again. "I don't think so."

Henry plopped onto the floor and put his head in his hands. "This is so weird."

He kept glancing around the room as if expecting one of the ghosts to jump out any moment.

"Henry, stop. You're making me nervous."

"*I'm* making *you* nervous?" he asked incredulously.

"Yes." Sadie laid the diary on the bed. "This is so frustrating!" She moaned, chewing her lip. "I need to see her. I think she could help us. She knows so much about my family and this house. I know she's a ghost. So what? She could talk to me before, but now that I know the truth she can't? Is that some kind of ghost rule?"

"Who knows?" He glanced at the diary, then flipped it closed. "Bess or no Bess, as soon as the rain stops, I say we check out the well."

Sadie nodded. "Agreed. What do we do in the meantime?"

"We get some food. I'm starving."

Sadie grunted. "When are you not starving?"

They headed down to the kitchen and made waffles to take back to her room. Then they watched forlornly as the rain came down in sheets for the next two hours, accompanied by the occasional crack of lightning and rumbling thunder.

Sadie paced back and forth in front of the balcony doors, barely able to contain her frustration. "This is ridiculous! Is it ever gonna stop?"

"Give it up, Sherlock. It does this a lot."

"Maybe we should go outside and look in the well anyway!"

"And get struck by lightning? No thanks."

"Ugh!"

By lunchtime the thunder and lightning has ceased, but it was still raining. Meg showed up with sandwiches from Stella's and insisted that they eat together.

"Oh, Henry. I ran into your mother at Stella's. She has a few deliveries for you this afternoon and told me to be sure and send you home after lunch."

Sadie's face fell. "But Henry and I had things we were gonna to do this afternoon!"

"I'm sorry, Sadie. But you have the whole summer."

After they finished eating, Sadie walked Henry to the door. The rain had finally stopped, but now he was leaving. "I can't believe you have to go home," she whispered.

He shoved his hands in his pockets. "Yeah. We'll look in the well for the coins tomorrow."

"Okay."

Sadie watched him jog down the rain-slicked driveway onto the main road until he was out of sight.

Mr. Bones was cutting back some weeds next to the house. She hadn't noticed him before.

"Hey there, Miss Sadie."

"Hi, Mr. Bones." Sadie smiled.

"What are you and Henry up to?"

"Nothing right now. He had to go home."

"Did I hear you mention looking in the well for the treasure?"

Sadie had a sinking feeling. No one else was supposed to know. "Um… It was just talk. We thought a well would be a good place for Nathaniel to hide it."

Mr. Bones nodded. "A well would be a fine place, but it would also be a dangerous place. I don't want you and Henry poking around in there. If you fall in, you could drown before anyone came to pull you out."

"I promise we'll be careful."

"You remember what I said."

Sadie nodded.

Mr. Bones threw the shears over his shoulder and disappeared around the side of the house.

Sadie stood on the porch, thinking. Henry had said that the well was on the other side of the dense grove of magnolia trees near the kitchen. What harm would it do to take a quick look? She'd still go back with him the tomorrow.

She sprinted around the house toward the Magnolia grove. As she approached, she heard a man's hushed voice. It was the same familiar voice she'd heard before, but she still couldn't place it.

"Listen," he said in a growl, "you better do your job. I'm tired of coming up empty handed!"

"Why don't you do it yourself and leave me out of it?" Owen whimpered.

The first man's voice dropped to a more sinister tone. "It's going to take more than a boot print to scare that girl. That was just another stupid idea. It's time for you to step up."

"I don't think she knows where it is." It was Owen again. "I've been following her, and—"

"Then get rid of them both," the first man interrupted. "Do I make myself clear? Or do you want to keep that Simpson fella company?"

Sadie backed away from the trees, her heart beating wildly. She couldn't seem to catch her breath. She whirled around and flew into the house by way of the back door. Her mom was nowhere to be seen.

Sadie took the stairs two at a time, flinging open the door of her mother's empty room. She ran down the hall, looking in every other room with no luck. The room across from her parents' room had a window that looked down at the driveway at the back of the house. Sadie peered out to see if her mother's car was there, but all she saw was Owen's truck. She slid to the floor and put her face in her hands.

"Mom, where are you?" she murmured.

Just then, Sadie heard footsteps in the hall outside her mother's room.

"Miss Sadie? You in there?" It was Owen.

Sadie crouched on the floor behind the guest room bed, trying not to make a sound even though her heart was threatening to beat out of her chest. It sounded as if Owen was opening and closing doors as he made his way down the hall, looking for her.

On his way back toward the landing, he paused briefly at the guest room door. Sadie held her breath until she heard his booted feet trudging up the steps to the third floor. A short time later, he descended the stairs to the foyer, mumbling to himself all the way. As soon as the front door slammed shut, Sadie collapsed on the floor and sobbed. There was no doubt about it now. They weren't safe at Prophet House.

CHAPTER 22

A little while later, Sadie heard someone coming up the stairs again. She was still on the floor behind the bed in the guestroom. She held her breath.

"Look what I found in the cellar!" Meg called out. "It's one of the chamber pots, I can't imagine—"

"Mom!" Sadie bolted to the stairs.

"Goodness, Sadie! Where's the fire?"

"Where were you?"

"In the cellar, like I said. I was looking for more pots for the—"

"Mom, listen! I heard a man outside a while ago. He was talking to Owen about getting rid of us. We have to call Dad! He needs to come home! And we need to call the police!"

Meg frowned. "What on earth are you talking about?"

"Aren't you listening? Owen and some other man are after the treasure! They want us out of here so they can find it!"

"Sadie, calm down. You're not making any sense."

"I can't calm down. We're not safe here! Owen was in our house looking for me! He can't get out of it this time!"

Meg descended the stairs and marched out the front door with Sadie behind her. Owen was digging up some wilted flowers in a bed next to the driveway.

Meg raised her voice. "Owen, can I see you a minute?"

Owen came up the steps to the porch. "What is it, Mrs. Prophet?" His eyes darted over to Sadie. He looked frightened.

"My daughter says she heard you talking to someone

about us. She seems pretty shaken up. I'd like an explanation."

"I'm sorry, Miss Sadie. I was arguing with the tree man again. He says some of the magnolias aren't healthy. I've been taking care of them just fine, but he wants to get rid of them."

Sadie stared him down. "You're lying! You were talking about getting rid of my mother and me! The other man threatened you if you didn't!"

"No, miss." His voice was shaky. "We were talking about trees."

Sadie was seething. "Okay, where is this *tree man*? I haven't seen him!"

Owen's face was devoid of any color. "His truck was parked on the back of the property. He was headed that way last time I looked."

Meg spoke up, "Sadie, I think Owen has explained—"

"No, Mom! He's lying!" Sadie glared at Owen. "Why did the other guy bring up Mr. Simpson? Was that about trees too?"

He looked at his feet. "We got into it about some other stuff too. Things between him and me that go way back. It's nothing about you. Like I said, I'm sorry, Miss Sadie."

"I heard you come inside the house!"

"I was looking for you so I could apologize for the ruckus."

Meg shot Sadie a warning look. "That's enough!" She turned to Owen and smiled. "Thank you for explaining, Owen. I'm sorry we took you from your work." She motioned for Sadie to follow her inside.

As Sadie followed her mother into the kitchen, her anger boiled up and spilled over. "You can't tell me you believe him!"

"He's been nothing but polite and hard working since I met him. I think he's telling the truth."

"And I'm lying?"

"Of course not. I think your imagination has run away with you because of all the stories about this place. You misunderstood what you heard."

"It hasn't and I didn't."

"Sadie, this is the second time you've accused Owen of

something he didn't do. This has to stop."

"Mom, you have to believe me! Owen isn't the person you think he is."

Meg sighed. "Fine. I'll call the sheriff's office tomorrow and see if they have anything on him."

"Why don't you call them now?"

"I'll do it in the morning. Let's not talk about it anymore today. If we're going to be murdered during the night, I at least want my last day to be pleasant."

"Not funny, Mom."

They barely spoke during dinner. Normally, Sadie would've been excited about chicken parmigiana and Caesar salad, but she barely tasted it as they ate in silence. She couldn't believe her mother had been taken in by Owen's feeble explanation... again. She couldn't stop thinking about the man Owen had been talking to. She felt like his identity was on the tip of her brain, but it just wouldn't come to her. It didn't help that he'd been talking in a hushed tone the whole time.

When the dishes were done, Meg went upstairs to shower and Sadie used the opportunity to call Henry. His father answered the phone.

"Hi, Mr. Northrup," Sadie said. "This is Sadie Prophet. May I speak to Henry?"

"Sadie Prophet! It's nice to finally meet you, even if it's not in person. Henry talks about you all the time."

Sadie wasn't sure how to respond, but she could picture Henry listening on the other end, his face beet red. In spite of the fact that she was in mortal danger, the image made her smile.

"He's standing right here, trying to take the phone from me."

She heard Henry in the background. "Jeez, Dad!" A moment later, it was his voice on the phone. "Hi, Sadie." He sounded embarrassed.

Sadie lowered her voice. "Can you come over?"

"It's kind of late. Did something happen?" he whispered.

"Yes. Can you sneak out later?"

He didn't answer.

"Henry?'

"Sorry. I moved to another room so my parents wouldn't hear. Tell me what's going on."

Sadie told him about the conversation she'd overheard between Owen and the other man.

When she was through, he whistled. "You have to tell your mom."

Her eyes filled with tears that spilled down her cheeks. "I did. She didn't believe me."

"That sucks."

"I'm afraid to be alone here tonight."

Henry hesitated, then said, "I'll be over as soon as my parents go to bed."

Sadie's heart fell. "How late will that be?"

"It's eight o'clock now, so about an hour."

"Your parents go to bed at nine o'clock?"

"Yeah. They get up at five every morning," he said.

"Oh. Okay, I'll see you a little after nine. Come to the kitchen door."

"Will do. See you then, Sherlock."

Sadie bathed and pulled on sweatpants and a T-shirt. At eight forty-five, she went downstairs to the kitchen to wait for Henry, but found her mother at the kitchen table, going through receipts for all the garden supplies with Frank.

"Frank brought us this delicious cinnamon tea," Meg said. "Would you like some?"

"No thanks." Sadie's mind had kicked into overdrive. How was she going to explain Henry showing up? It was probably too late to call and warn him to wait.

"Frank and I are just about finished. I don't think I've ever been so sleepy."

Frank chuckled. "You've been up at the crack of dawn every day, working on the garden, Miss Meg. It's no wonder you're tired." He pushed back his chair. "I think I better head on home to get some rest too. I'll see you in the morning."

Meg smiled sleepily. "Thank you, Frank." As soon as he was out the door, Meg pushed her chair back. "I'm going to bed if you don't need me for anything."

"You go on. I'm getting water and heading upstairs too."

After her mom had gone up to her room, Sadie thought about going after Frank and asking him to stay. But as the thought crossed her mind, she heard a quiet tapping on the back door. When she opened it, Henry was standing there smiling.

"Henry…"

"What's the plan, Sherlock?"

Sadie threw her arms around him. "Thanks for coming."

"I won't let anything happen to you," he whispered, pulling her close.

Sadie felt safe with him there. She closed her eyes and listened to his heart beating.

When she stepped back awkwardly, he looked at her and smiled. "Maybe we should lock up? You know, in case Owen shows up to murder us all?"

Sadie nodded. They locked the back door and checked the front to be sure it was also locked.

"We have to be really quiet," Sadie whispered. "My mom just went upstairs. She won't be asleep yet."

They tiptoed up the stairs and down the hall to Sadie's room. Once inside, Sadie closed the door and breathed a sigh of relief. Henry dropped his backpack on the floor. That's when she noticed what was in his other hand.

"You brought your lacrosse stick."

He nodded. "Don't laugh."

She looked at him fondly. "I'm not."

Satisfied, he pulled three empty soda cans from his pack.

Sadie asked, "What are those for?"

"They're my sophisticated alarm system. We set them in front of the door, and if anyone opens it… clang, clang." He grinned.

"You're pretty smart."

He bowed. "Why thanks. That means a lot coming from you, Sherlock."

Sadie grinned. "Okay, Watson."

"So, what now? We just stay up all night?"

Now that Henry was here, Sadie didn't feel as nervous as she had before. She figured the two of them would be more than Owen could handle. Almost immediately, her intense desire to look in the well resurfaced, nearly snuffing out her fear of Owen and the mystery man.

"This might sound crazy, especially since I was so freaked out earlier, but I was kind of thinking about looking in the well."

Henry's mouth fell open. "Now? It's dark. And what about Owen?"

"He's probably back at the cottage sound asleep. It might be the only time we can look without him seeing us." Sadie scurried over to the wardrobe and pulled out her flashlight.

Henry seemed skeptical. "I don't know."

"Come on, Henry. I just want to take a quick look."

He sighed. "Okay, but I'm bringing the stick."

They tiptoed down the stairs again and slipped out the kitchen door. The grounds were dim and shadowy in the moonlight. The beam from the flashlight did little to cut through the murkiness. She realized that someone could be lurking among the magnolias and they wouldn't even know it. The reasonable side of Sadie's brain kicked in again, and she found herself having second thoughts. But now Henry was fully onboard. He took the flashlight from her and charged ahead.

The opening of the well was about three feet wide, with a wooden cover that was bolted down with a padlock.

Sadie looked over her shoulder and thought she saw a dark shape move through the shadows cast by the giant magnolias surrounding the well. She grabbed the flashlight from Henry and shined it around.

"What's wrong?" Henry asked.

"I thought I saw something."

"What'd you see?"

The beam from the flashlight revealed only trees and foliage, swaying in the breeze that wafted in from the ocean. "I guess it was nothing." She handed the flashlight to Henry and pulled on the well cover. "How do we get this thing off?" She asked anxiously.

Henry examined the lock. "I think we need bolt cutters. Do you know where any are?"

"Owen probably has some in the toolbox in his truck."

"Back in a sec!" Henry whispered excitedly.

"Be careful!"

He came back five minutes later with a pair of bolt cutters.

Sadie was seriously impressed. "Where were they?"

"In Owen's truck, like you said. He should remember to lock it." Henry started to cut the padlock off, but hesitated. "You think we should really do this? What if somebody falls in or something?"

"My dad has a toolbox too. I think it's in the pantry. No bolt cutters, but he has at least three of these locks. After we do this, we can put one of them on."

Henry was satisfied. "That works. Here we go."

"Mr. Bones definitely wouldn't approve of this," Sadie whispered.

Henry cut off the lock and pushed up on the cover. It fell backward off the other side, exposing the opening of the well. "Don't tell him."

Sadie hung the flashlight over the rim and switched it on. "See anything?"

Henry shook his head. "The beam doesn't go down far enough. We need a stronger light."

"Maybe there's one in the cellar. There's a bunch of stuff on the shelves by the door. I think I might have seen a few flashlights."

He took off around the side of the house, leaving Sadie alone by the well again. Somewhere off in the distance an owl hooted.

"Perfect," she muttered to herself. "What's next, crows?"

She thought of the story she'd read in her advanced English class this past year. It was "The Raven" by Edgar Allan Poe. She'd found it particularly chilling. Standing alone on the abandoned grounds of a haunted sea captain's house, during a full moon, she could imagine the kind of sinister tale Mr. Poe would come up with if he were here.

Minutes ticked by, but Henry still hadn't returned. Sadie fiddled with the coin in her pocket, wondering what it was worth. She thought about the chest in the painting over the mantle in the caretaker's cottage. It probably held thousands of gold coins. How much would a chest full of Spanish gold coins from the late 1700s be worth now? Or a dozen chests? Finding them would change their lives. Her mother would never have to work again. She could spend time in her garden and continue to get better. Her dad had a map in his office at the university, marked with all the historic places he wanted to visit in his lifetime. Maybe they'd buy a boat, twice the size of Stevie's, and take trips all over the world so he could check them off… one by one. But the best part about finding the gold would be that they could stay in Everleigh forever, because they wouldn't have to depend on people like Mr. Endicott ever again.

Unable to resist, Sadie leaned over the side of the well and shined the flashlight down into the dark hole again, hoping to see a glint of something shiny. But there was only blackness. Frustrated, she went up on her tiptoes and hung over the side as far as she could without falling in. Her eyes followed the beam until it seemed to spread out into a faint circle. Water!

Suddenly, someone shoved her from behind and she tumbled head first over the edge. Her wrist twisted as she frantically grabbed hold of the ragged stone rim, making her cry out in pain. Sadie reached up with her other hand, desperately trying to hold on. The flashlight had slipped from her hand and she heard a muted splash when it hit the water below.

"Henry, help!" she screamed as she tried to use her feet to scramble up the inside wall. It was no use. The sides were covered with some kind of slimy material, making it impossible to get any traction. With all of her strength, she gripped the rim around the mouth of the well, but the rough edges cut into her hands and her grasp was quickly weakening. "Henry, help me! I can't hold on!" she sobbed.

Something wet trickled down her arms—most likely blood. Her hands began to slowly slip over the edge. She was seconds away from dropping, perhaps plunging to her death. How would her mother cope with another loss? Maybe Owen had done something to Henry too, and no one would ever know what had happened to the two of them.

Sadie closed her eyes. *Please let Henry be okay...* Her

left hand slipped off the edge. Just as her other hand was about to go, someone grabbed her wrist and yanked, hard. She catapulted out of the well and hit the ground with a force that knocked the air out of her lungs. Lying in the grass, gasping, she looked up and saw Henry kneel beside her. He dropped two flashlights, presumably from the cellar, on the ground.

"Oh my God, what happened? I heard you scream! Are you okay?"

"Henry…" She choked out, trying to catch her breath. "Thank you."

"For what?"

"For saving me."

The full moon showed his obvious confusion. "Sadie, what are you talking about?"

"Someone pushed me into the well, but you grabbed my wrist and pulled me out."

Henry sat back on his heels. "I didn't pull you out. You were lying here when I got back."

Sadie sat up slowly and looked around. "If you didn't save me, who did?"

Henry swallowed hard. "I think the bigger question is who pushed you? We better go back inside. Now!"

"Wait!" Sadie stuck her hand in her pocket, and her stomach dropped. The coin was gone. "No!" She dropped to the ground and felt around frantically. "Henry, help me find it!"

As she crawled around in the grass, Henry looked around furtively, as if expecting someone to pounce on them any second. "Sadie, we have to go inside. We can look for it tomorrow," he whispered.

"I can't lose it, Henry!" she sobbed. "We need to—" Her fingers encountered something cool and hard in the grass. "I found it!" she nearly screamed.

Henry grabbed her by the arm and pulled her to her feet. She sprinted to the house with Henry on her heels, relief coursing through her. Once inside, they locked the door behind them and made their way silently up the stairs to Sadie's room.

"Your hands are bleeding!" Henry sounded alarmed.

"I'll wash them off."

Sadie trudged down the hall to her bathroom and lathered her hands. The soap stung the cuts on her palms and fingers, but she barely noticed. All she could think about was how close she'd come to dying.

When she returned to her room, Henry was waiting with the first aid supplies from the bin under the kitchen sink. None of Sadie's cuts looked deep enough for stitches, so she sat on the rug next to the fireplace and let Henry apply ointment and Band-Aids. When he was finished, he sat down next to her, concern written all over his face. "Are you sure you're okay?"

Sadie nodded. "I think so."

"We need to call the police, or at least tell your mom."

"I'll tell her tomorrow. We can call the police then too."

"Sadie, somebody threw you in the well. You could've been killed."

"I know. But I'm safe now." She laid her head on his shoulder. All she wanted to do was to sit on the floor with Henry and not think about anything else.

"Promise me we'll tell your mom first thing in the morning."

"I promise."

Henry pulled her hair away from her face and studied her. "You're really pale. You might be in shock or something."

Sadie shook her head. "I'll be okay."

"You don't think Owen might try something again tonight?"

"No. If he'd wanted to kill me he would've. I just need to rest." She lay her head on his shoulder again. "Talk to me about something else. Tell me what it was like to grow up in Everleigh."

Henry was hesitant at first, but once he got into it, he talked until almost two in the morning. Most of what he told her was about famous people who had visited Prophet House, unruly guests, and reenactments that had gone hilariously wrong. It was all interesting, some of it even funny, but no matter how hard she tried to listen, Sadie's mind kept going back to her harrowing experience at the well. She could still feel the jagged stone under her hands, her certainty that she was about to die.

"Why don't we see if Bess left any more notes in her diary." Henry suggested after he'd run out of stories.

Sadie took the book from the chest next to her bed and flipped through until she found the last entry she'd read. She turned to the next page and handed the diary to Henry. "I'm too tired. You read it."

Henry studied the script, then looked up. "Sadie, you're not gonna believe this."

Sadie leaned forward. "Tell me."

He read the words out loud…

"Be ever… something. I'm not sure what that word is. Oh… it's vigilant." He studied the words again before continuing. "This right here… It looks like 'stranger' but that doesn't make sense. Wait! I have it." He set the book in his lap and turned it to face Sadie. "Here's what it says…"

Be ever vigilant, as he is becoming desperate. But do not fear. You are stronger than most. Thank you for being the friend I have longed for.

Love, Bess

Sadie looked up at Henry, her eyes wide and filled with tears. After several minutes with neither of them saying a word, Henry spoke up.

"We need help."

Sadie nodded. "I'm showing this to my mom when she wakes up. I'm gonna tell her everything."

They were both exhausted. Henry yawned and leaned his head against one of the chairs on the rug. He could barely keep his eyes open.

"You should go home," Sadie said. "You can't be gone when your parents wake up. I think we scared Owen. It doesn't look like he's doing anything else tonight."

"I can't leave you alone after this."

"It'll be light in a couple of hours and Frank usually shows up around seven."

Henry yawned again. "Are you sure?"

Sadie nodded. "Yeah, I'm sure.

"I'll leave the cans. You can set them up again after I leave."

The key to the front door was still on the chest next to the bed where she'd left it. She picked it up and placed it in his hand. "Lock the door behind you. I'll get the key back tomorrow."

Henry hesitated before stepping into the hall. "I can make it back here in ten minutes if I run."

Sadie put her arms around him and hugged him tight, then watched him pad quietly down the hall. He looked back and smiled before disappearing down the stairs.

As soon as he was gone, she crawled into bed. All she wanted to do was sleep. The cans were on the chest beside the bed where Henry had left them. She'd forgotten to set them up again, but was too tired to do it now. The journal was also on the chest. She picked it up and noticed that it had fallen open to an entry she'd read before. Now that she knew what it said, it was easier to make out.

I have been such a fool. Blind to the truth. How can I forgive myself for the vile thoughts that have festered in my mind about him? I could not have been more wrong. He wants only to keep them from harm. But I am afraid that will not be possible. He is no match for the one who wants to finish us.

CHAPTER 23

Sadie awoke to the sound of a floorboard creaking. At first, she thought she was dreaming again. She reached for the lamp, but it flicked on before her fingers made contact.

Owen stood over her, a scowl on his face. "You and me need to talk, Miss Sadie."

Sadie tried to shake the fog out of her brain as the realization hit her that she was alone in her bedroom with Owen. Just like in her nightmare. But this time it was real.

She sat bolt upright and set her jaw, trying her best to appear calm. "Wha–what are you doing here?" Fully awake now, her mind scrambled to come up with a plan to escape him.

Owen leaned toward her. "We need to talk about that treasure."

Owen was about six feet tall, but he was practically skin and bones. She might be able to fight her way out of this. Her eyes darted to the lamp beside her bed. It was heavy brass. A strategic blow would probably knock him out cold—if she was able to lift it. Just because she had in the dream didn't mean she could in real life.

He leaned even closer. "Are you listening to me? I got to talk to you now! It's important!"

There was a sharp *thwack* and Owen's eyes flew open wide for a moment before he collapsed in a heap on the floor.

Henry stood over him, the lacrosse stick in his hand. He dropped it and gently touched her shoulder. "Are you okay?"

"Henry! You came back."

He smiled. "I had one of your funny feelings."

She threw her arms around him and sobbed into his shoulder. "I thought he might kill me."

"I said I wouldn't let anything happen to you. I've been on the stairs the whole time. I must've drifted off though. I'm sorry I let him get past me."

Sadie jumped up. "I need to check on my mom! Watch Owen!"

Sadie ran downstairs to her mother's room and found her sound asleep.

"Mom?" Meg didn't stir so Sadie touched her arm. "Mom! Wake up."

Her mother's eyes fluttered, then opened a little. "Sadie… go back to bed."

"I need to talk to you about Owen. He came in my room just now. He wanted me to tell him where the treasure was. I think he would've hurt me if Henry hadn't knocked him out."

"You had a bad dream," Meg murmured. Her eyes closed and she seemed to be sleeping again.

"Mom! What's wrong with you?" Sadie felt a wave of panic. "Wake up!"

The door creaked behind her and she looked back. Frank stood in the doorway, motioning for her. She jumped up and ran to him.

"Frank! Thank God! I need help. Owen's in my room. Henry knocked him out. And something's wrong with my mom. I can't wake her up!"

He pulled her mother's door closed. "Don't worry about your momma. She'll wake up tomorrow once the sleeping pill wears off. I might've dropped one in her tea when she wasn't looking." He snickered. "But if you put in enough cinnamon, there's no aftertaste at all."

The image of her mother sitting at the kitchen table, sipping cinnamon tea, popped into Sadie's head as she struggled to comprehend what was happening. "What?"

Sadie stared at Frank as a wave of intense anger overtook her. "You drugged my mother? You're supposed to be our friend!"

Frank grunted. "You and your momma are so gullible. I sure hope I don't have to hurt either one of you. But you're gonna tell me where the treasure is or I'll have to do just that."

Sadie glared at him. "All this time, I thought *Owen* was the one I should worry about!"

Frank's smile disappeared. "That useless nephew of mine couldn't get anyone to talk if his life depended on it. But fortunately for me, I can." He stepped toward her and Sadie noticed a pair of shears in his hand. "Now you tell me where those coins are or you, your momma, and Henry won't live to see the sun come up."

"I don't know where the coins are! I don't even know if there are any coins!" Sadie looked past Frank, hoping to see Henry show up with his lacrosse stick again.

Frank sneered. "If you're looking for your boyfriend, you can quit. I already took care of him."

Sadie's heart jumped into her throat. "What did you do to Henry?"

"Oh, he's not dead. Not yet."

Her mind was reeling. She had to stall Frank somehow. Her eyes narrowed. "Fine. I'll take you to the coins, but you have to promise not to hurt my mother or Henry."

His brow furrowed. "You just said you don't know where they are. Maybe you're lyin'. Maybe your momma's the one I should be asking."

"I'm not lying. I can prove it."

"Oh yeah?" He sneered. "Then prove it."

Sadie reached into her pocket and pulled out the gold coin.

Frank snatched it out of her hand and whooped. "I knew it! I knew you Prophets had the gold stashed somewhere!" He lowered the shears. "Lead the way, mistress."

Sadie slipped past him and walked slowly up the staircase, holding onto the railing so her legs wouldn't give way. He lumbered along behind her, huffing and puffing as if ascending Mount Everest. His revolting breath smelled of stale tacos.

"I thought you were our friend," Sadie said. "You had

meals with us and helped my mom get better because of the garden. Look at all you did for her. You don't have to do this. You can leave and we'll forget all about it. I swear."

His malevolent laugh didn't sound anything like the Frank she'd known. "I'm thinkin' all those years in theater helped more than I thought they would. And as far as the garden goes, if I never see another tomato for the rest of my life, I'll die a happy man!"

He shoved her up the stairs to the landing on the third floor. She looked down the hallway at the open door to the captain's room, wishing she could check on Henry. Instead, she opened the door to the attic and led Frank inside.

He pulled a cord attached to a single bulb hanging from the ceiling and it cast a dreary light over the cavernous space. "What are you playing at, girl? I've been up here a dozen times and so has Owen. There ain't any treasure here."

"It's not in the attic." She felt around the wall for the door that led to the stairs. When her fingers encountered the crack, she gave it a shove and the door opened. "You don't know everything about Prophet House. I do."

Frank whistled. "Well, what do you know?"

"It's down these stairs," Sadie lied.

He gritted his teeth. "After you, girl. And no tricks."

Sadie stepped onto the stairs and Frank followed, his meaty hand gripping her shoulder so tightly that the pain was almost unbearable. With his bulky build, he was barely able to fit into the narrow stairway and his arms rubbed against the bare wood walls as they descended. Sadie took the stairs slowly at first, but then subtly picked up speed with each step. When, according to her mental calculations, she was no more than two or three steps away from the broken one, she took a deep breath and elbowed him in the stomach as hard as she could. Frank grunted loudly and let go of her shoulder.

When he did, she bolted down the stairway, taking care not to fall on the broken step. Frank stumbled after her and screamed obscenities when his foot caught on the broken board and hurled him down face-first. Sadie shot ahead, putting more and more distance between them until she reached the bottom and the cellar door flew open. Bess stood in the doorway, waving frantically for her to hurry.

"Bess!" Sadie sobbed.

Someone grabbed her by the arm and pulled her out of the stairway, flinging her to the floor and slamming the door.

"Get up, miss!" Owen stood over her. He grabbed the wheelbarrow and shoved it against the door. "You have to get out of here! My uncle—"

Sadie felt as if her brain was going to explode. Was Owen helping her? "What are you doing?"

"I'm trying to get you to safety! My uncle means to kill you if he doesn't get what he wants."

"But I thought—" Sadie couldn't seem to move. Her eyes darted around the cellar. "Where's Bess? She was here just a minute ago!"

"What are you talking about? There's nobody here but me." He grabbed her shoulders and shook her. "Snap out of it, girl! My uncle's dangerous!" Owen took her by the arm and dragged her out of the cellar into the night air.

Sadie noticed that Owen's head was bleeding. "Y— You're not going to hurt me?"

Owen met her gaze. For the first time, Sadie saw kindness in his mismatched eyes. "I'm no criminal, Miss Sadie. Thomas Owensby was the caretaker here when Nathaniel and Sarah were alive. He was my third great granddaddy… a good man, loyal to the Prophet family. His brother, the one they called Crazy Eyes, was a bad sort, greedy and mean as a snake I've heard. Uncle Frank is cut from the same mold. I was trying to warn you about him before, but somebody banged me over the head."

Sadie hesitated as the truth clicked into place. "You pulled me out of the well, didn't you?"

Owen nodded. "We don't have time to talk about that." There was suddenly a pounding noise coming from the cellar. "That wheelbarrow won't hold the door for long. Run to the cabin and call the police!"

"Aren't you coming with me?"

"I better stay here and wait for Uncle Frank. Don't

worry. I can handle him. Now get going!"

"Be careful, Owen."

"You too, Sadie."

Sadie ran through the garden into the woods behind Prophet House, only stopping to catch her breath when she was out of sight. She'd been wrong about Owen the whole time! Her mother's impression of him had been right. He was rough around the edges, but a nice guy. He wasn't after the treasure at all. Frank, the friend who'd been over every day helping her mom in the garden and eating meals with them at their kitchen table, was the one all along.

Sadie heard footsteps behind her on the path, so she veered off into the underbrush and hid. But after several minutes, whoever had been running after her didn't pass by. She waited for several minutes more, then made her way back to the trail and took off for the cottage again.

Lights shined from the front windows when she got there, but all seemed quiet.

She pounded on the door. "Mr. Bones! It's Sadie! I need help!"

There was no answer, and the door was locked. She pounded on it until her hands hurt, but he didn't answer. Sadie's legs gave way and she crumpled against the door, sobbing. Frank must have done something to Mr. Bones too. She hoped it was the cinnamon tea and not something worse. Maybe he was buried somewhere on the property, next to the other caretaker. The thought of that gave her a terrible pain in the pit of her stomach. She rested her head on the door and cried.

CHAPTER 24

After a while, Sadie heard someone slam the door in the back of the cottage, followed by a sound from inside. She jumped up and pounded on the door again. "Mr. Bones, are you there?"

The door flew open, but it wasn't Mr. Bones. It was Frank. "Well, ain't this a nice surprise. Here I thought I'd spend the whole night tracking you down. But here you are, pretty as a picture." His voice was dripping with sarcasm.

"What have you done to Mr. Bones?" Sadie nearly screamed.

For a split second, Frank looked confused. His eyes darted around as if looking for someone else. Satisfied that they were alone, his wicked smile returned. "Who's Mr. Bones, girl?"

"You know perfectly well who he is! What have you done to him?"

Frank stepped back. "Come on in and see for yourself."

Sadie backed away. "I–I need to see him first!"

Frank stepped toward her. "Why don't you come in? I'll take you to him."

Sadie stumbled backward onto the cobblestone path and barely kept her footing.

"Mr. Bones! Are you in there?"

Frank stopped advancing and frowned. "You must be confused, or maybe you're just plain crazy. Who are you talking about?"

"You know perfectly well! The other caretaker, Mr.

Bones!"

"There's no caretaker but Owen."

Sadie glared at him. "You're lying. He lives here. I saw his room."

"You little snoop! You were in my room?" The veins in Frank's neck looked as if they were about to pop out.

"Y—you're room?" Sadie sputtered. "But I thought…"

I don't know what your game is, but there's nobody here but you and me." His wicked smile returned. "Now why don't you just come on inside with your old friend Frank?"

Sadie's anger and confusion were driving her closer and closer to hysteria. She stomped her foot hard on the ground. "What have you done to Mr. Bones? Where is he?"

Frank lunged forward, grabbing her by the arm, and Sadie punched him as hard as she could in the face. Her knuckles throbbed from the impact and she winced in pain. Frank released her and stumbled backwards, his hand over his eye. When he looked back at her, Sadie saw a blue eye where there had been a brown one before. In spite of the intensity of the moment, she remembered the receipt for contacts she'd seen in the caretaker's cabin when she and Henry had snooped around. The contacts weren't for Owen—they were for Frank.

He stepped toward her again, his gold tooth glinting in the porch light as he sneered. Suddenly, he seemed to look past her, his eyes wide and his face drained of all color. "What the—" His voice sounded an octave higher than normal.

Sadie spun around, and there stood John Barry, exactly as he'd looked in the painting with Nathaniel. He wore a blue waistcoat over a crisp white shirt and dark breeches. Her feet remained rooted to one spot as she struggled to wrap her head around the vision before her. Slowly, realization sank in. His normally gray hair was a neatly groomed medium brown, pulled back at the neck. His previously lined and weathered face was smooth and tanned. But his warm smile was exactly the same as it had always been. He was John Barry, Nathaniel's friend from almost two hundred years ago. But he was also her friend, Mr. Bones.

Sadie forgot all about Frank cowering behind her. "Mr.

Bones?" Her voice sounded strange. "Is it you?"

He smiled that familiar smile and bowed. "At your service, Miss Sadie."

"You look… you're young."

He raised his eyebrows and chuckled. "Well, not so young I'm afraid."

Frank backed into the wall of the cottage, his eyes fixed on the new and improved Mr. Bones. His jaw had dropped open and a tiny stream of saliva hung from his bottom lip. He was shivering so hard, the saliva string danced around with a life of its own.

Mr. Bones turned his attention to Frank. "What do you have to say for yourself?" he said in a forceful voice. "Speak up, man!"

"You—you…" Frank looked as if he was about to scream any second. Sadie was tempted to hit him over the head with something, just to put him out of his misery.

"Well, Frank, I've been meaning to ask you how the portrait of me and Nathaniel moved from the grand foyer to the caretaker's cabin."

The only sound that came out of Frank was a gurgle, followed by something resembling a hiccup.

"That's what I thought. See, Miss Sadie, there were only three paintings of the captain—the one that hangs in his room, the one of him and the missus that was destroyed in the fire, and the one he had this French fella paint of him and me right after we built the Sea Hawk. I think Frank here took that one, maybe thinking it had a clue to the whereabouts of a particular treasure. Isn't that right, Frank?"

Frank slowly raised his hand and pointed a puffy finger at Mr. Bones. "John Barry! You ain't real! You're dead!"

"Well, look who just made it to the party!" His booming laugh made Frank shrink into the wall again. Mr. Bones took a threatening step toward him. "I knew Luis Owensby, but most of the crew called him ol' Crazy Eyes. He was as low as a lizard's belly. Signed him on as a cook, but he had other reasons to be there. He's the reason none of us were ever seen alive again. Looks like his seed kept on growing the same weeds!"

Frank let out a scream that sounded like a screech owl's and ran for Owen's truck. Halfway there, he stumbled over his own feet and screamed again.

Once inside the pickup, Frank screamed again for good measure, then floored it down the driveway, kicking up a cloud of dirt and rocks.

Sadie stared after him, relief washing over her. "I hope he's gone for good."

John Barry turned to her. "Maybe and maybe not. Greed is a powerful motivator, lass. But I can promise this. You'll always have protection if you need it."

Sadie wanted to throw her arms around him, but she was afraid to. "I can't believe it's really you. Why'd you call yourself Mr. Bones?"

"Well now, there's a story about that. On our first time out with the new boat, Nathaniel and me stumbled onto an old deserted ship just floating along at sea, pretty as you please. I took a couple of men and boarded her, thinking there might be something valuable left behind. I found this big old chest, locked up tight, so we hauled it aboard and beat the lock off with an ax. Inside was…" He chuckled.

Sadie grimaced. "Bones?"

"Yes, ma'am." He laughed. "After that, the crew started calling me Bones." He looked at her fondly. "There's something else you want to know, isn't there, lass?"

Sadie nodded. "What happened to you and Nathaniel? Why didn't you ever come home?"

His expression turned solemn. "That coward's ancestor was Luis Owensby, but the crew called him Ol' Crazy Eyes. He figured there was some of the treasure onboard the Sea Hawk and he wanted it for himself. He started a fire in the galley so no one would notice him ransacking the captain's cabin. Every soul on board perished except Crazy Eyes. He took the jolly boat and left us all to die."

Something dawned on Sadie. "That's who Bess was afraid of. She wrote about him in her journal."

"Aye. She was right about him. By the time he made it back to Prophet House, the men he left behind on the ship had all perished." He shook his head sadly.

"He was the one who started the fire, wasn't he?"

"Aye, lass. He meant to kill them all, not just little Bess. There was Sarah and young Nate too."

"What stopped him?"

"We did. Nathaniel and me."

"But you were dead."

"Aye. He had a problem with that as well. Ran off the moment he saw us. But Thomas found him and hauled him back to face judgement for what he'd done." He shook his head. "Bess had a bad feeling about Crazy Eyes from the moment she saw him. We should've listened to her, but she was a wee girl and we all thought… it's no matter now."

"Owen said Thomas was a good man, even if his brother was Crazy Eyes."

"It's the truth. Thomas was a good friend."

"When you told me about Bess's father dying in a fire out at sea, you were talking about my great-great-great grandfather." Sadie said sadly. "But you were also talking about yourself. It must've been awful."

"Aye, lass. It was. But at Nathaniel's side was where I belonged. I have no regrets. Truly, it was fate that brought us together long before that day."

"What do you mean?"

"Like Nathaniel, I wasn't *on The Isabela* by my own choosing. I was snatched from my ship and forced to join the crew." He smiled wistfully. "Seems only right that the two of us ended up with their gold."

"I don't know how I'll explain all of this to my parents."

"I'll leave that to you."

"I think my dad will be okay with having…uh…"

"Ghosts?"

Sadie nodded. "But I don't know about my mom. I'll have to say something, though. She'll wonder what happened to you."

"Has your mother mentioned me, even once?"

Sadie thought for a moment, then shook her head. "No, I guess not. She's only talked about Owen."

He nodded. "Other than Crazy Eyes, you're the only living soul besides your grandmother, Mistress Mary Ann, who's seen me since *The Elizabeth* was lost. I was mighty surprised when you spoke to me that first day."

A fresh realization settled over her. "Like Bess. She said she didn't think anyone could see her when I caught her in the captain's room the day we moved in. But I saw her."

"To my mind, that makes you special. You have your grandmother's gift."

His comment pleased Sadie. "I'm glad." She thought of the first time she'd seen Bess, standing by the window in the captain's room, the day they arrived at Prophet House. "Mr Bones. Do you see Bess very often?"

"Aye. And her mother."

Sadie's eyes widened. "Sarah Prophet?"

"Mistress Sarah." He smiled. "A fine woman indeed."

"I wish I could've known her."

"You had the pleasure of meeting her daughter though, didn't you?"

Sadie nodded. "She was my friend."

"Miss Bess sees something special in you, I'd wager. I do as well."

Sadie felt a pang of longing. "Then why doesn't she come around anymore?"

Mr. Bones looked at her kindly. "She sticks close to her mother. But I expect she liked having a friend who thought she was like everyone else."

"And now I know the truth. So it's not the same."

"Aye."

Sadie's eyes filled with tears. "I miss her. But I'll never see her again, will I?"

"I can't say for sure, Miss Sadie."

"I don't care that Henry and I never found the treasure. I met Bess… and you. That's enough." She wiped a tear from her cheek. "But we might have to leave here."

"Perhaps not. Frank was right about one thing. There is a clue in a painting. Just not the painting he thought." He gazed at her fondly. "You've been close many times. Why don't you try retracing your steps? Maybe Henry can help you."

"Henry! I think Frank may have hurt him!"

"He's fine. Don't you worry, lass."

Sadie breathed a sigh of relief. "I'm glad you showed up, Mr. Bones."

"I'm glad too, Miss Sadie."

She looked down. "Owen helped me. I've been wrong about him all this time."

"Give him a chance. It's more than blood that makes a person. Just because his uncle is a bad sort doesn't mean he is."

Sadie felt a difference in Mr. Bones' demeanor all of a sudden, as his eyes shifted away from her. "You have to go now, don't you?" she asked, dreading the answer.

"I'd like to stay, but the captain calls."

"Will you tell him about me?"

"He already knows."

Tears welled in Sadie's eyes and spilled down her cheeks. "I know you're John Barry, but you'll always be Mr. Bones to me, if that's okay."

He touched her cheek, leaving it tingly. "Mr. Bones it is. You run along now, lass. I think you have some treasure to find." He studied her for a moment, then smiled. "You do the name proud, Sarah Elizabeth Prophet." He bowed and said softly, "Your servant, mistress."

Sadie stood perfectly still, tears pouring down her face, long after he'd disappeared. Suddenly snapping back to the present, she hurried back to the house and upstairs to check on her mother. She appeared to be all right and sleeping peacefully.

When Sadie placed her hand on her mother's cheek, Meg opened her eyes and smiled. "Is it time to get up already?"

"No, Mom. I just came to say good night. Go back to sleep. We can talk in the morning."

"Good night, Sadie." Her mother sighed, drifting off again.

Sadie kissed her on the cheek. "Good night, Mom."

Relieved, Sadie trudged up to her room, wondering what had become of Owen and Henry. She'd make sure to find them both in the morning so she could thank them.

As she reached the third-floor landing, she heard a loud crack, followed by a deep rumble of thunder. Another storm was descending on Everleigh. When she entered her room, the doors to the balcony were open and the first drops of rain floated in and hit the wood floor with a splat. Her brain was on overload and threatened to shut down if she didn't take a minute to get her bearings. She leaned against the four-poster and closed her eyes for just a moment.

It happened all of a sudden. She felt a presence in the room, followed by the smell of tacos. All of her senses came alive at that moment. She lunged for the spyglass, yanking it off the stand and holding it like a bat as she spun around.

Frank stood by the door wearing an evil grin. "Now ain't that just the scariest thing I ever got threatened with. But it don't hold a candle to this." He pulled a machete from his boot and pointed it at her. "Yours ain't the only family who's known about the treasure for these two hundred years. I been hearing tales of it since I was a kid. So has Cousin Willie. Of course, he's too high and mighty to get his hands dirty. He leaves that to me."

Sadie's eye caught a movement in the hallway, just outside her door. "You planning to talk her to death, Frank?" It was the voice she'd heard in the magnolia grove—the one she hadn't been able to place. But this time it clicked in her brain. She berated herself for being so slow to catch on.

Frank snickered. "Well missy, meet my cousin on my mother's side. Her maiden name was—"

"Endicott!" Sadie spat out. "So all this time…all he really cared about was the treasure!"

Mr. Endicott stepped into the room, his eyes narrowed. "Do you have any idea how much twelve chests of Spanish gold would be worth today?" he growled. "More than you can fathom! I spent two years looking for it before bringing those two idiots here to help me. As you can see, they've been useless. So I'm going to ask you one time, and you better give me the answer I want to hear. Where is it?"

Sadie glared at him. "I don't know where it is!"

Mr. Endicott pulled the gold coin from his pocket and

flashed her a wicked smile. "Does this look familiar?"

Sadie looked around frantically. "Mr. Bones! I need you!" She backed to the balcony doors as the rain outside came down in torrents.

Mr. Endicott sneered. "You might be able to trick my simpleton cousin into thinking this place is haunted, but I can assure you I'm not that gullible."

"I'm telling you, Willie, he was real!" Frank whimpered.

Mr. Endicott shot him a withering look. "Shut up, Frank! Do what I told you to do!"

Frank set his jaw. "Sorry, Miss Sadie. But Willie and me need those coins, and we ain't leaving until we get them." He took a step toward her, his machete glinting. Suddenly his stony expression changed to one of terror. "Stay away from me!" he screamed in a shrill voice.

Sadie whirled around and gasped, then stumbled backwards into the room.

Nathaniel Prophet towered over her, splendid in his dashing black waistcoat, deep brown trousers, and glittering sword that was secured at his side by a gold sash and sheath. With his flaming red hair and chiseled features, he was a fearsome sight to behold. Mr. Bones had been an impressive presence at the cottage, but the commanding figure before her was nothing less than magnificent.

"Captain Nathaniel Prophet at your service, lass," the specter before her said in a deep, resonating voice. "May I be of assistance?"

Sadie opened her mouth, but nothing came out.

Nathaniel Prophet directed his steely gaze at Mr. Endicott, who'd turned white as a sheet. The coin fell out of his hand and hit the floor, rolling around in a circle before settling against his meticulously polished leather shoe. Instead of picking it up, he stared wide-eyed at the captain for just a moment before stumbling frantically out the door. Seconds later, they heard him tumble down the stairs.

Nathaniel's expression turned dark and furious as he took a menacing step toward Frank and drew his sword. At that precise moment, another bolt of lightning flashed and the sword appeared to burst into flame. In a booming voice that dwarfed the sound of the storm, he bellowed, "BE GONE FROM THIS HOUSE AND NEVER RETURN, ON PAIN OF DEATH!"

Frank froze, his eyes as big as silver dollars and his mouth hanging open. Then he collapsed on the floor, unconscious.

Sadie crawled over and nudged Frank's shoulder, getting no response. She looked at her imposing great-great-great grandfather. "I–I think he's dead, c—captain."

Nathaniel threw his head back and laughed, then leaned down and smiled kindly. "No, lass. Only fainted. Men like this are cowards. It takes little to make them swoon."

Sadie stared at him, utterly mesmerized. "You're my great-great-great grandfather."

"That I am."

"I saw you on this balcony before, during a storm. But when I looked again, you were gone."

"I'm sorry I frightened you, little one. It was not my intention." He stepped back and sheathed his sword.

"And you were in my room. You said you were watching over me."

"Aye, lass. I've watched over you every night."

Sadie smiled. "Did you leave the boot print?"

He shook his head. "That was not I. It was left by the cur on the floor, hoping to frighten you."

Frank roused. Upon seeing the captain again, he scrambled to the door on his hands and knees and took off down the hall, leaving his machete behind and screaming the whole way.

Sadie looked back at Nathaniel. "What if he comes back again? And Mr. Endicott…"

He smiled broadly. "I believe your young man has summoned reinforcements and is speaking with several officers at this very moment on the front lawn. You'll not be seeing Frank or Willie again."

Now that the threat was gone, Sadie faced Nathaniel, her eyes brimming over with tears. "I can't believe you're here…" She paused, unsure how she should address him. "What should

I call you?"

"If it suits, you may call me Grandpapa."

Sadie smiled. "I'm glad to meet you, Grandpapa."

"Likewise, little one. It is my great joy."

He stepped closer and pulled out his sword again. "I believe this was meant to be yours."

With his heel, he stomped forcefully on the floor next to the bed post closest to the windows. Everything in the room shook, and a short floorboard adjacent to the post opened. He crouched and slowly inserted the blade into the hole while Sadie watched, mesmerized. Suddenly, a small panel at the base of the bed post popped open and a gold coin fell onto the floor. Nathaniel raised his booted foot and gave the post a kick. More coins poured out until there was a hefty mound of glittering gold at his feet.

Sadie could hardly breathe. "Oh my God… Bess's portrait! She was sitting by the bed post and there were coins on the floor! That was the clue!"

Nathaniel's hearty laugh filled the room. "Don't forget, lass, there are three other posts. They all open in the same manner." He stepped back. "I'll leave you to it."

He took another step back. Now fully on the balcony again, he seemed to become almost translucent.

"Wait, Grandpapa! Don't go… not yet."

"I'm afraid I must be off, my dear Sarah Elizabeth. But you may be sure I will never be far away."

Sadie called to him as a bolt of lightning struck overhead, spraying him with brilliant light. And in that split second, he was gone. She ran out onto the balcony, but there was no trace of Nathaniel Prophet.

The rain continued to come down in force, but she barely noticed as she gazed out at the ocean, hoping to see the ghostly image of *The Elizabeth* on the horizon. And for a fleeting moment, she did.

***

Mr. Bones was right all along. The summer did fly by,

and Sadie found herself in the middle of a tornado of energy as the town, and especially Mrs. Northrup, descended on Prophet House for the reenactment of life in Nathaniel and Sarah's time.

The microwave was safely hidden in the pantry under a stack of feed sacks. Antique rocking chairs, a butter churn, and an elaborately painted wooden rocking horse, with a mane and tail made of real horse hair, now graced the front porch. Children, dressed in period costumes, chased hoops around with sticks and played nine pins on the front lawn. All motorized vehicles were safely stowed on the old Ewing farm as horses and carriages were the only modes of transportation allowed within eyesight of the property. And the chamber pots were back.

As hordes of visitors toured the house and grounds, Sadie found her mother on the widow's walk, gazing down the road. Her auburn hair was hidden under a dark wig, with tightly wound curls on each side of her face. She wore a pale gold, high-waisted gown with a deep red sash and matching shawl. Sadie stepped on her own dress as she climbed through the trap door.

"I have a whole new respect for Sarah." Meg said. "I nearly killed myself getting up here in this dress. How she managed to do it every day without injuring herself is beyond me. Especially in this condition." Meg patted her stomach.

"Did the doctor say the baby's okay?"

Meg smiled. "He's fine. Looks like Prophet House will have another Nathaniel after all."

"I can't believe you didn't tell dad before he left for Italy."

"He wouldn't have gone, and all those students would've had no one to chaperone."

Sadie nearly tripped on the hem of her dress again. "Once a year is all I'll be able to take of this."

Meg laughed. "You'll survive."

"Barely." Sadie pulled her skirt up to keep from tripping again. "What time is Dad supposed to get here?"

Meg turned back to the road again. "Any time now," she said wistfully. "What was all the commotion with Stevie?"

Sadie grinned. "She's not happy with the last-minute change."

Meg chuckled. “She’s not happy she’s Elizabeth’s ghost?”

“Nope. I almost feel sorry for her.”

Her mother raised her eyebrows. “You do?”

“I said almost…”

Sadie leaned over the rail and spotted Henry, looking uncomfortable in his breeches and waistcoat. He looked up and waved awkwardly. Sadie gave him a thumbs up and he smiled.

“He makes a nice Nathaniel the second, don’t you think, Mom?”

Meg sucked in her breath excitedly. “Sadie, look! He’s coming!”

Owen’s truck pulled to a stop about a quarter of a mile from the house. Her dad exited, carrying a backpack and pulling a piece of rolling luggage.

“I’m glad he didn’t have to take a taxi this time, Sadie said. “That was nice of Owen to drive all the way to Davenport to pick him up. I can’t believe I used to think he was a murderer.”

Meg was beaming as she watched her husband jog up the road, dragging his luggage behind him.

Dean noticed them on the widow’s walk and waved excitedly.

Sadie smiled and waved back. “Did you tell him he has to change clothes when he gets here?”

Meg shook her head. “I spared him that detail.”

“I can’t wait to tell him everything that happened this summer—Bess, Mr. Bones, the captain… “

“Don’t forget to add Frank pushing you in the well and Owen pulling you out.”

“And Mr. Endicott getting arrested. I still can’t believe he’s Frank’s cousin and the whole benefactor thing was just so he could find the treasure. We sure messed up their plans, didn’t we?”

“We sure did.”

“They’ll both have lots of time to think about that in prison.”

“Yes, they will…” Meg sighed. “I thought Frank was a friend.”

"He had us all fooled." Sadie put her arm around her mother's growing waist. "When we talk to Dad, maybe we should leave out the part about the police finding the old caretaker in the well."

"No. We'll have to tell him everything… the whole story. He'd find out eventually anyway."

"He's gonna freak about the treasure." Sadie smiled. "Why did we leave all the other coins in the bed posts?"

"I think that's the best place for them right now. After all, they were safe in there for two hundred years. I was thinking of setting up a fund for the historical society."

"Mrs. Northrup will go berserk when she finds out. I can't believe you haven't told her yet."

Meg smiled. "She thinks Prophet House has a new anonymous benefactor. She's dying to know who it is. It's driving her crazy." Meg sighed. "Right now, I'm looking forward to some peace and quiet. I'll tell her eventually. Maybe we can put her in charge of how the funds we donate are spent. That should make her happy."

"She'll be shoving banana bread at us for the rest of our lives." Sadie laughed. "Speaking of baked goods, Stella brought cinnamon buns over this morning. They're hidden in the pantry."

Meg wrinkled her nose. "No cinnamon, please. I've lost my taste for it."

"Do you think telling the town about the coins will change everything?"

Meg sighed. "Maybe. But think of all the good we can do with the money."

"Yeah." Sadie watched Mrs. Northrup flitting through the crowd. "Henry's mom will be over here all the time, wanting to talk about ways to spend it."

Meg nodded. "Most likely."

"That doesn't bother you?"

"She's kind of grown on me."

Sadie nodded. "Me too. Weird, isn't it?"

Meg laughed. "Yes, it is."

Dean worked his way around Big Jake pulling a wagon

full of kids. Mrs. Northrup spotted him and ran over. Sadie watched him nod politely. Every few seconds, his eyes darted to the widow's walk.

"Maybe we should go down and rescue him," Sadie sighed.

"I think he can handle himself. Look."

Dean began walking toward the house again with Mrs. Northrup close behind, still chattering away. When he reached the porch, he gave her a mock bow before ascending the stone steps. Mrs. Northrup took the hint and resumed her part as hostess. She noticed a young couple studying their brochure and rushed over to introduce herself.

In a few minutes, they heard him climbing the steps to the widow's walk.

Sadie sucked in her breath. "Can we tell him now?"

Meg smiled. "No time like the present."

Sadie grinned. "He's never gonna believe it… "

THE END

EPILOGUE

The last day of the reenactment went off without a hitch. Sadie was surprised at how disappointed she felt now that it was over. Even so, she looked forward to sleeping in the next day. Her dad had promised them breakfast at Stella's in the morning. It was wonderful having him home. He'd entertained them all week with funny anecdotes from his summer in Italy. Life had returned to their new normal, and it was better than she'd ever imagined.

Sadie stood in the now empty foyer of Prophet House, soaking up the quiet. It almost felt strange to be alone in the house after it had been filled with visitors for the past ten days. Her parents were still outside with the last few townspeople who didn't seem to want to leave. Henry had promised to meet her in town after breakfast the next morning. Melanie and Cody were joining them too. All in all, it had been a perfect day.

Sadie's feet were aching from her lace up boots. She sat on the bottom step and slipped them off before plodding up the stairs to her room. Like every other time, she experienced a fleeting moment of hope that Bess would be there. But other than that brief encounter at the cellar door when Frank was chasing her, she hadn't seen Bess since the day she and Henry discovered her portrait hidden in the wall.

Sadie reached her room at the end of the hall, opened the door, and felt her heart skip a beat. A lovely woman in a pale blue gown was standing on the balcony gazing out at the ocean. Her dark hair was partially pulled up, the rest falling in gentle curls over her delicate shoulders.

Bess stepped out of the wardrobe and reached out her hand, smiling. "Sadie, I'd like you to meet my mother."

The woman slowly turned. Her kind eyes were the color of a vivid Autumn sky. "Hello, my dear. I've so wanted to meet you..."

www.ingramcontent.com/pod-product-compliance
Lightning Source LLC
Chambersburg PA
CBHW032006060325
23041CB00004B/173